The
PRODIGAL

The
PRODIGAL

Janice Parker

TATE PUBLISHING
AND ENTERPRISES, LLC

Published by Tate Publishing & Enterprises, LLC
127 E. Trade Center Terrace | Mustang, Oklahoma 73064 USA
1.888.361.9473 | www.tatepublishing.com

Tate Publishing is committed to excellence in the publishing industry. The company reflects the philosophy established by the founders, based on Psalm 68:11,
"The Lord gave the word and great was the company of those who published it."

Published in the United States of America

ISBN: 978-1-63268-285-7
Fiction / Historical
14.02.26

Chapter 1

Clint woke up in a small, filthy, smelly room that had only one dusty window. He groaned from the agonizing pain in his neck where they'd struck him. The thick rope binding his hands and feet was so tight, his skin was peeling off. He was huddled near the door; his legs were stiff and sore.

Where am I, he thought. Clint didn't know how long he'd been there.

He rolled over on his right side and moaned as he tried to sit up. He tilted his head against the wall; he could vaguely remember. A vision of Abby being shot pierced his mind. "Oh God, let her be okay," he said in a whisper. *I've got to get out of here.*

She's got to be all right. God please, let her be okay. Clint studied the room and noticed a wooden door. The glass window looked easy to break.

If I can just pry myself loose, I could get out of here. He leaned forward to try and free himself from the coarse rope, but it was useless. His heart was beating violently in his chest.

Hours passed and fear gnawed at his mind and he was heavy from torment as sweat poured profusely from his forehead down his body. October was scorching hot in the Democratic Republic of Congo.

Thoughts flooded his mind. *It will take a miracle to get out of here. Is Abby still alive? Will I ever see her again? I never got to say goodbye to my Dad. Tell him I love him. Ask him to forgive me.*

"God help me," he said quietly.

Minutes later, the sound of men yelling caused his stomach to jump. Waves of fear ran through his body as one of the voices got louder. He heard the sound of chains clanking. Suddenly, the door flew open.

Clint strained in the glare of the bright sun. The large black man who had held Chiamaka stood there, his face engulfed with rage. Clint froze instantly fearing that he would see death.

The man untied Clint's hands and his feet. "Get up!" His voice was deep and it was hard to understand him.

Clint rolled onto his knees, his body was stiff. The man yanked him to his feet and shoved him up against the wall before pushing him forward.

At first, it was hard to walk. He felt the roughness of the ground through the hole in his shoe. The man pushed him again, this time more forcefully. Clint fell to his knees. The man grabbed his arm with such force, it felt as though it would rip right out of its socket.

When he regained his footing, the man led him in front of a small hut. The leader of the group was standing there.

The leader began barking orders in his native tongue. The others, who seemed to fear him, stood almost at attention. Two of them left and entered the hut. One of them returned with a wooden chair, which he set before the leader.

The village looked deserted. There was one car that looked like a jeep. There must have been at least twenty men. They were heavily armed with guns, dressed in trousers. Clint wondered if the village was used as some type of military base. There was a heap of guns stacked up near one of the huts. He was being locked up in one of the wood houses. Three men were standing close to the leader.

"Sit," said the leader. His voice was calm and rational.

The large man who'd brought him outside pushed him down on the chair.

"I will ask you again. Where is the rest of the money?" There was intensity in his face.

Blinded by the sun shining directly into his eyes, Clint paused, straining to see the man's scowling face. His hand fluttered nervously.

"I told you. My father gave it to me. I don't have any more money."

The leader nodded to the large black man. The man punched Clint in the stomach. Clint cried out, feeling a deep wrenching pain in his gut.

"Where is the rest of the money?" Quietly he said, "That's all I have."

The man took two steps closer to him. He smacked Clint across the face with the back of his hand. The force sent him flying out of the chair and onto the hard ground. Clint could taste warm blood as it ran down his lips. The man kicked him in his gut. Excruciating pain shot through him as he let out a groan.

His words slurred this time, "I swear . . . I don't have any more money." The man balled his fist and before he could strike again, Clint yelled, "Alright, alright, I'll get you more money! I'll do whatever you say!" He could hardly breathe from the pain.

The leader walked over to one of the other men. He looked at Clint.

"I knew he would eventually talk. Lock him up."

The large man grabbed Clint's arm, dragged him back to the room, threw him down to the ground, and tied his legs and hands, again. Clint heard him lock the door. He lay down on his side shivering with his legs against his chest.

It was hard to believe he was being held like a common criminal. He hadn't done anything wrong. How could God let this happen? Was he wrong to think he cared? What kind of a God is he? Is he punishing me?

A glimmer of hope. Maybe he could bargain with them and they'd let him go. But the reality of that soon shifted his emotions. His stomach tightened and his body began to shake violently from pain and fear. Tremors swept over him like powerful waves, he cringed to get them to stop.

As the hours passed, depression descended upon him. It was then, that it hit him. He would probably die. At that point, he began to face the consequences of his past actions and the current situation. The loss of freedom and pain of separation from his loved ones, especially Abby; not knowing whether she was dead or alive became torture. Visions of Abby continued to resonate through his mind. He quietly said, "God help me . . . please." He leaned back against the cement wall his mind in a daze. Clint wondered how the path he'd taken led him to the devastating presence he now faced.

Are all my mistakes catching up to me? he thought. Visions of his past spread through his mind, back three years when he was fighting in the war in Germany.

Chapter 2

Clint sat next to his tent on a giant tree limb that had fallen from a storm. He was dressed in an olive wool cap, heavy canvas leggings under his trousers and a wool shirt, covered by a thick sweater, and a cotton jacket. Even with his layers of clothing, he was still freezing.

Clint belonged to the 106th Infantry. They'd been in Germany a little over a month.

Clint's basic training was completed at Fort Jackson, South Carolina, summer of 1944. His division was then moved to Tennessee to participate in army operations, and then on to Germany.

Clint breathed on his hands before striking a match on his shoe sole. The bitter cold air chilled his face. After taking a long deep puff of his cigarette, he leaned forward. Nick, an American, was sitting next to him with his belly bulging in his olive coat. Minutes later, Frazier, a young and slender British soldier he had met only two weeks before, sat down on a log and joined them. He looked to be about 22 years old and had a lean face, inquisitive and brown eyes.

Several weeks earlier, Clint's division, led by their 28-year-old commanding officer, Lt. Col. Thomas Riggs, fought outside St. Vith, against German forces vastly superior in numbers. With the help of Frazier's British battalion, they held their ground. Clint didn't think he'd make it out alive. They withdrew over the Saint River at Vielsalm, then assembled at Anthisnes, Belgium for reinforcements and much needed supplies. The previous morning, January 10, they a packed up and headed south. At sun down, they set up camp north of Caibehay.

Horrifying pictures of bloodshed, injury, and death tormented Clint's mind daily. He would have given anything to be back home in his father's mansion enjoying everything money could buy.

Clint was the youngest of three brothers. His brother, Paul, was fighting the war in North Africa and Europe. William, the oldest, belonged to the 99th Infantry Division in Germany. He hadn't heard from either of them in over two years. War was nothing like he'd ever imagined it would be.

Nick said, in a thick Southern accent asked, "Mind if I borrow a cigarette?"

Clint reached inside his jacket and pulled out a cigarette and a book of matches, handing them Nick.

Frazier rubbed his hands together several times to warm them. "I can't wait for this insane war to end," Nick said.

"Me too," Frazier said with a slight accent. "I can certainly think of better places I'd like to be."

"I hate the Germans," Nick said. "I'd kill every Nazi I see if I could." He blew a puff of smoke into the cold air. Clint kept silent.

"Where are you both from?" Frazier asked.

"I'm from Alabama," Nick said, before taking another puff of his cigarette.

Clint paused for a few minutes. "Grew up in Dallas, Texas with my father and two brothers. My mom died giving birth to my sister. She died too," Clint said. His mood was glum. It was a subject he tended to avoid.

"What about you, Frazier?" Nick asked.

"I'm originally from Africa. My mum was a missionary and my pop, an archeologist. He was there conducting a study when they met. They married, had me and my younger sister, and we moved to Wales when I was ten."

Nick took one last puff of his cigarette and threw it to the ground. "Got a letter from my girl back home confessing her devotion to someone else."

Clint sat still smoking his cigarette, emotionless.

"Sorry to hear that. There's someone better for you," Frazier said.

Nick bent his head. "I loved her. Was plannin' on askin' her to marry me when I got home."

"There's better fish in the sea," Frazier said optimistically. "Trust me. I've had my heart broke. You'll get through it."

"Have you ever been dumped, Clint?" Nick asked.

Clint stared at Nick. "No, but I broke a few hearts in my day." Though Clint was medium weight and stood only at 5'7, he had the confidence of a boxer. He was handsome and he knew it. He had brown sandy hair, fair complexion, and high cheek bones. He was the desire of every girl back home.

Clint threw his cigarette butt on the ground and stamped it out with his feet. "It's late, we should get some sleep."

When Frazier stood, a little black book fell out of his jacket. "What's that?" Clint asked.

Frazier bent down and grabbed the little black book. "It's my Bible . . . . ever read it?"

"No, but I been in church more times than I'd like to remember. My father made me go as a kid. Can't say I ever got much out of it."

"That's too bad. This book has saved my life. My relationship with God is the only thing that keeps me sane."

"I'm tired. Goin' to bed. Good night," Clint said. He headed towards his tent with Nick right behind him. "Goodnight," Frazier said who walked to the other side of the grounds to his tent.

The next day, Clint sat in his tent next to Nick finishing up some watery oatmeal. Nick glanced back at a group of black soldiers were sitting in the back of the tent.

Black soldiers had been segregated from white soldiers, however, General Eisenhower, faced with Hitler's advancing army on the Western Front, temporarily desegregated the army and called for urgent assistance on the front lines. More than 2,000 black soldiers volunteered to fight.

Nick said, "Least they can make em eat outside or somethin'." Clint looked back. "Never hurt me so don't much care."

He stood, grabbed his tray, set it down on a small table stacked with other dishes, then stepped outside and headed to his tent.

Clint's battalion had planned to move east toward Berlin. He was only five feet away from his tent when suddenly heard the sound of airplanes approaching. As he peered up to the gray, windy sky, bullets suddenly flew out of the plane and hit the ground only a few feet away from him. Clint felt his heart almost leaped out of his chest as the air raid occurred.

German dive bombers followed with an intense attack. Sirens went off instantly and men began scrambling, trying to find cover and weapons to fight back. Clint ran towards his tent for cover when a big blast went off, knocking him to the ground. Disoriented, he struggled to crawl to safety and he managed to stumble to his feet. Clint watched men crashing into one another, others wounded as they laid flat on their backs and stomachs. Many bled copiously. American and British soldiers were firing machine guns. He knelt for shelter beside an American armored car and gripped his M1 Garand, semi-automatic rifle.

Within minutes, U.S. Corsair fighter planes were flying above firing at the enemy planes. He pointed his gun, ready to fire when bullets flew out of the speed of lighting, shooting at the dirt ground inches from him. Then a bomb went off, flipping the car over and throwing him several feet away. He felt a sharp pain in his shoulder as he lay on the ground, stunned and scared, unsure of what to do. At that moment, his life flashed before his eyes. He thought for sure that he would die.

Blood began to pour out of his shoulder. He could barely move.

He looked to the right and saw Nick lying on the ground, unconscious. Clint tried to scream out but the words simply wouldn't come; he felt any minute he would faint. Within seconds, he felt a strong arm drag him into a nearby tent. Looking up, he saw a young Negro man holding him.

He vaguely heard the words of the man. "You gone be all right."

Clint felt the arms of the soldier hoist him over his shoulder and lay him down behind a tent. That was the last thing Clint remembered.

When Clint awoke, he felt relief strike through his bones. In spite of the excruciating pain shooting out of his arm and the massive headache creeping down his neck, he was happy to be alive. He reached up and felt a bandage wrapped around his head.

Clint was in a large tent surrounded by wounded men. This place was staffed with doctors, nurses, and assistants, and well-equipped with beds, blankets, candles, food-units, washing-rooms, a cabinet stacked with medications, and what looked to be operating devices.

There must have been at least 100 wounded men in the tent. He could hear the mumbling of voices next to him. Shifting his head to the right, two doctors were standing next to a patient's bed. The older doctor said, "It appears he has a blockage. The femoral artery was severely damaged causing insufficient blood supply to his thigh. Severe gangrene has developed and amputation is inevitable."

"Oh God, no," the man cried. "Please . . . don't take my leg, I'm begging you."

The same doctor said, "The limb can cause serious problems with infection. It could be a threat to your life. We have no choice."

"What about the right leg?" the other doctor asked.

"We may be able to save it. We'll administer an anti-coagulant drug. Hopefully we can by-pass surgery."

A red-headed nurse was passing by. The older doctor said, "Nurse, bring the gurney around."

They lifted the man from his cot and wheeled him away.

Clint cringed and closed his eyes, trying to blot out the desperate cries surrounding him. The man to his left had a bullet wound of the face. Next to him was a man who'd suffered a large blow to his head. He overheard a doctor telling him he had a traumatic brain injury that would take months to recover. He hoped the nightmare would soon end.

When the fog cleared, a nurse covered in blood was approaching. "How do you feel?" she asked, feeling his pulse.

"In a lot of pain," Clint said hoarsely.

As she lifted the wool blanket over Clint's chest, she said, "You have a slight concussion. The doctor performed surgery on your shoulder to remove the shrapnel from the bomb. You should consider yourself lucky because it could have been much worse."

"The doctor will be by in an hour to give you some more morphine."

Clint simply nodded. He tried to sit up and cleared his throat. "There's another wounded soldier, Nick Moore. Do you know if he's okay?"

"He's alive. There was a bullet embedded in his forehead and I'm afraid his right leg was badly wounded so we had to remove it."

Clint dropped his head back onto his pillow.

"Try and get some sleep. I'll be back and check on you soon."

Everything seemed so detached, as though it were happening to someone else. He just wanted this nightmare to end.

Five hours after eating half of a peanut butter sandwich, Clint lay on the bed staring at the tent wall.

He glanced up and saw a young Negro soldier standing at the foot of his bed, smiling broadly.

He stood tall in his olive cotton field jacket. "How you feelin', soldier?"

Clint squinted as he attempted to lean forward. In a bit of a daze he asked, "Are you . . . . the man that helped me?"

"Roy's my name. I'm with the 758th Tank Battalion. We came under heavy enemy fire. Forced us east and here we are."

Clint rested his head on his pillow. "Thanks for the help." "I'm glad you all right, man."

To the right of Clint on a small wooden table was the other half of his peanut butter sandwich. He looked back at Roy. "You want half a sandwich?"

"No thanks," Roy said, still smiling. "My Battalion's headin' out tomorrow. I wanted to make sure you was all right. Say, you ever get to Mississippi and want some good baby back ribs and corn bread, look me up. My mama makes the best in the state." He handed Clint a sheet of paper with his address.

Clint laid the paper on the table.

You take care of yourself and stay out the way of those bombs." "I'll try. Thanks again."

~⌘~

After four days, Clint stubbornly insisted on being released. The doctors were amazed by his persistence. He was too wounded to fight, so was scheduled to take the next ship home. Nick had to remain for two more weeks before being released.

Clint moved between beds, eyeing the wounded men before finally approaching Nick's bed. Nick was half asleep.

"Nick . . . Nick." Nick slowly opened his eyes and turned his head sideways and smiled at Clint.

Clint moved closer. "How do you feel?" "I've been better," he said. He tried to move.

Clint glanced at his leg. He tried not to show it, but the sight of him was frightening. Nick's entire forehead was bandaged.

"So, hear you're on your way home," Nick said, enthusiastically. Clint fidgeted before saying, "Yes."

Nick was trying to remain stoic, but Clint could tell he was scared.

"I'm not sure what life will be like for me. Guess it'll never be the same. Guess I should be glad to be alive, huh?" Nick said.

Clint nodded. "I'm sure it'll be okay." Clint wasn't much on compassion. It was hard for him to be empathic, even in the worst of times. But in spite of his shallow persona, he genuinely liked Nick.

"You're strong. You'll pull through this." "Think we'll ever see each other again?"

"I still have your address that you gave me a couple of months ago. You still have mine, right?"

Nick nodded.

"I'll keep in touch."

Just then, the doctor appeared.

"I should go," Clint said, moving backwards. "Write me, okay, Clint?"

"I will. See ya, Nick."

Clint gathered his things and stepped out of the tent. It was three o'clock in the afternoon and the ship was scheduled to leave at five. As he peered up at the cloudy gray sky, he heard his name being called.

"Clint!"

He turned around and saw Frazier.

"I heard you were leaving. If you ever get to Wales, give me a ring." He handed him a sheet of paper with his home address and phone number."

Clint stared at the paper for a second and then nodded. "Thanks." He stuffed the address in his wallet.

"I'm glad I got to know you. These are unfortunate circumstances of course, but it was good to meet you. I'm quite relieved to hear you're your going home. You take care of yourself."

He shook his hand. "I will. Bye Frazier." "Goodbye Clint."

Chapter 3

The ship landed in Baltimore on time. He de-boarded and took a train to Dallas, Texas. It was a four-day trip. He slept no more than two hours a night. The train ride was bumpy, stuffy, and noisy, making his injury that much more unbearable.

Clint gazed out the window, impassive and distant from everything and everyone around him. Although he was glad to leave Europe and escape the horrors of war, he wasn't thrilled to see his family. He never got along with his father, even though he knew that he was a good man.

Clint's rebellious and stubborn personality made it difficult for him to submit to any authority figure, which affected his Army career. He was reprimanded by his commanding officer for violation of military regulations. When first recruited in the army, he failed to wear a proper uniform. He refused to maintain clean barracks and destroyed army property. Verbal counseling and advice didn't help, which resulted in extra instruction and in some cases, punishment.

Clint was used to getting his own way. He'd been given everything money could buy, but it never seemed to be enough.

He leaned his head against the back of the seat and stared out the window. The words his father spoke to him before he left for war still rang in his ear.

"Clint, why must you be so rebellious? You've been kicked out of two boarding schools for fighting. You barely passed your classes. You've been thrown in jail twice; once for fighting and the other for stealing liquor from the corner store. As much as I hate to see you leave for war, I hope and pray this experience will mature you and that God will would protect you."

He meditated on the words. *The war changed me, Dad, but in more ways than you think. It taught me to hate. I hate Germans, I hate war, and right now, I hate life.*

The train arrived in Dallas Tuesday afternoon. Clint slowly de-boarded, holding his injured arm, carrying a small green bag. He was still wearing his uniform. His shoulder was still tightly bandaged. The sun was shining down on him, even though it was a cool day.

He squinted his eyes and looked up. His father, James Edison, was standing next to his black 328 Roadster, several yards away. There were at least ten jeeps parked in the lot.

The 5'6" man with light brown hair, showing strands of gray, smiled when he saw Clint. He moved quickly and wrapped his arms around him. His eyes were bloodshot.

"It's good to have you home, Clint. I've missed you."

Clint held his father, but his thoughts were whirling. It was hard for him to think.

James stared straight into Clint's eyes. "I was so scared to learn you were injured. I couldn't bear to lose you. I'm glad you're all right." His mood had dampened and his voice lowered.

Clint nodded. "It's good to be back." "Let's go home, son."

They climbed into the car and drove through downtown Dallas, through the Main Street district with its towering buildings, and then passed the City Center business district. Mostly men filled the busy streets. They drove past the Dallas Arboretum and Botanical Garden, and through the West Village.

There were jeeps everywhere.

"What's with all the jeeps?" Clint asked.

"Dallas serves as a manufacturing center for the war effort," James said. "The Ford Motor plant in Dallas has been converted to full-time war-time production, producing only jeeps and military trucks.

"You must tell me all about the past year. Your brothers wrote me, Clint, but I never heard from you. You couldn't know how worried I was."

"Sorry," he said, still gazing out the window. "I barely had time to write. Everything happened so fast, we were always on the move."

"I understand. I know the horrors of war. When I fought in World War I, I didn't think I'd make it out alive. It's nothing like it seems. Once you're rested, I want to hear everything."

Clint nodded. Exhausted, he leaned his head back on the seat and stared out at the huge river, which flowed only in Texas.

Clint was quiet most of the way home while James did most of the talking.

"We've had several trials and tribulations. Eight months ago we had a severe drought. It was the worst we'd seen in years. The land was dry and

12

the ground, hard. I thought we'd lose the cattle since there was little water for them to drink. God worked a miracle and it rained."

James shared how he'd been working diligently to assist the Japanese Americans to gain back their land and find employment. Clint nodded on occasion, somewhat listening, but his mind was far away as he visualized the distressing images of war.

They drove on a narrow dirt road through rolling hills of brown farmland for almost twenty minutes. Then they swept past acres of flatland surrounded by a white fence that looked newly painted. Clint looked up as they drove through the open gate and saw the sign 'Edison Ranch'.

I made it home, he thought to himself.

The ranch sat on 1500 acres of grazing pasture. They pulled up to a 33-room, Victorian mansion surrounded by five majestic oak trees. A large crystal clear pond sat right next to the house. Hundreds of Texas longhorn and Angus cattle were grazing what appeared to be endless pastures. Over a dozen horses were browsing and eating hay behind an enclosed fence, next to a brown large warehouse that was used to house the cattle. Several ranch hands were working.

Clint stepped out of the car and studied the land. Everything looked the same. There were at least 15 men, some feeding cattle, others handling the horses. Clint never thought he'd be relieved and ecstatic to see some ranch hands. He never appreciated them until now.

"Hey Clint. Welcome home," Ray said, a medium height blonde man, with a cowboy hat and faded jeans. He was standing next to the warehouse.

Hi," Clint said.

Clint had known most of the workers all his life. Prior to working on the farm, Ray's wife died giving birth to their first child. He was distraught and turned to alcohol to consume the hidden grief. He lost everything. James met him at one of the homeless shelters where he volunteered. He ministered to him sharing the love of God, gave him a job, and a few years later, Ray re-married. He has two children and works as one of James managers.

"Clint, good to see you," said a large Negro man, who was sitting on a horse. Clint assumed he'd just come from moving cows.

"You too, Bo."

Bo had worked with James for fifteen years. He was a friendly, un-married, faithful, strong, and committed. He is one of the few men that Clint liked.

James grabbed his bag. Clint had just started for the house when he was overtaken by his golden retriever, Trip. He knelt down while the dog profusely licked his face. Rubbing the dog's back he said, "I've missed you too, boy."

He stepped onto the extravagant stone terrace surrounded by green plants and an assortment of flowers, and entered the house. He walked under high ceilings near the oak staircase. Clint's mother had a love for fine things, so the home was graced with original art, antiques. Clint walked across the 100-year-old Persian rug, and gazed quickly at the elaborately carved mantles. He followed his father past the large and elegant dining room with an 8th century pear wood table, and passed the French-paneled library. He peeked his head into the reception hall with its cream walls, ebony hardwood floor. He noticed the new crystal chandeliers hanging from the ceiling. The reception hall was large enough to seat 200 people. Clint followed James into the 700 square foot living room, decorated with a blush beige sofa and chair, thick Persian carpet, and ebony coffee table. A portrait of his mother was hanging above the granite fireplace. She had light brown eyes, long black hair, tan skin, and ruby red lipstick covering her thin lips.

"Sit down, Clint. Sit down. You must be famished. I'll have a good meal cooked for you."

"I'm not very hungry. I ate on the train." He was aloof and distant. "I'm gonna' go to my room and put my bags down. I'll be down later."

"All right Clint. I'll have a late dinner prepared. Sleep as long as you need to."

James kissed Clint on the cheeks and held him tight. "I'm glad to have you home."

"Me too," he said. He grabbed the bag from his dad and headed upstairs.

Clint walked to his room and turned on the lamp. Everything looked the same. A poster of Greta Garbo hung on the wall behind his bed and next to it, several posters of model cars.

He dropped his bag on the floor then opened the dresser drawer, his clothes were neatly folded, the room was spotless. He reached for a photo on his desk of his older brother, William, who he called Will. It was a photo of the two dressed in overalls and holding fishing rods. Will was also holding a giant fish. That was the day they went fishing on the Colorado River. He was only 12. Clint couldn't wait for him to get back.

Next to the photo of Will was a photo of his mother. She was holding Clint at age two. A flashback of his father weeping at her grave came to him. That was the only time he ever saw his father cry. He was depressed for months. Life was never the same after she died.

Clint pulled off his pants and shirt, dropped them on the floor, then threw himself on his bed, closed his eyes, and within minutes, fell asleep.

James sat down on an oak rocking chair next to the fireplace. Tears came to his eyes. He was so overwhelmed with happiness that one of his sons had made it home alive. *God is merciful*, he thought to himself. With a deep sigh and exhalation of breath, he said, "Thank you God, for returning my son safely. I pray you do the same for the other two."

James was a strong man of faith who genuinely loved God. He was patient, kind and had attended church regularly at Grace Baptist Church for over 15 years.

He grew up in California with five sisters and a younger brother. There were too many mouths to feed with not enough food. His father died of a heart attack at the age of 42. At 16, James was the oldest and assumed the responsibility of caring for the family. He dropped out of school and worked two jobs to help his mother. She cleaned houses while he worked bagging groceries and as a bell boy in a hotel at night. At 22, he joined the army and fought in World War I. Once the war was over, he moved to Texas where he met his wife, Alice.

He worked three jobs to provide for his family and put himself through school. After earning a degree in business and finance, he managed to get a job at local cattle ranch. The owner liked James and eventually promoted him to head rancher. James saved money for over ten years and invested in 50 acres of land. One day, gas and sulphur were found in a water well, and paraffin dirt was found on the surface of his land. As soon as he'd heard that these were the first signs of oil, he took a risk by investing all of his money and taking out loan. Within the next year, oil was discovered on his land. He became one of the wealthiest men in Texas and built his oil and cattle empire.

Though James was rich and successful, he still found time to serve; working at the homeless shelter, helping out in his church. He gave to hundreds of charities and provided funding for several orphanages, which he visited often. One month before Clint returned, James had attended a meeting in Washington D.C., along with some of the most prominent and important people in the country to discuss assistance for underdeveloped countries. Vice President Henry Wallace was also in attendance.

James stood and walked over to the table and stared at the pictures of his three sons: William, Paul and Clint. William stood 6 feet tall, with dark brown hair and green eyes. He was intelligent and graduated first in his class. He planned to attend law school once the war ended. He had a gentle nature, like his mother.

He smiled remembering the last time he'd seen saw his son, Paul, who graduated from college with honors. Paul was strong, opinionated, honest, and hardworking. Once he returned from fighting in the war, he planned to help his father run the business.

James glanced at the photo of his youngest son, Clint. His mood changed as he became somewhat distressed. His relationship with Clint had always been strained. One year at war seemed to have toughened him, but James wondered if it had matured him. His attitude and demeanor seemed unchanged. Clint was spoiled and used to getting his own way. He took his studies less seriously than his brothers. What should have been a life of peace, prosperity, and gratitude for Clint, was instead a life of rebellion, gambling, drinking, and acts of violence. James would never forget the first time Clint was expelled from school for two weeks. He'd vandalized the newly painted private school. James had to pay to have it re-painted and after much pleading, managed to keep Clint from getting kicked out. Right before turning 18, he managed to fail three of seven final exams. After James spoke to the Board of Directors and made several threats to Clint, he managed to pull himself together and finish school with a C—average.

Clint had an unexplained opposition to anyone in authority and a strong stubborn streak. There was a deep-rooted anger that intensified every time things didn't go his way. James wondered if it came from his mother's death. He loved her very much.

James had raised Clint in the church since he was a little boy, and Clint loved it, especially Sunday school. He talked incessantly of the stories he learned of King David, and Solomon, and Paul and Peter. After his mother died, he became cold, reserved, and lost interest. He drew deep within himself, rejecting everyone except for his older brother, William. Clint idolized him and William adored Clint. He was the only person who seemed to understand Clint.

James went into the kitchen. Their housekeeper, Camellia, had prepared dinner: BBQ chicken, mashed potatoes, and biscuits. He checked his watch. It was eight o'clock. *Clint must be asleep*, he thought to himself. *We'll talk in the morning.* After eating, he went upstairs to take a bath, read for a while, and went to bed.

Chapter 4

James went into the kitchen reading the business section of the paper. Camellia walked into the bright room with her plus size dress covered with blackberry stains. She'd picked a bowl to make a cobbler for dinner that evening.

"Good morning, Mr. Edison," she said, with a Latino accent. "Good morning, Camellia."

As Camellia opened the beautiful crystal glass window to let the cool breeze in, James watched the cool air blow against the lavender curtains. Camellia opened the refrigerator and pulled out a jar of milk and some fresh eggs, then reached above the cabinet and grabbed a pan.

"Will Clint be joining us for breakfast? I'm anxious to see him. I can't believe it's been over a year."

"He'll be down soon," James said, checking his watch.

"He slept right through dinner last night," Camellia said. "He must be exhausted. It seems like just yesterday he was a small boy running through the kitchen tracking mud everywhere. And now he's grown into a young man."

"This is true," James said, smiling.

"I'll start a fresh pot of coffee, Mr. Edison." "Thank you. I think I'll go up and check on Clint."

Clint slept late and had a restless night. He stared at the ceiling. He had dreams of bombs blasting and men dying. Clint had a flashback of the bomb, it sent chills through his body.

He heard a knock then the sound of the door opening bringing him back to the present.

"Clint. Are you still asleep?"

"No, I'm awake. I'll be down in a minute."

Clint finally crawled out of bed. The clothes he'd been wearing the night before were thrown on his hardwood floor. He entered the large bathroom, stared in the mirror, and rubbed his hand over his shaven head. Other than his hair, his appearance hadn't changed.

First thing I'm planning to do is grow my hair back.

Clint took a bath; clothed himself in a pair of faded black pants, a navy blue polo shirt, and a pair of sneakers.

It took longer than usual because of his wounded arm. He went down the stairs and strolled into the kitchen.

Camellia smiled, held her arms out wide and hugged him. "I'm so glad you're home. I've missed you."

"Me too," he said, still exhausted.

"I've made breakfast. Your father is out back. Go out and join him and I'll bring your food."

He stepped onto the back sun porch. It had a peaked roofline, columns, with a classical Georgian Colonial touch. James was sitting at the glass table reading the newspaper with a plate of half-eaten eggs and bacon in front of him. Clint planted himself down on the chair across from his father.

"Good morning. Did you sleep well?" James asked. He set the paper down.

"Yeah. I guess I didn't realize how tired I was." "It's to be expected. It was a long trip."

Camellia walked out and set down a plate filled with scrambled eggs, biscuits, and bacon, with a tall glass of freshly squeezed orange juice. He gulped the juice down, and began to devour the food.

James cleared his throat. "I thought we could go into town today and say hello to some friends. Everyone is anxious to see you. I need to stop by the Salvation Army to drop off another donation."

Clint ate the last of the bacon. He wiped his mouth with his hand then rubbed his hand against his pants. "I wanted to visit a few friends. I told Eddie I'd stop by this afternoon. You won't mind goin' into town tomorrow, would you?"

"Ah no . . . we can go tomorrow."

He heard disappointment in his father's voice.

Camellia stepped out on porch holding a pitcher of orange juice, "Would you like some more?"

Clint stood up, "No . . . . thanks for breakfast." Camellia nodded.

"I had Bo bring your car around in case you planned to drive it. He washed it earlier," James said.

"Thanks Dad," he said while eyeing the car. He flew into the house to grab his car keys. He past the parterre-style garden with lilacs and bay trees and jumped into his pearl white Lincoln Zephyr. It was professionally hand-built with leather seats, wool carpeted trunk, and suede headliner. Clint stopped by a corner store and purchased a couple of beers. He drove with his limp left wrist draped over the steering wheel, and held a bottle of bear in the other, arriving at Eddie's twenty minutes later.

Clint honked the horn twice and a skinny boy with a crooked nose flew down the stairs and ran towards him.

"Eddie!" Clint yelled.

The two embraced. Eddie, being two years younger than Clint, wasn't able to fight in the war.

"When did ya' get back!" He spoke with a thick southern accent. "Yesterday. My dad picked me up. I'm glad to be home."

"Come in," Eddie said.

Clint followed him into a small but pleasant home. They went into the tiny kitchen.

"Where's the folks?" Clint asked. "Dad's at work and mom's in town."

He reached up into the cabinet and grabbed two glasses and filled them with sweet tea. "You hungry?" he asked.

"No, I ate." Clint sat down at the kitchen table.

Eddie sat next to him and handed him a glass of sweet tea. "So . . . what was it like . . . war?"

"Like nothing you'd think. I still see images of men dying around me. And the weather . . . it was freezing. We were up sometimes 36 hours." Clint took a drink of tea.

"Was it hard . . . killin' people?"

"No," Clint said persuasively. He leaned forward on his chair. "We'd been recovering from what I call my worst nightmare. We were out-numbered by Germans soldiers in St. Vith. I thought for sure I was dead. My Platoon headed toward Vielsalm.

"I leaned back against a tree to smoke a cigarette with one of the soldiers I met, Timothy. He was barely 18 and had been there for two months. We talked about twenty minutes. Then I looked up and saw an airplane flying just to the east of where we were on the ground. At first, we weren't sure if it was one of ours. Our Master Sergeant started yelling to get us organized so we could move on. We started back up the same trail, when all the sudden, I saw a couple of Nazi's hiding in the brush. They were holdin' machine guns. Then more of 'em started orbiting around us, coming from the bushes and behind the trees firin' their weapons. We tried to take cover. There were bodies everywhere. One of the Nazis fired and hit Tim. I tried to help him, but he died instantly. I could see the smile on the face of the German soldier who killed him. I'll never forget it. I grabbed my weapon and started shootin' like a wild man. I killed at least five of 'em. We lost about 20 men in that raid."

Clint smirked. "From that point on, I had one mission . . . killin' Nazis. "I never saw it myself, but a soldier told me the horror he felt when he'd come face-to-face with that Nazi concentration camp. He said he'd thought he'd get sick."

Clint stared out the window, almost in a daze. "Seeing the people dying and the dead bodies stacked like cordwood. Just hearin' about it I wanted to see every Nazi dead. I'm just glad to be away from that sickening country. I never wanna go back."

They spent the afternoon at Eddie's house talking, laughing, and catching up on the past year.

At six o'clock, Clint said, "Let's get outta here."

Clint and Eddie jumped into the car. Clint drove recklessly to the west side of Dallas, the poorest part of the city. They parked in front of a bar in the basement of a faded four-story red brick building. Many of the surrounding areas were boarded up or vacant.

They walked into the smoke-filled dingy room. The place was noisy, dirty, and crowded. The men looked hard-drinking and rough, and the women beautiful and loose.

They headed towards the front of the bar. Women stared as Clint walked in. He glanced at a few with confidence and arrogance as though he were God's gift to women.

With his good elbow, Clint leaned on the crowded counter. The stout, muscular bartender asked, "What can I get cha?" "Two shots of whisky," Clint said.

The bartender placed two shot glasses in front of them and poured them full with whisky. Clint downed his with one gulp. "Another." he said.

His eyes lingered around the room and stopped at a striking blonde woman sitting at the far side of the bar. Her hair was long and sleek. Next to her was a gorgeous brunette.

He grabbed his drink and said to Eddie, "Follow me."

They weaved in and out of small round tables filled with people laughing and drinking. He grabbed a chair from a nearby table, and sat down next to the blonde.

"You don't mind if we join you?"

"It's a free world," she said, as she grabbed a cigarette from her purse.

She was wearing a red dress, thin black stockings covering her slender legs and a long pearl necklace. She looked to be 25. Her nail polish matched her dark red lipstick.

"So, ya gotta name?" she asked. "Clint. And this is my friend, Eddie."

Eddie nodded. He sat directly in front of the brunette.

Clint grabbed a matchbook from his pocket and lit her cigarette. She took a puff. "I'm Meg and this is my friend, Irene."

"Hi," Eddie said, smiling at Irene. "Charmed," she said.

"What are ya drinkin'?" Clint asked. "Martinis, dry."

Clint waved to a bar maid. "Two more martinis and two beers."

She leaned forward. "So . . . ya just get back from war or somethin'?" She glanced at Clint's bandaged arm.

"Yeah, a few days ago."

She blew another puff of smoke in the air. "What was it like?"

"People died, wounded men, freezing weather. It was war," Clint said, almost annoyed. He was sick of talking about it.

The bar maid arrived with their drinks.

"You're not bad lookin'," Meg said. "I bet you've had a lot of girlfriends."

"I've had my share."

Eddie grabbed his beer. "A toast." He held it in the air. "To Clint. Our very own war hero."

"Stop kiddin', I ain't no hero," Clint said, irritated. "We'll here's to his safe return," Meg said.

"Hear. Hear." Irene said.

The three of them tapped their glasses together. Clint, still agitated, lit a cigarette.

After a while, Eddie began spinning his lies about shooting, traveling, hunting, and riding, trying to impress the girls.

"One time, I met the President of the United States," he said.

Meg's mouth flew open. "What!" "You don't say," Irene said.

Clint shook his head in disgust. Eddie wasn't much to look at so he often exaggerated his adventures to impress women.

"What'd he say?" Meg asked, excited.

"We'll, he was at the state capital and I was there with my graduating class. He was wearing a suit, red tie and leather shoes, and came right up to me." Eddie leaned back a little, his voice deepened. "He said, "You look like a bright young man. Why, I see great hope for our nation with young bright men like you.'

Meg's eyes wide, she said, "Isn't that somethin'. The President." They looked in amazement as Eddie spilled one lie after another.

They'd been friends for 15 years, so Clint had grown accustomed to it. The girls were eating up every word.

They talked, drank, and laughed for hours. At ten o'clock Clint looked at Eddie and said, "Let's go."

"Yeah," Meg said. She looked at Clint. "Say, let's go back to your place."

"No . . . not tonight. It's late and I'm tired." Clint stood up.

He took a few steps. Eddie jolted towards him. "Are you kiddin'? Come on, don't be stupid. The night's only beginnin'."

Clint turned around. "I said no."

Eddie took a few more steps, tripped and fell. Irene laughed hysterically. He got up and wrapped his arm around her. "Come on, let's go."

Clint walked first, Eddie right behind him; Meg only a few steps behind them. Clint bumped into a large bushy haired man who was smoking a cigar.

"Hey, say excuse me," he said in his harsh voice, echoing through the bar. Clint turned around, gave him a stony look, and kept walking.

"Hey, did you hear what I said?"

Clint continued to ignore him and kept walking. He felt a strong arm yank him around. "What'd are ya deaf?"

"I accept your apologies," Clint said, mockingly. "Now get lost."

It was obvious the man was drunk. "Look, you low-life scum. You . . . ." Before he could complete his sentence, Clint jabbed him in the jaw with his good arm, knocking the cigar out of his mouth. People hustled to move out of the way.

The man punched Clint in the stomach. Clint threw another punch, this time sending him flying backwards. The man stumbled to his feet. He tossed a punch and knocked Clint down. People were yelling and cheering them on.

"Come on boy, get up," said the man. Blood was running down his lip. Clint stood, glaring into the man's face.

"What's the matter, you afraid?" said the man, sarcastically. "You wanna kiss and make up?"

For a minute, Clint forgot that his left shoulder had been injured. He rammed into the man and they both fell, breaking one of the tables. After a few minutes, they heard the sound of approaching police sirens. A minute later, two police officers stormed into the room.

One of the policemen grabbed the large man, the other grabbed Clint, who turned and looked at Eddie, dazed and drunk.

The police hustled him into the car and to the police station.

Four hours later, a guard approached Clint's jail cell. Clint was sitting on a narrow bunk, leaning against the concrete wall to ease his pounding headache.

"You made bail," the guard said.

Clint slowly stood up, his body aching. He had a cut across his face, right below his right eye. He held his bandaged arm; the pain was agonizing. The guard escorted him into the main office and stared straight ahead. Clint's father was standing next to the counter.

With his eyebrows arched and deep voice, James said, "Let's go home."

After twenty-five minutes of silence and they'd just driven onto their property, James finally spoke. "I know the horror of war and how difficult it is coming home . . . to civilization."

Clint turned his head away from his father and rolled his eyes.

"I'm going to give you the benefit of doubt and let this incident go." Clint's face showed no expression.

After arriving home near midnight, Clint started walking away.

"Clint, I will say one thing. You associate with the wrong crowd; you end up in a mess. By associating with wise people, you will become wise yourself."

Clint gave him a cold stare. "I'm tired. I'm going to my room." He climbed the stairs and went straight to bed.

Chapter 5

The next morning, Clint lay in bed half asleep with his eyes closed, recovering from the previous night. He imagined himself on a yacht off the coast of an exotic island, surrounded by lushly beautiful trees, exotic flowers, and miles of sand. The shoreline dropped precipitously into the surrounding waters.

A stunning girl with thick black hair, sun-darkened skin, and perfect figure was rubbing suntan lotion on his back. He rolled partly on his side, took a sip of champagne, kissed her on the lips, and rolled over on his stomach to continue letting her massage his back. He was deeply engrossed in his fantasy when he heard his name being called at a distance. The sound of his door opening brought him back to the present.

"Clint!"

He jumped up, almost crashing down to the floor, as he glanced up at James with one eye open.

"Didn't you hear me calling you? It's almost noon. Get up." James left his room.

Clint hesitated at first. Annoyed, he threw his blanket off and lay still for several minutes. He stared at the ceiling. He'd been so emerged in his fantasy he actually began to believe it was real.

Should have known it was too good to be true.

He slowly lifted himself from his bed.

After dressing, he went into the kitchen, drank a couple cups of coffee, and stepped outside to glance around the yard. A few of the ranch hands were feeding the horses. James sat on the porch, dressed in a three-piece suit and bow tie, reading some documents.

"If I would have let you, you would have slept all day," James said, agitated.

Clint didn't respond, but glanced at the papers on the table. "What are you doing?"

"Working."

Clint tried to have small talk with the hopes that the last night's fiasco wouldn't be mentioned. After all, his father had just bailed him out of jail.

"On what?"

"I'm planning to start shipping oil to Mexico early fall so I'm finalizing the details."

Clint glanced at Bo, who was standing next to a broken fence with paint peeling off from it. A fresh gallon of white paint and a paint brush were on the ground.

James took a sip of tea and glanced at Clint. "Make yourself useful. Go help Bo."

He walked over, bent down, and picked up a hammer.

He lifted a board up with his smooth hands, took a fresh nail, and hammered it into the fence.

"If you place the nails a half inch apart, you'll make the gate more sturdy," Bo said, eyeing Clint's work.

Clint gave him a cold stare, picked up another nail and banged it into the wood. "OUCH!"

He threw the hammer down and kicked the fence. Bo laughed.

"What's so funny?" he snarled.

"You," Bo said, still laughing. "You ever built a fence? Matter a fact, you ever done a decent days work in yo life?"

Clint stared at him, rubbing his hand. "I've done plenty of work. Why don't ya mind your own business!"

Clint picked up the hammer, making another attempt, this time successfully knocking the nail into the wood.

Bo asked, "You glad to be back?" "I guess," Clint said.

"Yo dad was so scared. Camellia said she could hear him cryin' himself to sleep."

Clint remained silent.

"He heard from Paul and William."

Clint, who was kneeling while mending the fence, looked up at Bo. His tone changed, intense now. He asked. "How's Will? What'd he say?"

"He's alive. In one of the letters, he said his platoon came under heavy fire by machine guns and rifles. They'd lost mo men than they could count. Fought for hours. William fired his machine gun, killin' one man and knockin' out the weapons of two others. He crossed open ground to capture two of the men. Guns was goin' off around him. He threw a grenade at a couple of Nazis, killin' em.

Bo smiled, "I can see it now. Our little Will, takin' out the enemy."

Clint listened intently to every word. His heart raced as he visualized the event, as if he was there.

Bo said, "Will and his battalion worked they way a quarter mile along a ridge, attackin' hostile soldiers in they foxholes with grenades. They captured two mo enemy soldiers.

"He said he was gon get some kind of award for his bravery. That's yo brother-puttin' his life on the line to help others.

"Every time he wrote, he asked how you was. Yo dad didn't want him to worry. He said you was fine and comin' home soon."

Clint bent his head. "When's Will comin' home?" "Yo pop says a few months."

Clint didn't admit it to Bo, but he was proud of William.

"Can't wait to see him. It's the only thing good about being home. Knowin' I'll be seeing him soon." Clint looked at Bo. "I miss him."

"I know you do," Bo said. "And you'll be seein' him real soon."

He and Bo worked for hours before finally finishing the gate. Dripping with sweat he said, "I'm going for a swim."

Clint drove to a nearby store, picked up a six pack of beer and went to a large, crystal clear lake on his father's property. He spent most of his time there, especially in the summer. There was a small dock and a V-bottomed fishing boat large enough for at least ten people.

Clint swam and lay out on the dock for hours. At times the images of war would torment his mind, but he'd quickly down a beer to try and sooth his soul. It worked for a few minutes.

After several hours, he pulled himself together and headed up back to the house.

Sunday morning, Clint attended church with James. They sat on the second row. Clint was dressed in a nice pair of brown slacks and a cream shirt. The church was large enough to hold 500 people but about 300 attended regularly. James never missed a Sunday unless he was ill or taken away by business.

Clint sat slouched on the wooden pew. *It's miserable in here. It's only 70 degrees outside, but stuffy in here. I can't stand it. Come on preacher, let's get this over with.*

They sang three worship songs. A pretty, slender girl with a white dress and brunette hair styled in curls, began reading announcements aloud. Clint's eyes were fixed on her.

Maybe I'll ask her out. Nah, too nice.

He liked his women stunning and loose.

Afterwards, a thin, slightly balding pastor approached the pulpit. He cleared his throat before speaking into the microphone.

"Before I preach my message, I want to thank God for the safe return of Clint Edison who was serving and protecting his county in Germany for the last year."

Everyone applauded. Clint forced a smile.

The pastor cleared his throat and then said, "Let's turn to Isaiah 54:17. I want to focus on seven words: 'no weapon formed against you shall prosper.' This word "prosper" in the Hebrew language has been translated to mean "to break out" or "to push forward" or "to effect." No weapon that has been formed by hell, using your own grief or sorrow, shall affect you. Many of you have been through terrible and harsh times. You've been betrayed, rejected, and abandoned. But today, God wants you to know that his presence can heal you. God is greater than your trials."

James nodded his head, often. Clint was bored stiff. He checked his watch, frequently.

Thirty minutes later, the pastor said, "In closing, I want each of you to know that God has a plan for your life. His plan is to prosper you in ways you may not understand. We must surrender to him and allow his presence to cultivate us. We must choose to put others before ourselves and believe the best about people. It's God's grace that helps us to endure the hard times. God's grace will help you to overcome and live a victorious life. Everyone, please stand."

Clint exhaled as he stood. The pastor said a short prayer and excused the members.

He stepped down the stairs, went over to Clint and extended his hand, "Glad to have you back, Clint."

"Thanks. It's good to be back," Clint said, he shook his hand. "We prayed daily for your safety."

"Will you join us for dinner? Camellia has fixed a fine meal; short ribs and roasted corn," James said.

"I'd love to but I already have an invitation. Maybe next time." "Of course. Good day, Pastor and a wonderful message."

"Thank you, James. And Clint, again, it's good to have you home." He patted Clint on the back before being distracted by another member.

Clint glanced at his watch again. He hated the endless, boring conversations his father had talking to one church member after the other. They left the church fifteen minutes later.

When they arrived home, Clint flew upstairs and changed clothes. Eddie came over and after dinner, they spent the day at the lake, drinking.

One month flew by. Clint's days and nights had been spent drinking excessively, either with Eddie, Meg, or alone.

It was Friday night, eight o'clock. Clint and Eddie staggered out of the bar, laughing. Eddie's arm was wrapped around Clint's neck; it was hard for him to stand. They'd been there most of the evening. Eddie slipped and fell, laughing at himself as he glanced at Clint's pants. Clint had a large tear on the bottom right side of his jeans. He had ripped them on a tree branch, while walking back from the lake.

"Your dad has all that money and can't afford to buy you a decent pair of pants?" Eddie laughed again.

"Shut up and get up," Clint said, annoyed.

Eddie, Meg and Irene were right behind him, as they approached the car. Clint heard his name being called. He turned to see his nemesis, Dean. Dean was wearing a black leather jacket and had a cigarette dangling from his mouth. He was standing next to a newly polished Chevrolet Master with a pretty blonde and another boy. "What'd ya say to a race?"

Clint smirked. "Last time I beat you by a landslide."

"This time you might not be so lucky," Dean said, flicking the cigarette to the ground.

Clint glanced at Eddie, who shook his head. "Are you crazy? You've had too much to drink." "Doesn't matter. I could beat him half sleep." "I got fifty bucks says you'll lose," Dean said. "You're on."

They drove five miles to an open field. Eddie and the girls jumped out of the car.

Dean said, "Same as last time. We'll drive straight to old man Davis's place and turn around. The first one to cross this finish line wins."

Clint was in his car, smiling. The blonde stood in front of the cars with a bright blue scarf draped around her neck.

"You ready boys?"

Clint started his engine and pushed on the gas pedal several times. The sound of both engines revving echoed through the air.

"On the count of three . . . . one, two, three!"

Clint peeled rubber as both cars took off, speeding down the narrow country lane. Clint's eyes were glued to the road, only throwing a quick glance toward Dean from time to time.

Clint stayed calm. Dean pulled in front by inches, but then Clint inched ahead. The cars were neck and neck. Clint glanced in his rearview mirror and saw his friends screaming and cheering him on. The screech of the tires and the smell of burning rubber on the road brought tears to his eyes. There was nothing like being in control of a fast machine.

They drove in a straight line for a quarter mile before they reached the turn-around point. Clint shifted as fast as possible taking a slight lead. They were only minutes away from the finish line when Clint's right pant leg caught on the right pedal. He couldn't stop. The car began to swirl side to side on the road. He gripped the steering wheel, trying to free himself, but lost control. The car slipped down a hill. He managed to pry himself loose, open the car door, and jump out. Branches scratched his face as he fell down the hill, the car tumbling below him. He landed flat on his face and watched the car fall to its destruction as it smashed into a large oak tree.

In a daze, he heard the voices of his friends. "Clint, are you all right? Don't move. We'll get help."

He tried to move but cringed from the agonizing pain coming from his leg. His friends carried him up the hill. The car had left tire marks along the road.

Within thirty minutes, an ambulance arrived and took Clint to Glen Oaks Hospital.

His injuries were minor, several cuts to the face, bruises, and a sprained leg.

Clint stepped out of the exam room and into the waiting area, where he saw his father, James, shaking his head and looking at him scornfully.

"I'm tired, let's go home. We'll discuss this in the morning," James said.

When Clint opened his eyes the next morning, the hangover was creeping up from the bottom of his neck to the top of his head. It felt as if his head would burst open at any minute. He moaned from the pain in his leg. His dog spun around wagging his tail, looking for a cozy spot on the bed.

"Stay down, I'm not in the mood," Clint.

He turned over to glance at the clock: 11 a.m. He pulled a pillow over his head to block out the blazing sun shining through his bedroom window.

His mind was radiated with visions of his father's face at the emergency room. Clint was hardly intimidated by James, but dreaded the overbearing, senseless lecture he knew he'd get.

Clint lay in bed for two more hours.

He limped towards his bathroom. *My leg is killin' me.*

The doctor told him he'd be fine in a couple of weeks.

Clint glanced at himself in the mirror. His eyes were bloodshot, so he ran some cold water, slipped his hand under it, and rubbed it against his face. Grabbing a towel, he wiped himself dry.

He walked down the stairs in the long johns he'd slept in, taking small measured steps and leaning against the banister. As he approached the bottom, he heard footsteps coming towards him. As soon as his feet hit the marble tile floor, James stomped into the hallway, frowned and waved his finger at Clint.

"Need I say how disappointed I am with you! As hard as it was to see you go to war, I had hoped that it would have matured you." He threw his arms up in the air and said, "Nothing has changed! You are as immature today as you were when you left."

Clint looked at his father stone-faced, determined not to speak. He wouldn't admit he was wrong.

"This is the third car you have wrecked in three years. You've been home for less than one month, and you've been in one mess after another. What am I to do with you? Do you know how dangerous street racing is? You were lucky you didn't get killed. You could have killed someone else."

Clint went into the living room and slid down onto the sofa to rest his pounding head. James followed him.

"Don't walk away from me when I'm talking to you and look at me." Clint stared up at his father, fighting to control his temper.

"You were kicked out of two boarding schools, you barely passed the last. How can you be expected to help run the business?"

Finally, Clint broke his silence. "It was an accident. I lost control of the wheel."

James rubbed his forehead in frustration. "Do I look stupid, Clint? Do I appear to have been born yesterday? You were out drinking with your friends. You are an architect of your own destruction. I swear Clint . . . you are your worst enemy."

Clint rolled his eyes, listening to the immovable voice of his father. "This is the last time, Clint. I'm not buying you another car."

Clint's eyes widened and he could feel the color drain from his face. He glared at his father and slammed his hand down on a table next to him. "What am I supposed to do without a car! I told you it was an accident. It could have happened to anyone."

"Watch your tone, Clint."

James was silent for a moment. "You're determined to destroy your life, aren't you?"

Clint turned his head.

"I'm going into town. We will talk about this later." James stormed out of the house.

Clint shook his head, turned around, and hopped up the stairs on his right leg. He yelled down. "Camellia! . . . Camellia!"

She stepped into the hallway. "Yes Clint, what is it?"

"Bring a glass of orange juice and two aspirins to my room, please." "I'll have it up in a minute."

Clint limped back into his room and fell flat on his bed. He pulled the covers over his body and closed his eyes, trying to blot out his father's agitating voice. Clint was used to irritating his father. He figured in time, he would forgive him like he always did.

Chapter 6

That evening, Clint sat outside the backyard with Eddie, smoking a cigarette. The ground was covered with lush, green dales, dahlias, and white tulips. They had just finished eating baked chicken and mashed potatoes. His father had returned home two hours earlier and had eaten his supper in his study.

"So, your dad went nuts, huh?"

"That's putting it lightly," Clint said, derisively. "You are an architect of your own destruction." Clint spoke in a mocking voice. "That's what he said to me." He shook his head. "Told me I'm my worst enemy. Okay Pops, whatever you say." He inhaled another puff of smoke. "Tell you one thing. When I die, I'll die havin' the time of my life."

"Your dad usually gets over it . . . doesn't he?" "Don't care," said Clint, snapping his words.

Camellia stepped out on the porch and threw out a pan of scraps for the birds.

"Thank you for dinner, Camellia. It was good, as always," Eddie said. "You're welcome" she said, as she stepped back into the house.

"Hey, whacha say we take your father's boat out on the lake tomorrow." Clint nodded. "Okay."

"I'm thinkin' of sailin' around the world some day."

Clint smirked. "Where do you get your ridiculous ideas? You can't sail around the world, Eddie."

"Why not? I could be famous. Go in that, what-do-you-call-it book, world book of records—somethin' like that. You could come with me. We'd be so famous that we could get any girl we want."

Clint took a puff of his cigarette and threw it to the ground. Crushing it with his foot, he said, "I already get every girl I want. Tell you what. You sail around the world and when you get to French Rivera, I'll meet you there. I'll be the one sittin' on the beach surrounded by beautiful women."

The doorbell rang.

"Wonder who that is at this hour?" He stepped into the house through the French doors. Eddie was not far behind him.

There were two men dressed in military attire talking to his father. Clint froze as fear gripped him. He crossed his arms and shifted his weight to his right leg. *Why are they here? Is it one of my brothers?* His heart began to pound.

His father fell to the floor, sobbing and dropping his face onto his hands.

The military men turned and left.

Clint slowly moved to his father. "What is it?" he asked.

James looked up at him, tears where streaming down his face. He could barely talk. "William . . . has been killed."

Stunned, Clint froze. The words felt like a knife cutting though his heart. He was silent at first. His voice shook as he finally said, "There must be some mistake. He was supposed to come home in less than two months." "Paul will be flying home from Germany . . . tomorrow," James said.

Rage flooded Clint's body. Gasping for air, he clutched his stomach and flew out the door. He heard Eddie yelling for him, "Clint! Clint wait!"

He ran around the pond, passing dozens of oak trees. After two miles, when he could go no farther, he stopped, slid to the ground and cried. The anger that had overtaken him had melted into grief.

Eventually, he regained his composure and went back home.

He went in his room and lay on his bed, gazing up at the ceiling. It was a nightmare. He felt a hole in his heart. Images of his strong, tough brother flashed through his mind.

He remembered when Will had taught him how to drive and shoot a gun. They went hunting four times a year. He took his first trip to the big city with Will.

Tears fell down his cheeks. *Life will never be the same,* he thought to himself.

That morning, the door flew open at ten o'clock. James, who was sitting in the living room staring out the window, rubbed his eyes and stood up. "Who's there?" He walked towards the entrance of the house.

"It's me, Dad." Paul stood in the foyer. His shoulders looked broad in his uniform jacket. His head was shaved. James knew he was only 5'9", but he looked taller.

Tears came to James's eyes as he grabbed his son and hugged him for a long time.

"I'm sorry. I wish there were something I could have done," Paul said. His eyes were bloodshot.

"There was nothing you could have done," James said, wiping the tears from his eyes. He's with God now."

"When is the funeral?"

"They are bringing his body back this afternoon. We'll probably bury him Saturday . . . or Sunday, I'm not sure. Come, let me look at you. I've missed you. Are you okay?"

"I'm okay. The war was hard. Harder than I ever dreamed."

Paul had spent the first three years with Patton's army, tramping in the forest in North Africa and then in Europe.

James wrapped his arm around his son's neck and led him into the dining room. Camellia had made some muffins.

"Have something to eat," James said.

"I don't have much of an appetite. I think I'll go and unpack my things. Where's Clint?"

"He's still asleep," James said. "So how's he taking this?"

James eyes narrowed and his voice softened. "He's quiet, but I know the grief overwhelms him. He and William were so close."

Paul nodded.

"We can talk later, Dad." "Of course. Get settled in."

He grabbed his bag and headed to his room.

That afternoon at two o'clock, Clint walked into the living room to look for his father. His eyes went directly to the photo on the ebony wooden table. He stared at it for some time; William in fatigues, and next to him, Paul, also in his uniform. He looked into the glass case filled with the shiny trophies his brothers had earned. Paul had trophies for both basketball and football from junior high through high school. He'd also won trophies at the annual Rodeo in town. William had earned a trophy from the National Football Championship, chess club, and several academic achievement awards which included a certificate from being the president of the Honor Society. He was in the top ten of his class, received straight A's in college and was planning to go to law school. But he wasn't always a model son; he was strong-willed.

Clint remembered a time when he saw Will climb out the window, jumped on his horse, and meet his rough-housing friends who were waiting for him down the street at two o'clock in the morning. He showed up around seven a.m. the next day. James was furious. William was on restriction for a month. That was not the only time Clint could remember him getting in trouble. Will didn't always get caught. Will could break from their father's instruction, but still have a deep respect for him.

Clint heard voices coming from outside. He stepped out and joined Paul and his father on the grounds. William's body was due to arrive at the railroad station in thirty minutes.

Clint walked up to his brother. "Good to see you." "You too," Paul said. They embraced.

"I want to go with you . . . to the railroad station." James nodded.

Clint slid into the back of his father's car. Although he hadn't seen or heard from Paul in over a year, they didn't talk the entire drive.

When they arrived at the station, Clint stood, staring as the train approached. He knew his brother would eventually come home, but he had never imagined it would be in a casket. *This is the worst day of my life*, he thought.

Once the train stopped, four uniformed men stepped down, carrying a casket. They took William's body to the morgue. The funeral was scheduled for Sunday at noon.

Sunday's gray morning skies and chill winds that blew down 14th Avenue in Dallas framed Clint's mood. It was March 18, 1945. Over 30 friends and family were present for the funeral, including Camellia. She pulled out a handkerchief and wiped her eyes. James and Paul sat on either side of her.

The minister said a few kind words. He spoke of how proud he was of William and the service he'd done for his country. William had been fighting with the 99th Infantry Division for over two years. He fought in "The Battle of the Bulge". It was the largest land battle of World War II the United States participated in.

William was awarded the Silver Star for his heroism of risking his life and capturing four enemy soldiers.

Several people close to William spoke about the kind, generous, caring man he was and how he would be greatly missed.

Clint stared at his father. He had a bewildered expression on his face. It was obvious the grief was overwhelming.

Clint slowly lifted himself off the chair and stood before their friends and family. He took a deep breath and said, "My brother was my best friend. He was my hero." His voice was trembling. "Will taught me so much. He was never afraid of anything. If I could turn out to be like anyone, I'd want to be just like him."

He sat down next to Camellia. She gripped his hand and wept.

After the funeral, everyone met at James' mansion and ate food prepared by friends of the family. Camellia was too grief stricken to cook.

Clint stood on the balcony with Eddie and a few of their friends. They shared the fond memories they had of William. Clint remained quiet for most of the time.

He went into the house and glanced at a photo of his brother in uniform on a round table. His heart felt empty, lost. Tears fell from his face. The pain of losing his brother was almost unbearable.

Chapter 7

Clint groaned. Agonizing pain pounded in his head. He was kneeling on the hard concrete floor in a jail cell at the downtown county jail. Clint had been there all night. He'd just finished vomiting for the third time.

His head whipped around when he heard metal banging against the bars. Paul was standing next to a police officer outside his cell. A look of disapproval swept over Paul's face.

"You made bail," the officer said.

Clint slowly lifted himself up. He rubbed his head hoping the headache would go away. The guard opened the door. Clint briefly glanced at Paul, followed the officer, and stopped at a desk where another said, "Here are your things."

The officer handed him his wallet, watch, and car keys.

He and Paul walked down the stairs. Silence receded between them at first.

"Where's your car?"

Clint could tell by the tone of his voice that Paul was agitated. He didn't want to make matters worse so he lied and said, "At Eddie's." He'd actually left it at the bar.

They got into Paul's car. Ten minutes passed with not one word spoken. Finally, Paul said, "It's a good thing Dad left for work early today. He wasn't home to witness another one of your stupid mishaps."

Clint didn't answer.

"I'm sitting at the table eating breakfast. I was planning to go into town with some friends, when I get a call from the police station. Your brother got in a fight at a bar. He's locked up in the jail . . . when you gonna grow up, Clint? I'm sick and tired of watching you humiliate Dad. You're the most selfish person I know."

"Whadda you care," Clint said.

"I don't! But I care about Dad, which is a heck of a lot more than I can say about you. You can't even blame William's death for the mess you bring on yourself . . . and this family. You were a nuisance way before he died."

"It ain't none of your business what I do with my life!" Clint yelled. "It's my business when I'm left to bail you out!"

Clint tightened his jaw. The veins in his arm began to show. "You should've left me in jail then! I'm sick and tired of the lectures. I'm sick of this place."

"We'll I'm sick of you!" yelled Paul "Stop the car. NOW!" Clint screamed.

Paul skidded over on the side of the road, jerking them forward. Clint got out of the car and slammed the door shut. He watched as Paul sped off.

Clint walked eight miles to the bar to get his car and drove home. He arrived home at six that evening and went straight upstairs and stayed in his room the rest of the night.

⁓᷍᥊᥊᷍⁓

Clint had slept in. He'd demolished two six packs of beer, drinking himself unconscious. After a shower, he dressed and went downstairs. He walked into the kitchen, opened the cabinet, and grabbed a bottle of aspirin. Pouring water, he swallowed three pills.

He glanced through the window out back. His father was walking out of the warehouse. Camellia was working in the garden. He remembered he had heard Paul say the day before that he planned to go hunting with some friends.

He wandered into the living room, plopped down on the green plush sofa, and leaned back on the pillow.

"Clint . . . Clint." It was his father's voice. Clint didn't respond.

Again, "Clint."

James walked into the living room. "Didn't you hear me calling you?" His eyes were arched, he was making a fist.

Clint remained silent.

"For years, I've worked like a field hand to get where I am. What haven't I given you? You don't care about the ranch, education, or your family. Tell me, Clint . . . what do you care about?"

Clint crossed his arms and looked at his father, coldly.

"Your brother has been gone for four months. How long will you continue to drown your grief with alcohol?"

Again, Clint didn't respond.

He sat down next to Clint. "Paul and I both grieve for William too. His voice was softer now. This has been a difficult year. The war has taken its toll on all of us, but William would want you to go on with your life. I don't know why God allowed your brother to die, but I know he's in a good place."

Not another lecture, thought Clint, shifting his attention away from his father; he looked outside. *What I wouldn't give for a shot of whisky right now.*

"Why can't you be more responsible and hard working, like your brother? Before he could say another word.

"I don't wanna be like Paul! I don't wanna be like you!"

James looked at Clint solemnly. "I don't know what caused such hatred and anger, especially for me. But in spite of your feelings, I love you, Clint. I pray for you daily. I pray that God will show you how much he loves you and."

"Enough!" Clint threw the pillow beside him on to the floor. "I don't wanna to hear it. I don't want to hear about your God. I'm sick of your religion, I'm sick of this place, I'm sick of everything!" Clint stood. "I need to get out of here. I want my money."

James leaned forward.

"You said when I turned 21, I'd could get my inheritance. Well . . . I want it, now."

"Clint, you're not thinking straight."

"Don't tell me what I'm thinking! I'm sick of you always analyzing me." He slammed his fist on the table. "I can't stand it here. I don't want to run a ranch, I never did. I need to go where I can be free."

In a disconcerted voice, James said, "And where do you suppose that would be?"

"I don't know . . . . Italy. Maybe Switzerland. I just need to leave."

"I need to go into town, Clint. We'll talk about this when you're sane." James was walking out the door.

"I'm not going to change my mind," Clint said. James turned. "We'll talk again after supper."

"No . . . now! I'm gettin' outta here. I'll be gone by the end of the week." Clint stormed up the stairs, grabbed his suitcase, and began packing his clothes.

A week passed and James was unable to convince Clint to stay. Deep down inside, James knew the day would come when Clint would venture out on his own. He dreaded the thought, knowing Clint's history and that his choices had led to destruction and danger. He'd almost gotten killed in the car race. He feared for Clint's safety, but he knew he wouldn't change his mind. His emotions were a mix of grief and pain. He felt as though he was losing another son.

James was affectionate and verbally declared love and support for his sons. Paul and William returned the affection, but Clint kept his distance. James wanted a real relationship and good conversation with Clint; the kind that fathers and sons have. The kind he had with his other sons. Clint had always been more reserved than his other children, but now, after a year at war in Germany, he was even more reticent.

James knew that losing their mother was hardest on Clint. He had become distant and hard. James tried to fill the void with gifts. He gave Clint everything money could buy, but it never seemed to be enough. As the years progressed, Clint became more and more distant and their relationship more estranged.

Clint had remained silent regarding his experience in the war. When James asked questions or tried to discuss it, Clint gave a superficial response like, "It was hard" or "I'm just glad it's over."

Paul on the other hand, talked incessantly about the war. James sensed it helped for Paul to express his emotions and fears. Paul talked about the time their battalion had stumbled upon an enemy camp. When the Germans opened fire, Paul thought for sure he would die. They fought for hours and lost 21 men. He told James that next to losing William, it was the hardest experience he'd ever faced.

James could only hope and pray that the time he and Clint spent apart might eventually bring them closer together.

On Friday, Clint dressed in a blue shirt, blue jeans, and nicely polished boots. He walked down the stairs carrying a suitcase and a brown duffle bag holding books, shaving cream, and toothpaste.

He walked onto the front porch. James and Paul were sitting at the glass table drinking coffee. Eddie was waiting by his black battered pick-up truck to take Clint to the airport.

James rose to his feet and strolled over to Clint with a grim look on his face. Not to seem too insensitive, he hugged his father. "I'll be all right. I promise."

"Where are you going?" "France."

"Why would you go back to Europe? The war is barely over." "I'm actually going to the French Riviera."

"Have you made all of your travel plans?" "I'll take a ship to France from New York."

James looked annoyed. "I still believe moving so far away is foolishness."

He regretfully handed him an envelope with $20,000 cash. "I will wire the rest of the money when you arrive at your destination."

Camellia stepped outside. Her eyes were red from crying. "I'll miss you." She hugged him.

"I'll to miss you too, Camellia."

Tears ran down her cheeks. "Write, okay? I'll expect to hear from you often. Be careful and stay out of trouble."

"I will."

"There is one more thing, Clint." James walked back over to the table, grabbed a little, worn out black book, a small notebook, and handed them to Clint.

"The Bible is to give you strength and the notebook is to write to us."

Clint nodded and placed both items in his brown duffle bag. The tone of James' voice deepened. "Son, I know how unhappy you've been here. But remember this . . . no one is in control of your happiness but you. You have the power to change anything about yourself and your life that you want to change. And remember, son. No matter what you've done or how far you stray. You can always come home. I love you, Clint."

"I know."

Clint hugged his father, again. "I'll write as soon as I arrive."

Paul ambled over to Clint. Clint shook his brother's hand and said, "Take care of Dad."

"I hope you know what you're doing. Whatever you do, be careful. I don't know if Dad can take losing another son."

"I'll be all right."

Clint threw his suitcase and duffle bag in the back of the truck and jumped into the passenger seat. He waved goodbye to his father as they drove away.

Clint stretched out his arms and clasped his hands behind his head. "Glad to be leavin' here. In one week, I'll be sitting on the beach on the French Riviera with more women than I know what to do with."

"How much did your father give you?"

"Twenty thousand. Once I get to France, he'll wire four hundred thousand dollars more."

Eddie almost veered off the road. "You gotta be kiddin' me. What're ya gonna do with all that cash?"

"I'm buyin' a Villa, a couple of cars, and a few women to go along with them," Clint said, haughty.

Eddie laughed.

"For the first time in my life, I'm actually excited about something. And losing William . . . well there's nothing for me here anymore."

"What about Paul."

"He can't stand me . . . never could. Honestly, the feeling's mutual. It's a new life of freedom."

"How long you gonna be gone?"

"I don't know. Not sure if I'll ever come back here."

"You're a rich man's son who plays with money and wants to taste the world, but it ain't like you had it bad. You got everything now.

"It's like livin' in prison," Clint said. "The sooner I'm free, the better."

Clint looked at Eddie. "You're the only one I'll miss." He patted him on the shoulder.

"Me too," Eddie said.

Thirty-five minutes later, they arrived at the Dallas Airport. Clint got out of the car and grabbed his luggage.

Eddie walked over to him. "I'll miss you. Write or call okay?" "I will." Clint hugged him.

He boarded the airplane one hour later. The flight from Texas to New York took about six hours.

Clint took a cab to the port where the cruise ship was docked. It was bustling with people of all races walking the wooden docks. The weather in New York was scorching so hot that his shirt was drenched in his own sweat. He glanced up and saw an enormous vessel. Clint studied the massive ship. There was a rounded stern and a richly decorated clipper bow. The ship was scheduled to leave in six hours, but they were allowing people to board early.

When he boarded the gangplank towards the luxurious ship, a sense of freedom overtook him. He was leaving one life behind to pursue another; filled with fun and excitement.

A stout, short captain with a white cap covering his sandy brown hair said, "Welcome aboard the Hamburg America Line. Enjoy your stay."

Clint nodded. "Thanks."

He evaluated the place. The lobby had marble floors and mellow wood walls. Dozens of people shoved their way past him carrying large suitcases.

He climbed the spiral staircase to the second deck where he walked into his elegant, first class cabin overlooking the magnificent deep blue ocean. Fully equipped with a full size bed, private bathroom, couch, coffee table and chairs, and a porthole view. Clint strode over to the sink and lifted a class pitcher of ice cold water and filled an elegant crystal glass. He gulped the water, then moved over to the bed and threw himself down. Landing on his back, he thought to himself, *This is the life. Where should I go first . . . Nice, Paris, Italy, or Britain?* A flashback of his comrade, Frazier, entered his mind as he sat up on the bed and grabbed his leather wallet from his back pocket. Clint opened it and pulled out the card with Frazier's address and phone number. Thinking, *if I get too bored, maybe I'll look him up? I doubt that will happen.* He smiled as he put the card back in the wallet and lay back on the bed.

He'd received a letter from Nick two weeks earlier. He'd been walking with the help of wooden cane, married his long-time girlfriend one month earlier, and hoped to start a family soon. Clint hadn't written him back.

After about fifteen minutes, Clint dozed off.

Chapter 8

A round six o'clock that evening, dressed in an expensive tailored black suit, Clint stood on the upper deck. The air was hot and the wind, crisp. The sky was filled with shades of orange, and the sun was gradually dropping. Though he felt a sense of freedom, loneliness and isolation loomed over him.

Not a day went by when thoughts of Will's death didn't torment him. The two people he loved most were gone; his mother and brother. He flashed back to a time when his mother held his hand as they walked acres of green meadows to the lake. They swam and played for hours. He almost hated her for dying.

Clint glanced at the gold Rolex watch he'd purchased at an expensive jewelry store several days earlier. It was six thirty in the afternoon so he decided to take a tour of the ship before dinner.

He walked past a dining room and out to the second floor deck. There was a 35-foot long swimming pool and people sitting at dozens of tables in the shaded areas. He climbed the stairs to the next floor and peeked into a game room. Decorative lamps hovered over each of the gaming tables where men in sophisticated attire smoked cigarettes and played poker and blackjack. Others tried their hands at roulette and dice.

Clint moved past a library and entered another elegant dining hall with ebony wooden floors. The room was spectacular. Ornate chandeliers hung from the walls. Waiters hovered over elegantly dressed men and women who sat at tables decorated with white linen cloth and crystal candle holder centerpieces. A live band with violins, trumpets, flutes, and saxophones played softly while several couples danced. A young pretty hostess approached. "Just one for dinner?"

"Yes."

She led him past the dance floor to the far side of the room. As she pulled out a chair she smiled. "Enjoy your dinner."

"Thanks."

Clint ordered fresh crab, lobster, and linguini. As he bit into his linguini, he glanced around room and noticed a beautiful woman with blazing red hair, sitting alone only a few tables away. He watched her take a bite of her salad and use a white silk napkin to gently wipe her lips.

Clint leaned back in his chair with confidence. *She's a knock-out. I wonder if she's alone. I'll make a move, soon.*

Twenty minutes later, he took one last bite of linguini, set his fork down, and was getting ready to get up when a slender young man dressed in a black suit walked up to his table. His jet black hair was slicked back with gel. He glanced at Clint with his striking green eyes. "Mind if I join you, I don't like eating alone."

Clint looked at the stranger, callously. He paused, studying him. With his outstretched hand he pointed to the empty chair. "Have a seat."

"Thanks."

The young man sat down and then yelled out to a waiter passing by, "Waiter, bring me a glass of Cabernet Sauvignon." He looked at Clint, "Would you like something?"

"No. I'm fine," Clint said.

"So what's your name?" the man asked. "Clint."

"My mom said I looked like a teddy bear when I was born, so she called me Teddy, but my friends call me Ted. Ted Ross. So Clint, where ya headed?"

"The Riviera."

Ted grinned. "We'll, that is where the ship is headin'. Actually, that's where I'm headed too. You got family there?"

"No."

"Me neither."

Clint turned the face of his watch towards him. It was eight-thirty. He analyzed Ted. He was nice looking, seemed friendly, kept a smile on his face, and spoke with a slight accent. Clint couldn't stop his gaze from drifting back to the redhead. He leaned back in his chair. "Where are you from?"

"I was born and raised in the Bronx. I moved." He paused for a brief moment. "I just got out of the hole."

Clint tilted his head.

"I was at the Great Meadow Maximum Security Prison in upstate New York."

Clint was surprised. The man had a clean-cut look and seemed to be a nice person. It was hard to believe he'd done time.

"I got in some trouble with the law—drugs. January of 1945, I was released. I am the younger of two sons. My mother raised us."

Ted glanced around the room for a brief moment. "My father committed suicide when I was ten."

Clint displayed no emotion.

"He shot himself. I guess he decided to take the easy way out. Guess he didn't care much about me and my brothers . . . not enough to live. I'll never forget the last words he spoke to me. He said 'son, sometimes the best way to end a problem is to cut it loose.' I'm guessin' he thought he was the problem. After that, I lived in fear that my mother would die too."

Clint wondered why a complete stranger would be opening up to him this way. He didn't know the man.

"I think that's why I was attracted to crime in my early years. When I was 18, I moved out on my own and got a job at a supermarket. I met a woman who introduced me to opium. I got caught up with the wrong people and landed in jail. So that's my life in a nutshell. Enough about me, what about you?"

Clint paused for a brief moment. "I fought the war in Europe, got injured, and went home. My father owns a ranch in Texas."

Clint looked over at the beautiful redhead. She was leaving. He looked at his watch. "It's gettin' late, I'm a little tired. Mind if I cut the conversation short?"

"Not at all. Maybe I'll run into you sometime . . ."

Clint heard his voice drift off as he hurried across the room, trying to catch up with the woman. He stepped outside, looked to his right, then left, and ran down the stairs to look around.

"I lost her," he said out loud, frustrated.

He went into a smoke-filled gaming room and sat at one of the blackjack tables. There were seven people sitting around the table. Thousands of dollars were piled high next to the dealer. A large distinguished looking man with a goatee sat directly in front of Clint. He was dressed in a three-piece stripe suit, adorned with a collection of two gold watches and a collar pin. He threw down at least $3,000 in cash. A tall, angular man in a gray suit and shiny black shoes sat to the right of Clint.

Clint reached for his wallet and opened it, pulling out a wad of bills. He threw $2,000 cash on the table in front of him, between two betting circles. He lit a cigarette. The smoke drifted into the air.

Chips were stacked next to the dealer. Red chips were worth $100, green $500.

"How do you want that?" the dealer asked. "Green," Clint said.

The dealer exchanged the cash and then he dealt the hands.

Clint took a quick glance at his cards. The distinguished man rolled the tip of his goatee several times, glaring at Clint with his piercing green eyes. Clint glared back at the man straight-faced and somber.

The tall angular man to the right of Clint said, "Hit." He laid down two jacks and an eight. "I'm out," he said. One by one people opted out of the game.

The redhead entered the room. She stepped over to the blackjack table and watched. Clint couldn't help staring. She was the most beautiful woman he'd ever seen.

"Hit," said the large man across from him.

After glancing at his cards, the man gave the dealer a cold stare look. He threw down his cards. It was an ace, ten and two.

"Stand."

Clint smirked as he slowly turned over his cards. He had one jack and an ace. The dealer turned over his cards, two jacks. "Winner," he said.

The redhead walked away. Clint collected $5,000 worth of chips, followed the woman outside and watched her walk up the stairs. She stopped to lean against the rails. Her long red evening gown complemented her slender figure. Her hair blew away from her face as she stared out at the deep blue ocean. She appeared unfailingly charming, and she looked like she came from money. She pulled a cigarette out from a small alligator bag. He moved closer to her with confidence and could smell her velvety rose fragrance.

"Light?" he asked. Clint had an easy cavalier way about him.

She looked at him with cynical brown eyes, full sensual lips. A sparkling diamond necklace on her neck glistened in the moon light. She moved towards him and tilted her right hand in his direction. She wore luscious pink fingernail polish. He lit her cigarette. She blew a large puff into the evening sky.

"What's your name?" he asked.

"Ava," she said, before taking another puff. "And you are?" "Clint."

She inhaled. "Well Clint, nice to meet you."

"Are you alone?" he asked. "Why do you ask?"

"No reason. Just curious." "Yes."

"Do you sail much?" he asked.

Her chin went up just a fraction. "Yes, I love the ocean." She glanced out at the sea. Her hair seemed to turn a deep auburn as the light of the moon shone on it. "It's an incredible view . . . wouldn't you agree."

Looking directly at her he said, "Yes . . . beautiful." She smiled.

"So, what's someone so beautiful doing on a cruise ship alone?" Clint asked, whose gaze was still fixed on her.

"I'm recently divorced. I came on the trip to celebrate and also for business. I'm meeting investors in France. My father is a commercial real estate tycoon. We own property in Las Vegas and New York City. I am planning to spend a couple of days in the Riviera first . . . to relax, shop, see the sights. My father thought it would be good to get away."

"Your ex-husband's loss is someone else's gain."

She grinned. "Tell me Clint, do you like to dance?" "Matter of fact I do." She watched him glance at his watch. "Nice watch."

"Thank you. Shall we?" He motioned in the direction of the club.

When they entered the large dining hall, an orchestra was playing and singing lively music. The conductor, a short black singer, was dressed in a white and blue striped outfit.

Clint and Ava stepped onto the floor and danced to the spellbinding American music. Will had taught Clint to dance. From there, they sat at the bar and drank. Clint was having the time of his life. He invited Ava to his room for a nightcap, but she declined.

She kissed him on the cheek and said "Goodnight."

He went to his room, stashed the money he'd won in a drawer next to his bed walked into the bathroom. He brushed his teeth, and threw himself on the bed. Clint couldn't remember when he'd had so much fun. He smiled staring at the ceiling. *I give her a week before she falls in love with me*, he thought to himself. *I'll keep her around for a little while. There are, however, better fish in the sea.* After a few minutes, he fell asleep.

Clint spent every possible moment with Ava walking along the deck, enjoying the fine shows. He found her vivacious, stimulating, and hauntingly beautiful. They ate, swam, danced and gambled. The days were filled with fun, and nights with romance.

He had run into Ted on occasion. He and a lady friend he'd met joined them for dinner a few nights. Clint was captivated by Ava and felt alive for the first time in his life.

~∞∞∞∞~

The date was Sunday, July 9, 1945. The ship was scheduled to arrive in France the next day.

It was four o'clock in the afternoon. Clint stood in front of the mirror of his bathroom, combing his hair. A stack of money, totaling $7,000 he'd won from gambling, was on the desk next to his bed. The rest of his money his dad had given him was hidden in his duffle bag tucked under his bed. He'd plan to deposit the money in the bank once he arrived in France. There was a knock on the door.

"Who is it?" "Ava,"

"Come in."

The door opened. He smiled as Ava stepped into his room wearing a white, full skirt made of pure silk, and a light green blouse. She looked at him teasingly with her deep brown eyes and smiled as she moved closer to him and kissed him on the lips. "This has been a wonderful trip. I'm starting to fall for you."

He kissed her and raked his fingers through her hair. "It's only just begun. There's much to see in Europe. We'll see everything together."

"Come on, let's go. I'm starved," she said.

She grabbed his hand and pulled him towards the door. They ate dinner on the deck. Clint was amused at everything she did. She was unlike any woman he'd met; electrifying, intelligent, she lived life on the edge. They danced and drank all evening. It was almost midnight and the casino was still bright, airy, and lively, and filled with people.

"Let's go back to your room," Ava said.

He slurred his words. "That sounds like a good idea."

Clint could barely walk. He stumbled to his feet, laughing the entire time until they finally arrived at his room. He slipped and fell as he searched for the keys. She laughed feverishly as she tried to help him up. He finally managed to open the door, took three steps, and passed out.

Chapter 9

With a groan, Clint rolled over on his stomach. He felt light headed. Bleary-eyed, he used his hands to shield his eyes from the glaring light entering his room through the white sheer curtains. He was still fully dressed. *I must have passed out.*

After a few minutes, he lifted himself up, and stumbled into his bathroom. He splashed water on his face, reached for a towel and looked down at his wrist to realize there was nothing but a pale band of skin where his expensive watch had been. He went back into his bedroom, glanced at the table next to his bed. The stash of cash from his winnings was gone too. His heart began to race as he searched for the money and watch.

Frantic, he looked under his bed, grabbed his duffle bag, opened it, and breathed a sigh of relief. The money his father had given him was still there.

Rage flooded his body. *How stupid can I be? She robbed me.* He said aloud, "That worthless, no good . . . ."

He kicked at a wastebasket near the bed. His face felt hot and he could feel the blood flow through his veins. *When I get my hands on her . . . I should have known she was too good to be true. When I find her, I swear I'll kill her.*

He simmered down after a few minutes. *Maybe there's another explanation. Maybe we were both robbed. Or maybe she left and someone else took the money.* He tried to convince himself she wasn't only interested in his money. Embarrassed to admit it, he was falling for her.

After packing his clothes, he left the room and knocked on Ava's door, but heard no answer. He searched the decks and dining room, but couldn't find her. It was as if she disappeared, along with his 7,000 dollars.

Hours passed as Clint stood on deck staring out at the rich blue-green sea. He felt empty.

Clint prided himself on being able to get any woman he wanted. Ava was unlike any woman he'd ever known. She had an overpowering magnetism. He re-played the times they'd spent together at the late nightcaps, brunches, dancing and drinking in the casino and thought surely she'd fallen in love with him. But it was all an act. He was angry with her for robbing him and angry with himself for having feelings for her.

How could she do that? I'm guessin' she's not rich and her father's not a *successful entrepreneur . . . she's a common thief.* He shook his head. *Did she have any feelings for me? I can't believe I let myself fall for her. Never again,* he thought.

From a distance he could see Nice; with its hilltop perched villages and neighboring Alps. The scenery was breathtaking but his mind was fixed on Ava.

The ship docked and he disembarked at 2:00 p.m. He stood on the dock for almost an hour, hoping to see Ava. She was nowhere to be found.

He grabbed his bags and looked for a taxi. He heard his name being called.

"Clint, where ya headed?"

Clint turned around. It was Ted. "To a hotel."

"Mind if I share your cab?" "No. Taxi!" Clint yelled.

A cab pulled up.

He climbed in the car. "Hotel La Perouse." Ted got in on the other side. "So where's Ava?" Still burning with anger, he turned his head. "Let me guess, you dumped her."

"Something like that. Settling down isn't a priority," he murmured. He leaned back in the seat. "I'm not a one woman man."

Ted shook his head. "You're heartless," he said.

"She'll get over it," he said, arrogantly confident.

They arrived at the hotel forty minutes later. The hotel was at least 15 stories high. It was tucked into the hillside below a chateau and just a short walk from the Old Nice.

Clint handed the driver 30 francs and got out of the car.

"My bags are in the cab, he said to the skinny red-haired bellboy as he entered the lobby.

He walked up to the front desk. A stout, bearded clerk was behind the desk helping two guests.

"Bonjour."

"Hi," Clint said. "Do you speak English?" "Of course. How many?"

"One. I'd like a suite, if you have it."

"We can accommodate you." He checked his book. "Yes, we have a nice suite on eleventh floor overlooking the ocean. How will you be paying?"

"Cash."

Ted was given a room on the fifth floor. The bell boy led Clint to his room, set his luggage onto the floor, and was handed three francs.

"Have a nice stay, sir."

Clint stepped onto the thick white carpet. The room was filled with antiques, tapestries, and art. He studied the handcrafted furniture as he moved into the bathroom. There was a shiny white tub and a double sink with marble tile. He stepped outside onto the terrace. The room overlooked the Mediterranean. It was beautiful, but Clint wasn't impressed. Clint was used to the finest money could buy.

Clint walked back inside and stretched out on top the white comforter covering the King-sized bed. He put his hands behind his head and stared at the ceiling. Anger welled up inside him.

*I can't believe I was*ted *my entire trip on her. I hope I never see her again.*

Minutes later, the telephone rang. He reached over to the desk next to his bed and picked up the receiver. "Hello."

"Hey, you hungry? Wanna get something to eat?" Ted asked. "Yeah, I'll meet you in the lobby in twenty minutes."

After a quick shower, he dressed in a in a pair of white pants and blue shirt and left the room.

They ate at a quiet restaurant overlooking a pretty fountained square in Old Nice. A waiter with jet black hair spoke in French. "Monsieur, may I bring you something to drink?"

Ted responded in French. "Two glasses of Cabernet Sauvignon." The waiter nodded and walked away.

"I ordered a couple glasses of wine. Hope that's okay." Clint nodded. "Where you learn to speak French?"

"College. I went for two years. I don't speak it that great, just enough to get by."

Minutes later the waiter returned with their drinks. "Merci."

Ted insisted on paying the bill. Clint wondered how he could afford it. He seemed to have money to burn yet he never spoke of an authentic job. But as long as it didn't affect him, he didn't care.

They ate tiny fried ravioli with gazpacho sauce and cocottes.

After dinner, they toured the city. It was filled with expensive shops and fashionable people. They headed east towards old town. The streets were narrow and the alleys, windy, lined with faded 17th and 18th century buildings. Families were selling crafts and produce.

There were neo-classical, arcaded buildings painted in shades of red ochre and a flower market with a flamboyant array of carnations, violets, jonquils and roses.

Rows of grand cafes and villas were lined a quiet, un-crowded beach on the edge of the main road. Light traffic whizzed past as they walked on the sand mixed with pebbles before returning to the hotel.

At night, they went to the Cabaret du Casino Kuhl. When they entered the room, they were surrounded by glitter and the chatter of sophisticated glamorous people. Clint led Ted to the bar.

He leaned forward with his elbow on the bar, "Two beers."

The bartender poured two beers and handed them to Clint. Clint slid him a few bills, then turned towards the direction of the stage where he watched a juggler tossing rings through the air with skill, catching them one at a time. When he was done, he took a bow and walked off stage, as the audience applauded.

Then a skinny tall comedian appeared from behind the curtains.

"Hello everyone, welcome to Nice. I had a dream last night, anyone ever have a dream?" His eyes searched the audience for a response.

"You ever have a good dream, and then wake up right in the good part and they you're back in your stinking life again? You fall asleep and try to dream it again. That never works. Always end up with some weird mutation of my original dream. Like, in the first dream, I was having dinner with Greta Garbo, and we were gazing in each other's eyes. Then, I woke up. So, I fell asleep again and ended up gazing into the eyes of a bulldog, named Bo Jo. Horrible thing is, when I woke up, there he was staring and licking at my face."

The sound of laughter filled the room.

The comedian went on to say, "A completely inebriated man was stumbling down the street with one foot on the curb and one foot in the gutter. A cop pulled up and said, "I've got to take you in, pal. You're obviously drunk."

Our wasted friend asked, "Officer, are ya absolutely sure I'm drunk?" "Yeah, buddy, I'm sure," said the copper. "Let's go."

Breathing a sigh of relief, the wino said, "Thank goodness, I thought I was crippled."

Again, laughter filled the place. He told one joke after another. They made their way to the formal gaming room as applauses for the comedian died down. There was an exclusive area for slot machines to the far right.

Clint played black jack while Ted watched. At midnight, they left the casino. Clint had lost a little over $1,000 at the black jack table, but he didn't care. The adventure was invigorating and he loved it.

Clint had crepes and fresh fruit for breakfast on the terrace of his hotel room, then drove to a lively pier and shopped. He bought another expensive watch to replace the one that was stolen.

He visited the Musee de Arts Asiatiques. He strolled the aisle, eyeing the brilliant artwork. He examined a piece called "Cloche Boy". It had the shape of a gold bell. He couldn't read the writing below because everything was written in French. Next to it a piece of art called "Robe de cour". It looked like a silk gold dress from the 18th century. From the accessories, it looked Chinese.

There were tons of ceramics and devotional carvings. After an hour, he left and joined Ted for dinner back at the hotel.

Clint found France exciting; everything he had dreamed. He'd written his father a brief note shortly after arriving saying he was okay and that he'd received the money. Other than that, he hadn't contacted him.

Chapter 10

Clint dumped a handful of lotion on the palm of his hand and rubbed it on the sun-darkened back of a French model he'd met the previous night. Clint had commitment issues. He never dated a woman longer than a month.

He rented an extravagant 80-foot yacht for a week. He and Ted sailed along an exclusive waterfront. The coastline was striking, with a beach that rested beneath a hillside of heavy shrubs.

Ted's date, Anna, who he met several months ago at a nightclub, dove into the cool, blue ocean. Ted stood on the deck of the ship getting ready to jump. They had been in France for almost five months, the weather was hot, but Ted's legs were still pure white. He avoided the sun because he burned easily. Clint watched as he took a giant breath and then dove into the ocean.

He and Anna splashed around in the water.

"Hey," Ted yelled, coming up for air. "Get in. The water's great."

"Later," Clint said.

Clint reached up for a slab of cheese on a marble sideboard next to him and his date, took a bite, and then he took a sip of Dom Pérignon Champagne. He set the glass down and lay on his back with the sun was glaring down on his face.

Life was on a plateau. Clint spent money like that day was his last. He surrounded himself with gorgeous people, visited the finest places, and dated only the most beautiful woman. Could life get any better?

"Lunch is ready," the white-uniformed waiter said.

"Good, I'm starving." Clint lifted himself up, stretched out his arm motioning for Gina to take his hand and helped her up. He yelled down to Ted, "Lunch is ready. Let's eat."

Ted and Anna both climbed up the ladder. After drying themselves off, they followed Clint and Gina inside the boat. There was a lavish dining area with a long glass table and a marble bar sitting on an ebony hardwood floor. The bar held another bottle of Dom Pérignon, beer, and a bottle of Chateau

Petrus. There was an assortment of seafood: halibut, salmon, and fresh crab, mustard herb roasted potatoes, moules frites, and warm French bread. For dessert, mousse au chocolat.

Clint plopped himself down and piled his china plate high. He dipped the cracked crab in the melted butter, stuffed it in his mouth, and bit into the warm bread.

"The food's great," said Ted to Evrard, the waiter with thick black locks falling across his face standing next to the bar. He was also the cook. "Merci, Monsieur."

Gina rubbed her hands through Clint's hair and said, "I hear the Monte Cristo Casino has the best cuisine. I also hear that it has the most sophisticated club in town. They say it's a playground for the rich and famous." She spoke English with a deep accent.

Clint wiped his mouth with his napkin, gulped down his champagne and yelled up to the top deck, "Captain!"

"Yes Monsieur." The slender well-built captain was dressed in a white uniform and had thick black wavy hair.

"I want to go to Monte Carlo." "Yes Monsieur."

They arrived that night, at the Hôtel de Paris. The off-white curtains surrounded the large dining room moved charmingly in the evening breeze. Flowers were positioned to perfection at every table. Eighteenth century paintings that looked like they belonged in museums hung on the walls: one of a young girl reading, another of a dance class, and several of the ocean.

The food was fabulous; it was Mediterranean cuisine at its finest. The halibut topped with basil and fresh vegetables was the best Clint had ever eaten.

After dinner, they went to the popular Monte Carlo Casino that included an opera and ballet house named the Grand Théâtre de Monte Carlo. Rich women with diamonds dangling around their necks and men flashing wads of cash were engaged in what Clint found to be meaningless conversation; discussing parties and charities and simply how they became so rich. He found it nauseating and annoying.

The problems of the rich were of no interest to Clint. He'd been around the socially prominent for years and found them boring and dull. He rarely sympathized with anyone's problems and his only concern was the model to date, where to party, and what to buy next.

One of the rooms had a three-piece ensemble that was playing American music. They spent the first half of the night dancing the jitterbug to American swing. The latter half of the night at the casino, gambling and drinking. Clint lost $2,000.

~∞∞∞~

The next twelve months were filled with excitement, energy, and thrill. The climate was balmy, with long, dry summer days, moderate breezes, and mild winters with plenty of sunshine.

Clint flashed around a lot of money, spending carelessly. He'd spent almost half of his money gambling, purchasing the most expensive clothes, cars, staying in five-star hotels and traveling to some of the most beautiful places in the world.

He was often accompanied by Ted and a few female friends. They took weekend trips attending concerts in Italy and London. He'd gone to the opera the previous night. It was the first time he enjoyed it. The voices of the singers twined together with grace and beauty.

~∞∞∞~

Bored with Nice, he decided to move to Cannes. Free-spirited Ted went with him.

They packed their things and jumped into Clint's red BMW's 328 Roadster, and drove through spiraled hills and the mountains, jutting up high above the water. The hills were covered with umbrella pines, thyme, flowering laurel trees, giant cactus plants and olive groves.

They arrived that evening. They drove down the craggy coastline with the Alps plunging straight down into the blue sea.

He maneuvered the car down a narrow road, and drove onto a beach. The light from the sun was intense. Clint jumped out of the car.

"I'm going for a swim in the sea."

Clint ripped his shirt off, pulled his pants down, and raced towards the water. Wearing blue boxer shorts, he plunged into the deep blue ocean, and poked his head above water. Clint swam for twenty minutes while Ted watched from afar. The surge of the ocean finally drove him ashore. He jolted back to the car on the sweltering hot sand with his feet covered in sand. He shook the water from his hair.

Ted shielded his face with his hands. "Thanks, I needed that," he said, laughing.

Clint tilted his head side to side, trying to clear the water from his ears. "You should have gotten in. The water was refreshing."

"Tomorrow. I'm hungry, let's get checked into a hotel and eat."

Clint dried himself off using his shirt. He jumped into the car, turned on the ignition, and peeled rubber, driving to the closest hotel.

The next day, Clint found a villa to rent. A big square-shaped house painted in soft yellow had a large kitchen with all new appliances, a grandiose wood-paneled dining room with a glass table, and an antique china cabinet.

Elaborately carved 18th century French furniture, a magnificent marble fireplace, filled the living room. The balcony provided a view of the deep azure sea.

Clint went into his enormous bedroom with rose-marbled flooring. He sat down on the bed, lifted his brown duffle bag, and opened it. He rummaged through the money for several seconds; there was close to $200,000 left.

I gotta get this money in the bank.

He pulled out $5,000. *I'll stash this in case of emergency.*

He searched a couple of drawers until he found a white envelope. He lifted the mattress, stashed the envelope with the money under it.

The next day after going to the bank, he joined Ted for lunch. Ted was staying in a nice three-bedroom apartment with a terrace facing the ocean only ten miles away.

Clint enjoyed Cannes more than Nice. He swam at his private beaches, shopped at resorts buying designer brands only, visited historic spots like the Le Chateaus, a garden with pines and exotic flowers, and attended the opera. This was the life he'd always dreamed of.

Chapter 11

Clint maneuvered his way past the stack of clothes covering the carpet in his bedroom. It was the only room in the house where his maid wasn't allowed in. He put on a white cashmere robe and strolled into his kitchen. "Good morning Alberteen . . . my coffee please."

The stout dark-skinned maid said, "Good morning, Monsieur." She spoke English with a strong accent.

She poured hot steaming coffee into a Royal Albert china cup. Clint insisted on the finest of everything, even down to the dishes.

She handed the cup to Clint. "Did you sleep well?" "Well enough."

He opened the sliding glass door and made his way to the wicker chair and glass table on his balcony.

Minutes later, Alberteen set two over-medium eggs, croissants, and sautéed red potatoes in front of him. He added a touch of salt to the potatoes and took a bite, then, glanced down at the beach. Ted was running down the water in his red boxer shorts. They'd gotten home late and Ted was too tired to drive home, so he crashed in one of the spare bedrooms.

Clint's thoughts escalated as he studied his scrawny timid friend. *Ted looks terrible. His hair is long, all crazy looking, eyes are blood shot most of the time. He doesn't even look the same. Ted's normally a poster boy for punctuality, but all a sudden, he's showin' up for stuff late.*

During the last couple of months, Ted seemed restless, sometimes confused, had lost weight, and complained he had trouble sleeping and concentrating. Clint could tell something was wrong. One minute he was happy, laughing, having a good time, the next, he appeared depressed. He was often distraught, overwhelmed, and cried easily; especially when he talked of his past. Clint remembered learning about post-traumatic stress disorder in school and wondered if his dad killing himself might have caused it.

Besides Ted's split personality, he talked excessively. He didn't have a private bone in his body. At times, Clint found it relaxing. He could sit and listen and when disinterested, zone out.

I wonder if Ted is back on drugs, he thought.

Clint had pumped him for details earlier that week, but he didn't get much.

As long as it doesn't affect me.

He took a bite of his food, set the fork down, propped his feet up on a small stool, and continued to read his paper.

He and Ted spent the day sunbathing, eating, and sleeping.

Later that night, Ted joined Clint for dinner at a lively upscale Italian restaurant. Clint noticed Ted's eyes were glassy and fidgeted nervously, dropping his fork to the floor.

Clint bit into his grilled chicken linguini and leaned back on his chair. His eyes narrowed, "Ted, are you on drugs?"

"Ah . . . no . . . why would you think that?"

"You've been acting weird for months . . . confused and anxious like you don't know where you are. And you slept almost 15 hours last night."

Laughing nervously, Ted said, "I gave up that stuff along a long time ago. You think I wanna' chance going back into the hole?"

He gulped water and began to perspire.

"I don't need any trouble," Clint said, his eyes narrow, his chin lifted.

Ted looked directly into Clint's eyes. His mood changed, more serious now. "Do you ever pray?"

"Where'd that come from? Why are you askin'?"

"Just curious. My mom used to pray a lot and I wonder if it really helps."

"No, I don't pray. Look Ted, if you're in some kind of trouble . . . ." Ted jumped out of his seat before Clint could finish his words. He had a look of fear in his eyes and the color had drained out of his face. Clint glanced over at the entrance of the restaurant and saw three shady-looking men. Clint stared back at Ted.

"I'm not feelin' well, let's go."

Clint watched Ted weave his way in and out of people, his eyes recurrently glancing at the men to the far side of the restaurant. Clint watched the men canvass the place. A hostess approached to seat them, but they ignored her, still searching the restaurant.

Clint threw fifty dollars on the table to cover the bill, grabbed his jacket, and walked to the car. Ted was standing at the corner a block away, smoking a cigarette.

Clint got into the car and Ted joined him.

"Ted, I'm going to ask you one more time. You in some kinda' mess?" "Trust me, it's nothin'. I've got it all worked out."

Ted barely said a word the whole drive back, which was unusual. He dropped Ted off and arrived home half past nine o'clock. It was hard for Clint to sleep that night.

I hope I don't have to get rid of Ted. It's nice having a friend, but I don't need problems. I'm here to have a good time. The last thing I need is excess baggage.

After a couple of hours, he fell asleep.

The next day, they ate dinner at a little French restaurant not too far from the villa. Ted picked at his food and muttered nervous chitchat. Clint could barely understand him but hoped he'd pull himself together.

After leaving the restaurant, he and Ted, along with their dates, headed straight to Théâtre Lumière, to attend the 1st Annual Cannes Film Festival. Twenty films had competed for an award at this event; mainly the Palme d'Or. The films celebrated the heritage of film; American, Italian, Portuguese, Indian, and French, to name a few.

Clint had spent a fortune to assure them good seats and a walk down the red carpet.

They strutted across the carpet surrounded by the rich and the famous. Clint was dressed in an Italian black tailored suit, a white rayon shirt, and polished black oxford shoes. His tall slender date, an Italian actress he'd met at a party, was dressed in a long strapless dark red gown. Ted's date, a petite French brunette who worked as a barmaid at a local hotel, wore a stunning yellow gown that complimented her thin figure. They'd been dating for three weeks. Ted wore a gray designer suit with grey leather shoes.

The crowd around them was going wild as black cars swept past, carrying rich and famous people. A woman, whose arms were wrapped around a handsome silver-haired gentlemen in a tux, smiled and waved at Clint. She looked vaguely familiar but he could not place her. Then he remembered she was a model that he'd dated several weeks past.

Clint caught a quick glimpse of Humphrey Bogart when he stepped out of a black limousine. People were screaming and aiming their camera lenses to get a glimpse. When more car doors opened, the large crowd surrounding the red carpet went wild. They were enclosed by immensely successful stars and some of the wealthiest people in Europe.

Ingrid Bergman walked the carpet elegantly dressed, waving at the crowd as she paraded past. People strained to get a glimpse, but Clint was only a few yards away. He thought she was even more beautiful in person.

They made their way into the theater and sat in the balcony.

"I can't believe I'm here," Ted said, as his eyes roamed through the theater. "And I still can't believe you managed to get us tickets. How'd ya do it?"

"Pay the right price and you can get just about anything," Clint said, eyeing every beautiful woman that passed.

Everything went dark. The loud voices of people simultaneously murmuring instantly silenced and the curtain flew open. A conductor standing below the stage raised his baton and waved it as the orchestra began to play elegant classical music. When the screen lit up the audience applauded.

The credits were read by a French man after the film, The Lost Weekend, was over. His thick accent obscured the names. The man cleared his throat as he prepared to announce the winners of the Grand Prix. Eleven films were named including The Lost Weekend, Neecha Nagar, and The Red Earth. The audience applauded.

Clint, Ted, and their dates walked down the stairs when the ceremony was over. There were numerous parties. Clint's date had heard that most celebrities would be at Hotel of Cannes from La Croisette Beach, so they attended that one. They drank and danced. It was a spectacular night that even Clint would never forget.

The next evening, Ted and Clint arrived at one of their favorite Italian restaurants. Ted got out of the car first. As they approached the entrance, Ted peered right. Clint watched the blood drain out of his face. "What's wrong, Ted?"

Clint glanced right and noticed the same shady men they'd seen only one month before at the restaurant.

Ted grabbed Clint's coat and yelled. "RUN . . . RUN!" He started to run. Clint not far behind yelled, "What's happening? Why are they chasing us?"

Ted kept running as the men sprang after them. They dashed into an alley and across a busy street. A French man, who swerved his car around Clint and Ted, honked his horn and yelled, "Watch where you are going!"

They flew down some stairs; Clint tripped and fell on his side, hitting the hard concrete like a brick. Pain shot through his arm down his legs.

"You okay?" Ted said, breathing heavily.

"Yeah," Clint said, picking himself up. They ran down a narrow alley. "In here," Clint said. They entered a store where rich old women were admiring dresses. A pretty young French girl was straightening some blouses.

"May I help you?" She spoke cheerfully, and in French.

"You speak English?" Clint asked. He was panting. It was hard for him to talk.

"Yes, how may I help you?" "Is there a back door?"

She tilted her head; eye's narrowed, "Excuse-moi."

"Never mind." Clint swung his legs over the counter and vaulted to the other side, with Ted following right behind. The young girl looked frantic. Clint held up the palms of his hands and gasped, "It's okay. We've got to get out of here. Please help us." She gazed at them for a few seconds before glancing towards the street.

"This way."

They followed her towards the back of the store. She climbed a couple of stairs and opened a back door. "You may leave this way", as she pointed towards the dark alley.

"Thank you," Clint said.

"Di niente . . . I mean, you're welcome."

They ran down the narrow, filthy alley, passing a garbage bin and a bum lying right next to it. Clint peeked out onto the street, looking intently for the men chasing them. "I think we lost them, but we better stay put for a while."

Clint bent over, breathing heavily and looked up at Ted. "What's goin' on Ted? Why are those men chasing us?"

Ted leaned against the brick wall. He hesitated, then bent his head and took a deep breath.

"About six months ago, I met a woman in one of the bars near my apartment. We went out a few times. One night she offered me some opium. I thought . . . what would it hurt? At first it started out for fun but then . . . I guess it got outta control. I started gettin' high . . . daily."

Clint seized upon every tiny facet of information he could get from Ted. "Where'd all the money come from?"

Ted was silent at first. Finally he said, "Sellin' . . . opium."

"Back in the states, I sold it for a couple of months just to get some cash, but I was runnin' a little low, so she introduced me to a few of her friends and I started dealin' again. The people I worked for have a long-term partnership with Mafia drug distributors who supply heroin to Europe, South America, and Mexico. Petra, the man I work for, told me about a shipment comin' into the docks. I stole a few kilos and found a buyer who would pay more money. Somehow, they found out and must've been following me. We gotta' get out of here because they won't stop until they catch me. It was dumb!"

"You're an idiot! I could beat you myself," Clint said. He shrugged in disbelief and said, "What are we supposed to do? Are these guys gonna' kill us?"

"I'll come up with the money. I just need a little time. In the meantime, I say we get outta Cannes."

Clint's eyes darted down the street. His stomach was tense. He thought to himself, *What did he get me in to? I gotta' get rid of him. Tomorrow, I'll break the news and then I'm off to Paris.*

After twenty minutes Clint said, "I think it's been long enough. They're probably gone."

Ted nodded.

They walked backed towards the car, looking around, peering in and out of street corners the whole time. They were almost at the car when the men who had been chasing them stood a few feet away from them. He saw a big man with bushy black hair, a short fat man with broad muscular shoulders with two fingers missing, and a tall man with a big mustache and very white skin. Clint felt his stomach drop. They wanted to run the other direction but were surrounded.

The mustached man looked at the shorter man. "Take care of him."

The short man grabbed Clint and gripped him tightly around his neck, making it hard for him to breath. The other grabbed Ted and clamped his hand over his mouth. They dragged them both into a nearby alley.

Clint clenched his jaw tight. The mustached man said in a coarse voice, "Teddy, Teddy, Teddy. Where you been. Why'd you run? I just wanna talk." He spoke with an Italian accent. "I swear, I'll get your money. I just need more time," Ted said, his legs were trembling.

The man took two steps towards him. "Frankly Ted . . . you're outta' time. I told you we'd find you."

"I'm sorry. I swear . . . I'll pay the money back."

The large man punched Ted in the stomach. He gagged and coughed as he dropped to the ground with tears gushing out of his eyes.

The man kicked him in his chest over and over again. Clint tried to free himself but the grip around his neck was too tight. He felt numb and like air was being choked out of him.

Ted was gasping for air. The mustached man knelt down beside him, lifted his chin, and stared into his eyes. "You got 24 hours to come up with the cash or else!"

He smashed his fist into Ted's mouth. Blood dripped from his face.

The man holding Clint threw him to the ground. Clint struggled to his feet and knelt by Ted. He laid his right hand on Ted's back and gently rolled him over. He watched as the men left the alley.

"I gotta get some help. I'll call an ambulance and get the police."

"No!" Ted said, hoarse. "No please, I'm beggin' you. They'll probably arrest me. Besides, the mob owns half the police."

Clint grabbed Ted's arm and carefully helped him to his feet. Ted groaned clutching his ribs as Clint wrapped his arm around Ted's waist. Ted struggled to stay on his feet and limped the whole way to the car.

Clint drove to his villa and helped him into the guest bedroom. Ted staggered to a chair next to the bed. Clint went into the bathroom, grabbed a wash cloth and bandages from the glass cabinet, and gently wiped the blood from Ted's face. Once the bleeding stopped, he wrapped a bandage around his chest with a roll of gauze.

"Can you move? You need to lie down."

"I can't, hurts too much," he croaked. "I need to sit up."

"You look pretty bad. You sure you don't need a doctor? You might have a broken rib."

"No." He coughed, cringing from the pain. "I'll be okay."

Ted slowly picked himself up from the chair and sat on the bed.

Clint went into the kitchen, grabbed a glass of water and pulled out a blanket to cover Ted.

Ted leaned up against the headboard and closed his eyes. After realizing there was nothing else he could do, Clint went into the kitchen.

Clint mixed himself a stiff scotch. Then went into the living, sank into a chair, and downed the drink in one gulp. He stared out at a full moon, still in disbelief, his heart pounded thinking about it.

Those men could have killed me. Everything seemed like a bad dream. *I never thought I'd end up running from drug dealers in Cannes. What kind of mess did Ted get me into? I don't need to associate with this guy. I should have dumped him in Nice.*

Visions of the men chasing them still penetrated his mind. He got scared just thinking about it. His heart was still racing. *What have you done, Ted?*

After wrestling with his thoughts, he set his glass down and went to bed.

Chapter 12

That morning, Clint opened the door to the spare room and poked his head in. Ted was asleep. Normally, Clint slept soundly. It would have taken an earthquake to wake him, but he tossed and turned all night.

Clint went into the kitchen, sat down, and stared outside for several minutes. He ran his hand through his hair and settled his chin into his fist as his thoughts whirled. *Ted is draining me. I feel sorry for the guy, but I've got to get him out of my life. It's time for me to move on. Switzerland, Ireland, there's a whole world for me to see. How do I break the news to him? This is one attachment I don't need.*

An hour past before Ted slowly made his way into the kitchen, still wearing the clothes he had on from last night. He limped, gripping his side. His lips were swollen.

"How do you feel?" Clint asked. "Like a ton of bricks dropped on me." "Want some coffee?"

He shook his head. "Just water."

Clint grabbed a glass from the brown cabinet above the kitchen sink. He filled it and handed it to Ted.

He took a deep breath. "So what are you gonna do?" Ted stared up at Clint with a look of anguish.

"Not sure."

He took another drink.

"Sorry . . . about last night. Everything got out of hand."

Clint sat back down and after pumping for details, Ted reluctantly admitted to his long addiction to drugs.

"I never got off the stuff. I don't know what happened. It seemed so innocent to me at first. I never felt so good before—free, so alive, in control, you know . . . like a child again.

"My best friend was a dealer so I got the opium whenever I wanted it. My mother knew I was addicted and felt there was nothing she could do, so she just gave up on me. She got cancer and died six months later. I had no family, and the few friends I had were addicts. I thought I was on top of the world but in reality . . . I had nothing. The stuff is really is addictive. I felt like I had lost my soul. Like darkness would engulf me and leave me with only pain. It was like living in World War III. I don't know how it got so bad, Clint."

Tears ran down Teds eyes. "Then I got busted and went to prison. Once I got out, I needed the money, so I started sellin', right away. When I made enough money to live comfortably for at least a couple years, I took the cruise to the France.

"I guess I spent more than I expected in Nice so when we got to Cannes, I started dealin' again, but I was clean for a long time."

"Why did you get back on the stuff? Clint asked.

"I don't know. I'm sorry I got you into this mess, Clint." Clint nodded. "It's okay."

Ted closed his eyes and started to cry.

Uncomfortable and unsure, Clint said, "I'm sure everything will be okay. I wish I could help. Maybe you should leave town. Go back to America or somethin'."

He hoped Ted would agree.

Ted looked at Clint with his bloodshot eyes. "I need to borrow some money."

Clint scratched his head and stared down at the floor. "Ah . . . how much?"

"$10,000."

His eyes widened and jaw tightened as he stood to his feet and moved away from Ted to lean against the wall.

I only got about $125,000 left. I can't blow it on this loser.

"I know I have a drug problem and I'll take care of it, but I'm beggin' you. Just this once."

Clint hesitated. "I'd like to help, but I'm already short. I don't know if I've got enough to make it for one more year."

"I'm scared and you're all I got, Clint."

Clint fidgeted, unsure of what to say. *I knew I should've dumped him in Nice. This isn't my problem.*

"I wish I could help, but I can't." Ted bent his head.

"Look . . . I'll buy you a bus ticket and give you a little cash to get a hotel or somethin', but that's the best I can do. We'll get you out of town today. They won't find you."

Ted slowly picked himself up. "Thanks anyway."

He went back into the room. A few minutes later he returned holding his coat in his hand. "Will you take me home?"

"Yeah, of course."

Clint drove Ted back to his apartment. Silence loomed between them the entire way.

They pulled up to the driveway and got out of the car. Clint opened his wallet and started to pull out some cash. "Here, let me give you some money to get outta' town."

Ted smiled and held out his right hand, palm up. "No, it's okay." He climbed out of the car. Clint got out.

"You know something? My mom always told me I was a perfect picture of my dad. For the first time in my life, I think she's right. Sometimes the best way to end a problem is to cut it loose."

Clint didn't know what to say. Ted seemed strange and smiled.

"Do me a favor, Clint. If you feel like it, say a prayer for me." "Look, I hope things work out for you."

"Don't worry about me. Things have a way of working themselves out."

Ted embraced him, fiercely. Clint was perplexed; he patted Ted gently on the back, hoping he would release him soon.

Ted's eyes were filled with tears. "I'll miss you. Take care of yourself." "Bye Ted."

Clint got back behind the wheel. He watched Ted limp into his apartment building. His emotions scrambled as he pulled out of the driveway.

Maybe I should've helped him, but he could've never paid me back.

He drove almost five miles with his mind racing the entire time. *I wonder what he meant when he said the best way to end a problem is to cut it loose.*

Clint had a flashback of a conversation he'd had with Ted when they first met. They were sitting in the dining room of the cruise ship. Ted mentioned how his father, before killing himself said to him, *"Son, sometimes the best way to end a problem is to cut it loose."*

Clint pulled over onto the side of the road. "He wouldn't . . . would he?" he said out loud.

He spun his car around and sped down the road, pulling up to Ted's apartment complex within minutes.

Dozens of people were standing outside, looking up in shock. He glanced up and saw Ted standing on the ledge of the building right outside his window, about ten stories up. It looked like he would jump any minute.

Clint darted up the stairs and tried to open the door, but it was locked. He moved back and slammed his body against the door, knocking it open.

He ran to the window and stuck his head out. Ted was standing at the edge several feet away.

"Ted!" he screamed. "Don't do it!"

"It's easier this way, Clint. I miss my dad and my mom. I'll be with them now."

Clint's body flooded with fear. "I'll give you the money, I swear. Just don't jump."

Ted started to cry. "I can't stand it anymore."

Clint climbed out the window. "Ted, we can talk about it." "Clint, will you pray for me."

"I'll pray for you, Ted. Just get down."

Clint looked down and froze. He felt paralyzed clinging to the stone wall. His right arm gripped against the window ledge.

Ted had his left arm wrapped around an iron rail.

Clint tried to ease his way towards Ted but he was afraid. He held his hand out motioning for Ted to grab it. His voice was calm and his demeanor gentle. "Ted, you're my best friend. We'll get through this. Let's leave here. We'll go to Ireland, Paris, anywhere. There's still more to see. We can leave today. You'll never be found, I promise."

Clint thought he was getting through since Ted appeared calm. He took a small step towards him and suddenly, Ted let go.

"TED!" Clint screamed.

He heard the sound of his friend falling hundreds of feet to his death hitting the hard concrete below.

"Nooooooooo!" he screamed.

He heard the voices of men and women screaming in terror.

Clint climbed back inside and fell to the floor. *What just happened?* Tears fell down from his face as he screamed, "TEEEED, No, Oh God No!" It was like a terrible nightmare. His heart was pounding as he gasped for air.

He heard the voices of people still screaming below. He lay on the floor and cried, bitterly. Finally, he pulled himself up and went down the stairs. Still in shock, he felt numb and scared. He didn't know what to do.

The police arrived. Tears streamed down his face when they interviewed him. After an hour, he drove up to his villa, laid his hand on his steering wheel, and cried. The grief was unbearable. It was horrible with William, but this was different. He blamed himself.

He went into the house and stepped into the hallway.

His maid asked, "Are you okay?" You look as though you've been crying. Clint nodded, "I'm fine."

"Would you like something? Can I fix you something to eat?"

He shook his head, went outside, and stared at the ocean for hours. Clint was still in shock. Visions of his friend falling tormented his mind. Ted had lost the battle for his soul.

Clint spent the next three months drowning his emotions in alcohol and gambling; losing almost everything. He sat at a poker table in a scummy dilapidated building in a poorer part of Cannes. Cigarette smoke loomed throughout the small dingy building. Prostitutes wandered the room strolling back and forth, looking for customers.

The dealer shuffled the cards. The man to the right of him cut the cards. The dealer then dealt Clint five cards. Clint had a two, three, seven, and two queens.

"Draw, Clint said."

I can fake these guys out.

"Raise," said a heavy short man.

Clint shoved all his chips in the pot. Several betting rounds occurred. At the end, only three men remained, Clint was one of them. Each of them evaluated their hands. Again, the short man said, "Raise."

The other man and Clint were forced to fold. The man won the pot.

A large musty-smelling man with shoulders the size of a football player was standing only a few feet away from Clint. He approached him.

"Pay up. You owe $8,000."

Clint stared at the man, stone-faced. "Just one more hand."

"You ain't playin' another hand until you pay what you owe." The man crossed his arms and moved closer to Clint.

Clint got up, grabbed his wallet, and pulled out a wad of money. He threw it down on the table. "That's all I got."

The man stared at Clint, coldly. After counting the money, he said, "You owe $3,740 more. Pay up, now!"

Clint's words were slurred. "I said that's all I got."

The man eyed Clint's gold watch. "Take off the watch." Clint took it off and handed it to the man.

"How'd you get here?" the man asked.

Clint stared at him, irritated. "How do ya' think . . . I drove!"

The man grabbed Clint by the collar and dragged him outside. "Which car is yours?"

Clint pointed to the red convertible Lincoln Continental. "Hand me the keys."

"How am I supposed to get home?" Clint argued.

"You wanna' leave with all your body parts workin', then you'll hand me the keys."

Clint reluctantly gave him the keys.

"That car is worth $4,000. At least give me money to get a cab."

The man threw five Francs on the ground and then shoved Clint out on the street, sending him falling face first.

"I see you in here again, I'll kill you." He slammed the door shut.

Clint picked himself off the dirty ground and rubbed his face. He picked up the money, wandered around the cold, dawn streets, then took a cab home.

He entered his room and sat in the dark on the edge of the bed with his hands folded and pressed between his knees. Clint was drunk from alcohol and stricken with grief. He didn't care what happened to him; he was lonely and miserable. He fell back on his bed and passed out.

It was bleak and dreary at ten o'clock that morning. Clint sat outside at the table. The fun and excitement that had soothed his soul had been overtaken by depression.

Alberteen walked outside. "Would you like breakfast?"

No . . . thanks," Clint said, solemnly as he moved indoors towards his bedroom.

When he opened the door, a wave of insecurity swept over him. He paused several seconds before entering. What once was an elegant bedroom was now looked empty and dingy.

He sat down on his bed. Overwhelmed and lonely, memories of the time spent with Ted clouded his mind. How could everything so perfect go so wrong? The French Riviera had been exciting and glamorous but it was the most depressing place he'd ever been in. A flashback of the dreadful events engulfed his mind: bloodshed, injury and death from the war in Germany, the military men at the door announcing Will's death at his father's house, and Ted falling from his apartment building. Though he knew that Ted had been battling in his soul for years, he felt was partly to blame for his death.

Clint remembered the last words Ted spoke. "Say a prayer for me."

I don't know how to pray. Besides, God wouldn't listen to me.

A spectacular life was suddenly shattered by the horrific event in one day.

I've got to get outta' here. Where should I go?

He was broke and fell a month behind on his rent. All he had was the $5,000 stashed under his mattress.

Clint pulled out the white envelope and opened it up. He opened a black bag to put the envelope in, and eyed the bible his father had given him. He sat on the edge of the bed and fanned through a few of the pages, then set it down next to his nightstand.

Taking a deep breath, he lifted himself up, opened his wallet, and pulled out a sheet of paper. The words read, *I'll miss you, Clint. If you're ever in Wales, look me up. Frazier'.* Frazier's address and telephone number was also on the sheet.

Clint studied the paper for some time. He moved into the living room, picked up the telephone and dialed the number. After three rings, a deep male voice spoke.

"Ah, do you speak English?" Clint asked.

"Yes, who is this?" he asked with a deep Welsh accent. "My name is Clint . . . I'm looking for Frazier Brown." "One moment." The man yelled, "Frazier."

Seconds later Frazier picked up the phone. "Hello, this is Frazier." "Hi, it's me, Clint . . . from Germany."

"Clint, how are you? It's so good to hear your voice. Where are you?" "Cannes."

"What are you doing all the way out there?"

"I was vacationing. Look, I'll be in your area, so . . . I thought I'd drop by."

"That'd be grand. My parents would love to meet you. When can we expect you?"

"I can be there on Thursday."

"Good, we'll see you then. Call when the arrangements have been made and I'll pick you up at the dock. You'll need to catch a boat."

"Oh okay, I'll make the plans today." "Goodbye for now," Frazier said.

He hung up the telephone.

That night, he packed his things and went to bed early.

The next day, he hugged Alberteen goodbye and turned to face the villa he'd called home for almost two years. A feeling of grief struck him. What started as an exciting, adventurous life had ended in horror.

He took a train to Paris and traveled to Cardiff, Wales by a boat holding nearly 100 passengers. He sat staring out the window in the dining area towards the ocean. A feeling of deep regret filled his spirit because he hadn't written his father. He reached down into his duffel bag and pulled out his notebook. As he sat trying to compose a letter with words that could never express his feelings, he felt a large black cloud of depression begin to settle over him. He missed his mother. He missed Will and Ted. He even missed his father.

He sat staring at the blank sheet of paper for almost ten minutes. Finally, he put the notebook away. *I'll write my father in Wales.*

He leaned back and rested.

Chapter 13

James was sitting at the back porch at his oak table, drinking sweet tea as the cool breeze from the spring air blew against his face. He'd just finished reading the last chapter of the Book of John. He loved reading the bible and found it invigorating and strengthening to his soul.

He settled his chin on his fist, looked up, and studied the sky. As the sun began to set, it was filled with shades of orange and yellow.

It's been over a year and still no word from Clint, he thought to himself. *I don't even know if he's alive. Why won't he write?* "I miss him," he said out loud.

He exhaled loudly and leaned back on his chair. "He's in your hands, Lord. I pray you keep him safe and bring him home, soon."

Minutes later, he heard the sound of a car approaching. Paul drove up in his brand new silver truck, stepped out, walked over to the passenger side, and opened the door. A young Japanese woman of medium height got out. She straightened her slender blue rayon skirt and light blue blouse and took Paul's hand. He led her up the stairs.

James stood. "Hello Aiko."

"Hello, Mr. Edison." Her voice was soft, and her smile, graceful. Her long silky black hair fell perfectly behind her back.

"Hi Dad."

"Hello Paul. Did you have a nice dinner?" "Very," she said, smiling.

"Sit down. Please, join me."

Gazing up, Aiko said, "It is a beautiful evening. I love the color of the sky this time of day."

"Yes, it is," James said.

"You're very kind Mr. Edison; all that you are doing for my family. We are so grateful that you hired my father to work on your ranch, even though he has so little experience. Not many people would hire Japanese people. They are still angry over the war."

"Hiro Yoshi is a good man and a good worker. We are lucky to have him." James took a sip of tea.

"Would you like some tea?" James asked. "No thank you."

"You have a very sweet nature. I can see why Paul is so captivated by you."

She smiled, shyly. "I am equally captivated." She stared at Paul with her thick naturally long eyelashes. "He is a great man."

"Yes, I'm very proud of him."

Paul glanced at her. "Aiko is wise, and intelligent, not to mention beautiful. She plans to become a lawyer."

James lifted his chin upward. "Impressive. What made you decide to go into law?"

"I'm not sure how much my father shared with you about his life. He went to medical school in Japan and became a doctor. He came to America in 1925 and settled in San Francesco when he was 30 years old. That is where he met my mother. Soon after, they married.

"He provided much needed medical care to the Japanese community in the city, working long hours, and caring for the sick and desperate. People had very little money to pay, but he didn't care. His priority was the people first.

"Me and my brother were born in San Francisco. It was a good life. We were very happy.

"I was 17 years old when Pearl Harbor happened. We were devastated. At that moment, our lives were never the same. My family lost everything. We were American citizens but that didn't make a difference. We were sent to a camp in Idaho."

James leaned forward.

"We were surrounded by sagebrush. The winters were bitterly cold and summers, sweltering hot. In a distance, I could see a small town. I looked through the barbwire and wondered what it would be like to go there.

"Once we were released, we managed to find odd jobs working in fields picking corn, cleaning houses, and gardening. My father wanted a fresh start so we took a train to Texas. We were hungry and forced to live in an abandoned building for almost six months until he found work at a grocery store. My mother and I cleaned houses while my brother, who was 16, attended high school.

When I was 18, I started school at the University of Texas. My father sometimes worked 20 hours a day to pay the tuition. My brother joined the Army and is stationed overseas in Europe.

"Two months before I finished my first year of college, my father heard of a job on your ranch, so he applied. We are so grateful that you hired him."

"It was a great injustice what happened in Pearl Harbor, but also for what was done to you," James said.

"I agree. That is why I decided I would fight for people's rights for the rest of my life, no matter how much money I make. I want to make a difference."

James shook his head. "That's a remarkable and heartbreaking story. It's still hard to believe. You and your family have been through great hardship. I couldn't imagine having to live through that, but I'm happy you are here. Your father is a good worker. He does double the work on the ranch than most men, and he is a wonderful person as well."

"Mr. Edison, you have helped in more ways than you think. We could never ask for more."

She looked at Paul. "I should be getting back, it's getting late." Paul rose from his chair. "I'll walk you home."

James stood up. "Good night, Aiko. Thank you for sharing. I have even more respect for your father."

"Thank you and good night." "I'll be back soon, Dad."

James nodded and went into the house.

He went by the window in the living room and watched Paul gently run his fingers through Aiko's hair as they walked home. They'd only been dating for two months, but James could tell it was serious. He couldn't be more pleased with Paul's choice.

He climbed the stairs and went to bed.

At noon the next day, James watched as Paul returned home from moving cows to a livestock auction 12 miles north of the ranch. Bo had gone with him. He reined the horse and rode a few yards from the fence and said "Whoa." He dismounted and dropped the reins to the ground and tied the horse to the gate.

James couldn't help but notice the transformation the years had created in Paul. He was stronger, more serious, and even his appearance had changed. His face seemed to have aged and streaks of gray lined his sandy blonde hair. He was always built solidly, but his shoulders had broadened.

James strolled out onto the porch after finishing breakfast. He saw Aiko's father feeding a horse panel. Paul was not far away.

The short, gray-haired, Japanese man said, "Good afternoon Mr. Edison."

"Hello Hiro," James said.

"Hello Mr. Yoshi," Paul said, walking over to them. "How was the auction, Paul?"

"Good, sold 50 cows." "Good. Good"

"I need to go into town to buy a couple of saddle racks, a new feed storage, and some stall mats, but I have a meeting across town. All the ranch hands are busy. Do you have time, Dad?"

James scratched his head. "I guess I could go. It'll do me some good to get out. Why don't you come with me, Hiro?"

"I would like that."

They drove Paul's truck into town. James pulled up to the small, but crowded hardware store where dozens of men were purchasing tools and equipment. James pointed to silver stall mats. "I'll take those."

They grabbed the feed storage and saddle racks, paid the store owner, and began loading them in the truck.

"Hey there James." James turned around to see his neighbor, Mike Marshall, a big man dressed in jeans and covered in dirt, who stood next to a tall, tan broad shouldered younger man.

James walked towards them while Hiro continued to load the car. "Hello, Mike. Haven't seen you for a while."

"Likewise. You remember my son, Marcus." "Howdy," Marcus said.

"Why you've sure grown. Where have the years gone?" "How's business?" Mike asked.

"Never better."

Mike's eyes narrowed as he looked at Hiro. He asked in a tense voice, "What's he doin' here? Don't tell me he's workin' for ya?"

James turned around. "I hired him several months ago. He's a great asset to my business. Hard worker."

"They killed my boy in Pearl Harbor. I can't see how you'd hire the likes of them."

"What was done was a horrific thing, but not all Japanese people are too blame, especially, Hiro Yoshi. He is a good man."

Marcus spit chewing tobacco on the ground. "I hate the likes of em'." "That kind of prejudice is what destroys our country," James said, agitated.

"Tell em' he comes near our property, we'll kill em. Just like they did my brother."

"I don't have to listen to this." James stomped off. "Is everything all right, Mr. Edison?"

"It's fine, Hiro. Let's go."

Later that evening, Paul and James went horseback riding. The sun was starting to fade and the cool breeze had brought some relief from the heat. They rode through miles of valleys in the brown hills; Paul on his chestnut horse named Mister and James on a white stallion named Thunder.

About a quarter mile from their house, Aiko appeared with her mother walking along the side of the road carrying grocery bags.

Within minutes, Marcus and a few of his friends pulled up from behind them.

"Look Dad" Paul said, alarmed. James turned.

Marcus jumped down from his horse. He spoke to Aiko then grabbed her by the arm.

Paul took off instantly with James only a few feet behind him.

Marcus pulled Aiko towards him. She was struggling. Her mother tried to intervene, but one of the other men shoved her to the ground. Aiko slapped Marcus and then he knocked her down.

Paul rode right up to them, then jumped down to grab Marcus and slammed his fist into his face, sending him flying backwards. Marcus's friend ran over to Paul and punched him. James arrived and got off his horse to pull Marcus's friend back, then with his string arms, gripped him around the neck.

Once Marcus regained his footing, he slugged Paul in the stomach. Paul smashed his fist into his face once again and knocked him flat on the ground. Marcus held his mouth as blood streamed down his lips.

Paul stood over him. "Touch her again and I'll kill you!" Paul helped Aiko up. "Are you okay?"

"Yes, I'm okay." Her voice was shaking.

He looked at Aiko's Mother, Kameko. "Are you all right?" She wiped tears from her eyes and nodded.

He wrapped his arms around Aiko and held her. Then took her by the hand to lift her onto his horse, while James helped Kameko. The long leather thong that held her pure white hair in a bun fell out of her hair. James picked it up and handed it to her. Paul and James grabbed the bags of groceries. As they began to leave, Marcus pulled himself off the ground and yelled, "Get your Japanese whore and her mother outta' here."

Paul turned around, his face burning with anger. He balled his fist and started towards them again, Aiko yelled, "Paul, please no. Let's just go."

"Paul, let him be." James gave Marcus a hard stare. "He will reap what he has sown."

Paul turned back around. They took the women to the ranch.

James helped Kameko off the horse. He could tell her nerves were beginning to calm. She placed both hands together, bowed and said in a deep accent, "Thank you for your help. We are grateful."

"You're welcome," James said.

He invited both women to join them for a late lunch. They ate black bean soup, corn bread, and sweet tea outside on the patio. Hiro was finishing up a few chores and was planning to join them later.

Camellia walked out on the porch carrying a tray with four slices of blueberry pie. "Would anyone like dessert?"

"We'd love some," James said.

She handed each of them a slice of pie. "Would anyone like more sweet tea?

"I would," Paul said, right before he took an enormous bite of pie.

"I will speak to Mike Marshall about his son's behavior in the morning." Paul set his fork down. "Not sure what good it'll do. That kind of hatred can't be cured by a good talkin' to."

"Nevertheless, it won't be tolerated." James was getting ready to take another bite when he heard his name being called.

"Mr. Edison, Mr. Edison." Hiro ran up the stairs to the balcony. He was breathing heavily.

"What is it? What's wrong?" James asked.

Our home . . . It was vandalized. I had just finished feeding the cattle. I went home to change and that's when I saw someone had broken in."

James jumped to his feet. "Get the car, Paul."

They pulled up to the house within minutes. James entered first since it was on his property. He shook his head. The furniture was trashed.

"Paul, call the police," James said.

Aiko covered her mouth with her hands. Kameko began to cry. They went into the kitchen where they saw pieces of broken plates and cups all over the sink and floor. In the bedrooms, clothes were thrown everywhere.

The sheriff arrived fifteen minutes later. Nothing appeared to be missing so it was evident it was an act of vandalism. After interviewing everyone, he completed his report and left.

Aiko wrapped her arms around Paul's neck and had trails of tears streaming down her face. "We were lucky no one was in the house when it happened."

"We'll find out who did this. Trust me."

"They will be brought to justice. You and your family will stay at our house tonight," James said.

Aiko moved close to her mother, who was silently weeping, and grabbed her hand.

Paul turned to James. "You know who's responsible? Mike Madison's son, Marcus, and probably a few of his friends."

"Yes, it is obvious. But unfortunately, we have no proof." "When I get my hands on him!" Paul's face was beet red.

"Paul, don't do anything foolish. Like I said, we can't prove anything." "I say we confront them now," he said, firmly.

"We'll drive out to their place first thing tomorrow morning."

~~~~~~

When James, Paul, Bo, and Hiro arrived at the Marshall ranch. Marcus was sitting on the back of a pick-up truck with a friend holding a rifle in his hand. He aimed and fired at an empty whisky bottle sitting on a tree trunk about 20 yards away. The glass shattered.

Marcus and his friends burst into laughter. He took a swig of whisky and handed the bottle to his friend.

Mike was standing next to the fence wearing a pair of oversized blue jeans and a cowboy hat watching a hired hand break in a new horse.

They got out of the car.

"That's far enough. What's he doin' on my property?" Mike said. "Yesterday, someone vandalized his home. Do you know anything about this?"

"You accusin' me of somethin'?"

"Where was your son yesterday afternoon? Now wait one minute." His face turned red. He took three steps closer to James and waved his finger. "You don't come on my property with that good-for-nothin' worthless Japanese trash. I suggest you get off my land!" Mike's breathing was labored and he was sweating profusely.

"You heard my pa. Get off our property!" yelled Marcus, running towards them.

Bo took a couple of steps towards him. Marcus stopped. "Not until we have the answer," James demanded.

"Look, I'm not gonna' say it again." Suddenly, Mike grabbed his chest, gasping for air, and fell to his knees.

"Mike, are you all right?" James asked. Mike fell flat on his face.

"Pa!"

James ran to him with Paul right behind. They rolled him on his back. Hiro knelt down beside him.

"Don't touch my Pa," Marcus said.

"He's a doctor. He can help him. Go call for an ambulance."

Marcus flew into the house. Minutes later, he returned with his mother. Hiro was still trying help Mike.

Mike looked up at him. He whispered, "I'd rather die than have you touch me." Then, he went unconscious.

Hiro stood. Mrs. Madison knelt beside her husband. "Mike." She began to cry.

Within 15 minutes, the ambulance arrived and took him to the hospital.

James and the others went back to the ranch. Five hours later, they heard news that Mike Madison suffered a massive heart attack and died on the operating table.

James attended the funeral several days later. Mike's loved ones gathered to mourn his loss. Mrs. Madison stood quietly, staring at the casket. Her eyes were red and full of pain.

James prayed silently, asking God to comfort her during this time of grieving and for the hatred to end.

A parade of emotions filled James with happiness as he sat in the front row at Paul's wedding. He glanced at his son in his new black tux and shinny cowboy boots with great pride. Paul had asked Aiko to marry him a month earlier. He knew they'd only known each other for a short period of time, but it was obvious they were in love.

Paul was standing next to the pastor, a friend, and Aiko's brother, who had flown in from Germany in time to attend the wedding.

Paul was calm, but James could tell he was nervous. Even though the temperature was at 70°, Paul's sweat was dripping from his forehead.

Lights that hung from the trees lit up the entire back yard. A small orchestra of two violins and a guitar played on the gazebo which was surrounded by daisies.

Paul turned as Aiko moved towards him. She was dressed in a white kimono made of elaborate rich patterned silk and finely embroidered with scenes of flowers and pines. Her hair was styled in a Japanese style bun called a bunkin-takashimada, and adorned with beautiful gold combs.

James watched Paul dance with his new wife. Seeing his son marry the woman of his dreams brought him unspeakable joy. Only one thing was missing: Clint.

Clint should be at his brother's wedding, thought James. Not knowing his whereabouts made his face grim. He said a silent prayer as his emotions overshadowed with sudden despair, "God, please bring my son home safely. Please."

Chapter 14

Clint got off the boat late morning. The trip took longer than he thought it would. The sun was breaking through a collection of clouds. The light breeze fanned his cheeks. He pulled off his cap and wiped his forehead.

Clint checked his watch nervously. He'd arrived there with mixed emotions of anticipation and dread. In a strange land, he was meeting a man he barely knew and his family. He wasn't sure what to expect. Clint's eyes peered right and left, searching the 200 foot long dock for Frazier.

How am I going to find him?

He started to walk in the direction of a parking when he heard his name being called.

Frazier, dressed in a pair of blue pants and a plaid shirt, was standing not far away from a tall red building. He dashed towards Clint.

"It's good to see you. Welcome to Wales." He hugged Clint. "You look well."

"So do you. Almost didn't recognize you; your hair is longer and you have a mustache," Clint said.

"I could say the same thing about you. You look good with longer hair and a lot darker than I remembered. It must be all that time you've spent on the beach." He patted Clint on the back. "Let's go, my parents are quite anxious to meet you. I live only an hour away."

Frazier grabbed Clint's suitcase. "I'll put it in the boot."

He lifted the trunk of his black Ford Anglia and tossed the suitcase in. Clint threw the duffle bag in and jumped into the passenger side of the car.

Clint noticed a large stadium to the right as they drove out of the station.

"Do you play rugby?" Frazier asked. "I've never heard of it."

"It's great fun. It's like your American football, only a bit rougher. We often go to games at that stadium. You'll have to join us while you're here."

Frazier headed towards the center of the city. They passed large buildings that looked to be made of white rock. The shaded streets were clean and neat. Men dressed in double-breasted suits and women in knee-length skirts and simply cut blouses, strolled by casually.

They passed a handful of retail shops, restaurants, and a nice clean park. Frazier talked about his planned become an architect. He'd taken a few college courses but was out on summer break. The conversation was pleasant, but at times awkward.

He seems personable, thought Clint. *Boring, but personable. I know he's pretty religious.* Clint remembered Frazier carrying a bible everywhere he went in Germany. *I wonder if he's ever had a drink in his life.*

"My parents can't wait to meet you. My sister's quite excited too. They're good people; you're going to love them."

Clint nodded. "Yeah, it'll be great to meet them."

He wasn't sure what to expect from Frazier's parents. He could find himself sitting at the table, sipping bad tea, being preached out by a couple of extremists. He figured they must be as religious, if not more, than Frazier. And when he thought of Frazier's sister, visions of a homely girl, pursuing him day and night, pleading for his affection, suddenly began to raid his mind.

On the other hand, the past few months have been the worst of his life. Maybe this trip would be a welcome change. He figured he could stay long enough to figure out where he could go or what he would do next.

Clint asked, "How long did you stay in Germany after I left?"

"One month. I got injured in an air raid: two broken ribs and a concussion. The pain was unbearable but to be honest, I didn't mind it. I was elated to be going home."

"Yeah, I know what you mean. That was the worst nightmare of my life. I'll never fight another war as long as I live."

"I could feel the prayers of my parents. They saved me," Frazier said.

Clint didn't speak.

"What about you? I can't wait to hear of your travel. France is an exciting country. I've been there once and found it quite captivating."

"It was." Clint peered out the window. His mood shifted to the horrible events of the past few months. He wanted to forget he was ever there.

They drove through a rich residential area and rolling green hillsides. "Beautiful country," Clint said.

"Yes, we'll have to do a bit of sightseeing while you're in town."

They went down a narrow sandy road and drove up to a lovely two-story white house with green shutters on the windows.

They got out of the car. The home sat on what appeared to be several acres of land. Everywhere Clint looked there was something to catch his eyes. There were cherry trees, apple trees, pear trees, and thick shrubs. An antique wheelbarrow was filled with a seemingly impromptu display of flowers. The lawn looked as though it had been cut within the past few days. A stunning arrangement of wild roses, poppies, and a rock garden were to the right of the house.

"You must be hungry. My mum's prepared a small feast." Frazier grabbed his suitcase and his duffle bag. "Come in."

They climbed three stairs and entered the house. They walked on the light brown hardwood floors. Warmth and friendliness filled the room. A light orange sofa and chair sat in the small living room. They went into the bright clean kitchen with black appliances, a green rug covering the tile floor, and a small wood kitchen table, decorated with a glass vase and yellow tulips. A pleasant aroma of roasted chicken filled the room.

A stout woman, with her gray hair swept up in a bun, was standing near the stove. She smiled broadly, her round face beaming when she approached them.

"Clint, this is my mother, Sarah."

She wrapped her arms around him. "Hello, hello, welcome to our home. We're so happy to have you. How was your trip here?" She had a slight accent, but not as strong as Frazier's.

"Fine," Clint said.

"Good. Good. Frazier told us what a nice young man you are. We were delighted that you phoned. We'll make sure you have a wonderful time. Frazier, show him to his room so he can freshen up a bit. I know it was a long trip."

"I wasn't planning to stay. I was going to get a hotel room," he said. He hoped she would disapprove since he was low on cash and needed a place to sleep.

"Nonsense," she said. "You're our guest and we insist you stay with us." "You won't win a battle against my Mum. I'll show you to your room."

They walked up the staircase. He followed Frazier into the second room on the right. He noticed a green and blue embroidered quilt lay on the bed, blue linen curtains blowing from the open windows, and a colorful striped rug covering the floor.

Frazier set the luggage down. "I'll let you freshen up. The loo is two doors down to the left."

Clint arched his eyebrows. "Loo?" "Bathroom. Lunch will be ready soon."

Clint nodded. He walked over to an oak dresser and picked up what appeared to be a photo of Frazier's father and mother in Africa. They were surrounded by dozens of African children. He remembered Frazier talking about how his parents had met there. His father was an archeologist and his mother lived there.

After setting the photo down, he went into bathroom to wash his face and brush his teeth, then went back downstairs.

He walked past a small but pleasant dining room. Several flower paintings were hung on the wall.

When he entered the kitchen, a tall man wearing a pair of wire-rimmed glasses, stood next to Sarah. He turned around.

"You must be Clint." "Yes sir."

He shook his hand. "It's nice to meet you. Welcome." "Thank you Mr . . . ."

"Alistair Brown. You may call me Alistair.

"You must be famished, Clint. Lunch will be served in the dining room."

Just then, Frazier appeared and said, "Follow me." Clint sat directly across from Frazier.

I'm starving. I hope the food's as good as it smells.

Sarah and Alistair walked in minutes later, carrying an assortment of foods: pate', cheese, corn, and roasted chicken.

Alistair sat at the head of the table and reached out as Sarah placed her hand on his. Frazier grabbed Clint's hand.

"Father, we thank you for the food you have set before us. May it give us strength and nourishment to accomplish your will. Bless the hands that prepared it. Amen."

"Amen," said Sarah and Frazier. "Amen," said Clint, quietly.

"I do hope you're hungry," Sarah said. She piled Clint's plate high.

Alistair put aside his glasses, crossed his arms over his considerable paunch. "So, how long have you been in Europe?"

"Almost three years. I stayed in Nice and then moved to Cannes."

"What brought you to Wales?" Sarah asked.

"I've always wanted to visit Britain and told Frazier I'd stop by if I was in the area."

"Well, we're so glad you did," Sarah said. "Frazier and Abby will take you sightseeing tomorrow. It's a beautiful city, you know. You're going to love it."

"Abby?" Clint asked.

"My younger sister," Frazier said while chewing on come chicken.

Clint leaned back. *Oh yeah, the sister. I hope she doesn't fall for me. The last thing I need is some ugly chick following me around.*

"Where does your family live?" Alistair asked.

"My brother and father live in Texas. My mother died when I was eight, and my brother died fighting the war in Germany."

A soft gasp hurdled from Sarah's lips. "I'm so sorry to hear that. That must have been quite terrible for you."

Alistair frowned, "That treacherous war. All those young soldiers lost and the massacre of the Jews."

"I cried just thinking about it," Sarah said.

"War was an experience I'd like to forget. I'm glad it's over," Clint said. "So am I, and so glad to have my love back safe and sound." She glanced at Frazier who was stuffing chicken into his mouth.

They talked for almost an hour. The incessant chatter of Frazier's father was agitating at times. He spoke of his business, world affairs, but mainly archeology. Clint tried to appear interested.

On occasion, Frazier would discuss his studies. Clint found it to be equally as boring. He had to admit though; it was nice being around them. They were warm and welcoming.

Frazier stood up when they finished eating. "Clint, fancy a walk?" Clint tilted his head. "Pardon."

"Would you care to go for a walk? I'd enjoy showing you the property." "Yeah, sure."

"Wait." Sarah walked into the kitchen and came out minutes later carrying a bag full of garbage. She handed it to Frazier. "Take this to the bin on your way out."

After unloading the garbage, Frazier gave Clint a tour of their property. While the sun dipped below the horizon, they walked past a pond surrounded by a flowerbed of tulips and primroses.

"So how long are you planning to stay?" Frazier asked.

"Maybe a week or two."

"What's next for you? Where will you go?"

Clint was at a loss for words. "Well . . . I've always wanted to see Greece. I'll spend a few weeks there and then on to Rome."

"Sounds quite exciting. I've never been myself."

Truth was, Clint was low on cash and had no idea what he'd do.

They stopped at a large lake surrounded by pine trees. Frazier waved at a red-faced farmer who smiled and waved back.

They walked for a couple of hours and talked about their memories of war and life after. Clint shared about his time at home, his brother's death, and how he decided to leave. He spoke of a companion who often traveled with him, but didn't discuss the details about Ted.

He thought it was odd how comfortable he felt with Frazier. Frazier seemed like the type of man he could trust; he was kind, friendly, and honest. He had a presence that made Clint want to be honest. He spoke often of his faith. When he talked about God, he spoke naturally; not preachy or overly religious. It was almost like God was his friend. He remembered that Frazier had always been uplifting, not condemning.

They stepped into the house a little past six.

Sarah swept into the hallway. "It's about time you two made it home. I was beginning to think you got lost. Go and get washed up. Dinner will be served in a half hour."

After a quick bath and a change of clothes, Clint joined Frazier in the living room. They moved into the hallway and almost to the dining room when a bedroom door upstairs burst open. Clint froze when he looked up and saw a young woman dressed in a slender gray skirt and a white top standing at the top of the stairs. She had dark brown hair that lay down her back.

She's beautiful, he thought.

His gaze was fixed on her. As she moved down the stairs, he felt his stomach drop. When her feet hit the floor she walked straight towards him. She looked at him with her stunning eyes.

He expected a sign of approval and a glimpse of excitement from her, but she simply smiled and said "Hello."

"Hi."

"I'm Abby, Frazier's younger sister." She spoke with a sweet accent. You must be Clint." She held out her hand to shake his.

"Ah yeah," he said. It was strange, he was almost nervous; emotions surfaced that he'd never felt for a woman before. He wanted to get to know her, be around her.

"It's lovely to meet you." She swung past him. "I'm starving. What's for dinner, Mum?"

"Beef stew, baby red potatoes, and peas." Sarah said. "Everyone, let's eat."

After saying grace, Alistair sank his fork into the savory beef stew. Clint's focus was on Abby. She looked to be 19 years old. He was baffled by her reaction towards him because he was used to women flocking after him, but she seemed almost uninterested.

Maybe she has a boyfriend, he thought. *Must be serious.*

"Pass the bread," Abby said to Frazier. "Please," he said, somewhat sarcastically.

"Oh stop being so coy dear brother and hand it over." "Where are your manners," he said. "Say please."

"My manners are exactly where they're supposed to be. Now hand over the bread or I'll be forced to bite your arm. You know I can take you."

"Hah," he said, jokingly.

"Oh stop it you two," Sarah said. "For goodness sake."

"I'm sure Clint doesn't fuss with his siblings the way you too do. Isn't that so, Clint?"

"Um . . . I'd be lying if I said no."

"Oh, we're only playing mother. Trust me, you'd know if it was a fight." "Sibling rivalry," Alistair said stuffing his face. "In one month, we'll have a peaceful house all to ourselves. Isn't that right, my darling?" He smiled at Sarah.

"That's correct and I'd be dishonest if I said I wasn't looking forward to it."

Clint wondered what they meant, but wasn't comfortable asking.

Abby asked, "So Clint, how was the French Riviera? I've never been myself but I heard it's quite exciting. I'd love to go someday." "It was great. Beautiful beaches; the weather was perfect." "Clint went to the Cannes Film Festival," Frazier said.

Abby's mouth flew open. "Did you see movie stars? I read about it in the paper. I would have fainted at the sight."

"I saw Ingrid Bergman. She was beautiful." "I would have went bonkers," Abby said.

"I was two feet away from John Wayne once when I went on my trip to Italy. Women were gazing. I simply nodded and smiled," Frazier said.

"You do know it wasn't you they were staring at?" Abby said, somewhat sarcastically.

"Allow me the delusion," Frazier chuckled as he leaned back and laced his fingers behind his head.

"Are you an early riser Clint?" Sarah asked. "The grounds are quite lovely in the morning. I'm sure Frazier only showed you a glance."

"Not usually."

"I'm up early. I love to walk in the morning air," Abby said.

Sarah said, "Yes, Abby is up with the birds. Frazier on the other hand could sleep all day."

"You know what the good book says. 'emor we which have believed do enter into rest'."

Abby laughed. "Talk about a misinterpretation of the word of God. Good one, brother. You're just plum lazy."

"So what is it you want to do with your life Clint?" Alistair asked.

Clint was at a loss for words. "I'm not sure. My dad wants me to run the ranch."

Sarah picked up the bowl of potatoes. "We'll I'm sure you'll decide soon enough. Whatever it is, you have to love it. Care for some more?"

"Just a little, thank you." She filled his plate.

"I wanted to be a famous scientist," Frazier said.

Abby leaned back in her chair. "Someday I'll be a famous poet. You can all say you knew me when."

"Hah, you should be so lucky."

"We'll just see, brother. I could be an ambassador or maybe a prime minister."

"That's a bit dramatic don't you think?" Sarah said. "We'll, I'm a dramatic person."

As the evening progressed, Clint shared more about life on his father's ranch; their wealth and privileged upbringing, hoping to impress Abby. She was more interested in the animals on the ranch than anything or anyone else. Clint found her endearing and light-hearted. She had a soft face but seemingly strong persona; confidence and an inner strength sprang from her.

After dinner, his eyes followed her as she climbed the stairs. He felt Sarah's arm rest on his shoulder. "Care to join us for a spot of tea before bed?"

"Yes, that'd be nice," he said, hoping Abby would join. They sat outside for two hours and talked but Abby never appeared. At ten o'clock, everyone went to bed.

Clint lay in bed. His thoughts were focused on the beautiful young Welsh girl.

I can't understand these feelings. I can't stop thinking about her. I want to get close to this girl. I've only known her for six hours and all I can think about is being with her.

He dozed off to sleep as the exhaustion of the day finally caught up with him.

Chapter 15

It was Sunday morning when the sun streamed into Clint's room. He heard a knock on the door as he lay in bed, half asleep. He stumbled out of bed and opened the door.

"Will you be joining us for church today?" Frazier asked. He was dressed in a pair of brown slacks, cream shirt, and a brown tie.

"Ah, oh ya, of course. I'll get dressed," he said while rubbing his eyes. Thirty minutes passed and Clint joined the family downstairs.

Abby emerged in a beautiful yellow dress that flared at the bottom, holding a cream wool jacket. Her hair was wrapped in a bun.

She looks gorgeous, Clint thought.

They ate a quick breakfast and then left for church. They arrived at the small brown building at nine o'clock.

Thirty wooden chairs sat in rows; 15 on each side. There were only about 20 people in attendance.

They moved slowly down the aisle. Hoping to sit next to Abby, Clint strategically walked behind her. Abby sat between Clint and Frazier in the third row right behind a tall black man. He looked back and with a deep African accent said, "Good morning."

"Hi, Kpassi," Abby said, smiling.

The tall, gray-haired Pastor, dressed in a long black robe, held a black book as he walked down the aisle. He turned around a few feet away from them and asked everyone to stand and sing a hymn. Clint watched Abby from the corner of his eye as she sang. She had a sweet voice and was always in tune.

After two worship songs, the Pastor moved in front of the pulpit. He spoke for thirty minutes about God's love, grace, and forgiveness. Clint felt Abby's arm brushing up against him. He couldn't stop focusing on her. Her face was fixed on the Pastor. It was clear she was listening to every word.

After church, Abby, Clint, and Frazier stood outside talking. Alistair and Sarah were talking to the Pastor. The huge, black man who had been sitting in front of them approached. His white teeth were shining bright in between his deep dark complexion. He held his hand out.

"Frazier, it's good to see you." Frazier hugged him. Abby hugged him and said, "Hi Kpassi. It's good to see you in Church. We missed you last week."

"Yes, I was visiting a sick friend in France."

Clint stared up at the six foot five inch African man, who he thought was odd to meet in Wales. He figured African people only lived in Africa, wore grass skirts, and carried spears, not dressed in three piece black suits.

Kpassi seemed friendly. He had a compassionate face, but eyes that looked as though they had known suffering.

"Kpassi, this is Clint, a friend of the family," Frazier said. He reached out his hand. "It's nice to meet you."

Clint shook his hand. "You too."

Kpassi looked at Abby. "Soon we will be on a long and wonderful journey. I can't wait to get to the homeland."

"It's all I think about. I've never been so excited."

He spoke to her in some sort of an African dialect. What was even more surprising was that Abby spoke the language back.

Clint was impressed that she could speak African. He wondered what he meant when he said 'emong wonderful journey'.

Alistair and Sarah approached.

Sarah said, "Let's go, we need to stop by the house and get the food. I hope you like to picnic, Clint. Once a month on Sunday, we go to this spectacular beach."

"Yeah, I love picnics."

They got back to the house and changed clothes. Earlier, Sarah had prepared baked chicken, French bread, potato salad, and peach pie. After packing the food and blankets, they drove along the dunes into a small deserted beach.

The sun glared down on them as they ate, talked, and laughed. Abby stood up and removed the light blue cotton summer dress she was wearing. Clint gazed at her slender figure in a white and red bathing suit.

"Abby, do be careful. Don't go in too far," Sarah said, waving her finger. "Mum, you worry too much. Last one in is a rotten egg." She sprinted on the sand and dove into the water. Clint and Frazier soon joined her, dressed in swimming trunks.

They played, splashing water on one another. When they made their way back to the blanket, Abby said, "Now where do you suppose they went?" Her eyes roamed the beach looking for her parents.

Frazier plopped down on the blanket. They probably went for a walk."

She grabbed a towel and rubbed it though her hair to dry it. "We should go for a walk. It's such a nice day."

"Sounds good," Clint said, excited at the thought of getting to know her better.

"You two go ahead. I'll sit this one out. I'm plum whopped." Frazier rolled over and lay flat on his back.

Clint and Abby walked on the sand near the edge of the water. "So, Frazier tells me you're planning to attend college this year." "Yes, I'm so excited.

"At one time, I wanted live in a flat at the French Riviera and be a writer. But that dream was short lived by mother's lectures and father's common sense. I've always wanted to study abroad, but mother almost fainted at the thought of me going far away. I'm planning to attend the University of Wales. We did agree that I could live in the dormitory."

"What do you plan to study?"

"I'm not sure. I want to be a nurse or a teacher. I love children, but I'm also considering creative writing."

He loved her accent. She giggled often. She was one of the happiest people he'd ever met. There was an easy rapport between them. She was the first woman he'd enjoyed talking to.

"Have you always liked school?"

"Yes . . . . well, maybe not always. There was my fifth grade teacher. He was a mean one; first time I ever got D. When he announced he was going camping with his family, I remember asking God to smite him with a severe case of poison ivy long enough so he'd miss school. Afraid it wasn't quite pleasant of me."

Clint laughed.

"What about you. Are you planning to attend a university?" "No . . . never cared much for school."

Clint's mood shifted—more serious now. Do you . . . have a boyfriend?" "No. I dated a boy once, a while back. It lasted two weeks. I'm afraid I don't have much time for dating."

Something caught her eye. She stopped, smiled and pointed. "Look," she said. "Isn't it beautiful?"

Just over the horizon on the water was a large rainbow.

"There is another sky, ever serene and fair, and there is another sunshine, though it be darkness there," Abby said, staring at the sky.

Clint looked at her.

"Emily Dickinson. I find her utterly inspiring. Have you heard of her?"

"I remember reading her poems in one of my English classes.

Unfortunately, it wasn't one of my best subjects."

"I love poetry. It's true literary works are written in verses with such great beauty and emotional sincerity."

Clint moved closer to Abby. "So, what's the nightlife like here? Do you go out much?"

"Not me. I'm afraid I'm a bit dull and aloof. And you? "On occasion. I'm sort of a night person."

"So, do both of your parents live in Texas?"

"My dad. My mom died when she was 32, giving birth to my sister. I was eight."

"Oh my gosh, how terrible. That must have been difficult."

"Yeah. I never realized how much. My mom really paid attention to me. She knew me. The only other person who knew me was my brother William, and he died fighting the war in Germany."

"I'm so sorry. Frazier told me about war; young men dying. How do you ever get over it?"

Clint paused, collecting his thoughts. "You don't. I never imagined war would be like that. I watched men die around me. There were times when medication for the wounded and food was scarce. It was a nightmare that went on and too long. The worst was feeling helpless. I lived in terror, just waiting for it to end. It's hard to get the images out of my mind."

"Did they ever get more medication or food?"

"Yeah, it did eventually arrive." He shook his head. I know one thing for sure is, I'll never fight in a war again."

"I pray we never have another war," she said.

They spent a few more minutes strolling along the sand before finally making their way back. Alistair and Sarah still weren't there. They lay down on the blanket. Clint was next to Abby. He'd never felt nervous around a girl before, but Abby was different. She seemed innocent and vulnerable, yet confident and secure.

They lay silent for a few moments listening to the motion of the waves as they rolled onto the shore.

"What are your plans for tomorrow, Frazier?" Abby asked.

"Why?" Frazier's eyes were closed and right arm was shielding his face from the sun.

"I want to take the car into town and do a bit of shopping. I need to get clothes for school."

Frazier turned toward her, half-sitting, his head propped on his hand. "You're not leaving for four months."

"I know. But have you forgotten, we're leaving for Africa in two weeks and I don't want to do it when we get back."

Clint's propped himself up on both elbows. "Africa?"

"Oh, didn't Frazier tell you? He and I are going on a mission trip with a few others from our church to a small village in the Democratic Republic of Congo. We're going to minister to them and help them in every way we can by working in their farmlands and providing much needed medical care."

Frazier swung around and nodded, confirming Abby's words.

"One of the men going with us is a doctor; a very good one. I'm so thrilled I can hardly stand it. This will be my second trip to Africa. My father took me when I was 12," Abby said.

So that's what that black man meant when he talked about a long journey. Clint's heart plunged. *What am I supposed to do? I really like this girl. And where will I go?*

"For how long?" Clint asked. "Three months."

Three months, he thought. Clint was shocked and disappointed. "But how will you understand them."

Abby speaks Swahili and French," Frazier said.

"My mother taught me. She was a missionary there for many years." "That's right, you spoke African to . . ."

"Kpassi," Abby said.

"Yes, Kpassi." The corner of Clint's mouth twitched upward as though he were trying to break a smile, all the while, a sense of loneliness began to hover over him.

She plopped down on her back on the blanket. "He's one of my best friends."

"How'd he end up here, in Wales?"

"My father met him when he was only a boy. His parents were killed so he lived in an orphanage for many years. The teachers were very mean and mistreated him. He ran away at the age of 16. My father met him on a mission trip. He was starving and living on the streets. With all the hardship he'd endured, he still had a thirst to live, so my father helped him back here. He taught him how to read, and helped him to get a job. He travels with my father on many trips."

Alistair and Sarah walked up to them chatting.

"Hello my loved ones," Sarah said. "It's getting late. We should go." Frazier jumped up. Clint stood and reached his hand down to Abby.

When she took it, he felt a warmth flow through him.

They arrived back at the house at eight o'clock. Mr. and Mrs. Brown went straight to their room, as did Frazier. Abby bathed, changed her clothes, and went downstairs. Clint took a long hot bath and peered into Abby's room afterwards.

The room was painted mossy green and the wooden floors were light brown. Silk curtains with green leaves hung from the window and paintings, mainly landscapes of nature, were placed on the walls. Beside her bed was a warm and cozy champagne sofa. There was also a painting right above her bed with an assortment of pink and purple flowers.

She jumped when Clint walked into the kitchen and pressed her palm against her chest.

"Oh Clint. You gave me a fright. I must have been concentrating too hard."

"I'm sorry. I didn't mean to scare you." "Oh, it's okay."

Abby was dressed in pink pajamas and hair tied back in a ponytail.

She was reading her bible. A glass pitcher of lemonade sat in the center of the table.

"Join me." She gestured for him to sit down while she got up, then took a glass from the cupboard and poured him lemonade. He took a sip.

"It's good, thank you."

"Freshly squeezed. I picked the lemons myself." "So, did you have a lovely day?"

"Yeah, it was great." His mood was grim. He was upset about the thought of Abby and Frazier leaving because he really liked it there, and memories of the past few months still haunted him. The death of Ted made his time in France a nightmare. He just didn't want to talk about it. His gaze swung over to the window.

"Is something wrong? "Uh, no. Why?"

"You were quiet the whole ride home and you've barely spoken a word since we've been back."

"I guess I have a lot on my mind."

"What is it? You seem reserved. Are you sure everything's okay?"

His heart began to beat faster and he squirmed in his chair. *Maybe talking about it with Abby will help. She's kind and I feel comfortable around her.*

He sighed. "I didn't have the best experience at the Riviera. It started out fine. I took a cruise from New York and met a woman, but the relationship didn't work out."

He wasn't about to tell Abby the truth about her stealing thousands of dollars from him.

"It wasn't meant to be."

She stared at him intently. Clint leaned back in his chair.

"Nice was spectacular, better than I could have imagined. Cannes was even better. It was a life I always dreamed of. I've never had so much fun.

"I met a friend on the ship, Ted. He was a good companion. We both had money to blow so we stuck together.

"He'd been in trouble with the law before . . . drugs. I didn't think much of it, but while we were in Cannes, but I began to notice a difference in him and wondered if he was back on drugs. One night, we were walking into a restaurant when some men started to chase us."

Abby's eyes widened.

"I thought they were gonna' kill us. They beat Ted up . . . pretty bad. Apparently, he'd stolen some drugs from them or somethin'. I'm not sure I even have the whole truth."

"What happened?" Abby asked. She leaned forward, hanging on every word.

Clint bent his head and silence loomed between them. A vision of Ted falling off the apartment building occupied his mind for several seconds. He placed his elbows on his knees. "He killed himself."

"Oh my gosh!" said Abby, stunned.

"He jumped off his apartment building. I tried to talk him down, but it was no use. I guess he figured he was better off dead. I watched him fall hundreds of feet."

She gently touched Clint's arm. "How horrible for you. I couldn't imagine having to go through that."

She gave him comfort. He leaned back in his chair.

"I blamed myself."

"Clint, it wasn't your fault. You can't blame yourself. There was nothing you could have done."

He narrowed his eyes and leaned forward on his elbows. "Why would a person kill themselves? No matter how bad things get, it's not worth ending your life." The tone of his voice changed; almost angry.

Her eyebrows rose as she said, "I don't understand it either. I guess people don't feel they have any other way out. Feelings of wounding and defeat overpowered your friend's hope for the future. If he would have given God access to his heart, He could have healed him. So many people need emotional healing. They suffer from feelings of loss, so much that they don't want to go on. They don't know how to cope. It's a shame, but it wasn't your fault, Clint."

She was wise beyond her years. There he was spilling his guts about a friend who took his life and all he could think about was grabbing and kissing her passionately.

"It's getting late," she said. "I have to be up early tomorrow. Thank you for sharing, Clint. I'll pray for you." She hugged him.

He wanted to grip her tighter. "Good night," she said. "Good night."

She left the kitchen and closed the door softly behind her.

I'm dying for a drink and a cigarette, he thought.

He went for a walk outside. The dew of the moist grass soaked the tips of his toes. He lit a cigarette. His thoughts were filled with visions of Abby.

Clint wondered why she wasn't in love with him yet. Back home, it took him less than an hour to win a woman's heart. He had dozens of women, but none of them made him feel the way he felt around her.

Why do I have this growing need to be beside her? I can get any woman I want. Now she's leaving. What am I going to do?

He threw the cigarette butt down and went to bed.

He tossed and turned at first, reliving the day's events. He enjoyed being here with Frazier and Abby, and it was coming to an end soon.

Where will I go? He thought. After hours of uneasiness, he finally fell asleep.

Chapter 16

Clint stared out at the Bristol Channel in the village of St. Donat's from the outer court of St. Donat's Castle. Mrs. Brown insisted Abby and Frazier take him to the medieval castle in the Vale of Glamorgan. Earlier that week, they'd toured the National Museum and hiked the cedar-studded hills.

The castle was located to the east of a small valley opening to the sea. Clint peered up at the tower. "How old is this place?"

Abby, who was only a few feet in front of him, turned around. "It was built in the 12th century."

"Hard to believe it's still standing," Clint said, eyeing the square gatehouse on the east side.

"Careful. Any minute a ghost may emerge and frighten the living daylights out of you," Frazier said, jokingly.

"Oh hush," Abby said. "No, it's true," Frazier said.

Clint slightly laughed. "That so."

"It's a preposterous rumor that the castle is haunted," Abby said.

"Yes." Frazier's voice changed; softer and deeper. "One minute you're touring the magnificent old castle and the next, an image appears. An eight feet tall beast, with fierce jagged claws and the face of a wolf, dashes out of know were, and attacks it prey."

"A ghost with jagged claws and the face of a wolf. Have you gone mad? Abby said. "I've never heard such nonsense. Stop it with your ridiculous stories."

Clint laughed.

"All right, all right, but don't say I didn't warn you." "Come on, let's go. I'm famished," she said.

They drove through wild and rugged coastlines. Clint gazed out the window as they passed an enormous body of water.

"This is one of Europe's largest waterfronts," Abby said. "It's beautiful here, isn't it?"

Clint nodded, "Yes."

They ate at a quaint pub, called the Bunch of Grapes, near the back end of the Glamorganshire Canal. Clint stuffed his face with a hearty Welsh meal consisting of venison faggots with pea purée and deep-fried whiting in beer batter. Abby had home-smoked duck breast with green tea oil, and Frazier had herb-flecked tuna, and baby potatoes. They enjoyed gingerbread cake for dessert. It was one of the best meals Clint had eaten in a long time.

When they stood to leave, Frazier said, "Perhaps one day we'll explore the nightlife here."

Clint got a glimmer of excitement. It'd been a long time since he'd had a drink.

"There are grand films showing at the theater. Then oh course there's my favorite ice cream shop."

It wasn't exactly what Clint had in mind. "That sounds good," he said, before putting on his jacket.

This trip had been like an oasis for Clint. He'd found more peace here than anywhere else.

Clint loved being around Frazier and Abby. They were a constant source of encouragement. And soon, it would end.

~~∞∞~~

Saturday morning, at six o'clock, Clint ambled down the hallway and knocked on Frazier's door.

"Frazier, you up?" No answer. He poked his head in the door. "Frazier, you awake?"

"Come in," he said in a groggy voice.

Frazier was lying in bed. The white linen sheets covered half his body and his pale chest lay bare. His wavy hair was chaotic, sticking out in different directions, and his eyes were half shut.

Frazier's room looked like a tornado had hit. The hardwood floor was covered with the trousers he had on the day before, several shirts, and a few pair of socks. Clint was surprised. Frazier was so clean-cut and proper.

Clint sat down on a chair next to his bed. "I'm sorry to bother you so early."

Frazier rubbed his eyes, "No worries. What is it?"

"I was wondering. Uh . . . I've been thinking about this all night." He paused for several seconds. "Can I go to Africa with you and Abby?"

Frazier propped himself up on his elbow. "That's an ace idea." His voice more assertive. "Now, why didn't I think of it?"

Clint smiled with relief. "Thanks."

"No bothers. It'll be a grand trip. Now be kind and close the door on your way out, will you."

"Oh course. And sorry again for waking you so early. Oh, is there anything I need to bring? How much money will I need?"

"There's plenty of time to work out the details. We're not leaving for a couple of weeks. What do you say you let me get a bit more shut eye."

"Uh, oh yeah." He left the room.

A weight lifted off him. Excited about the trip to Africa and thrilled about being with Abby, he rushed to his room to take a shower and got dressed.

Wearing a pair of black slacks and a t-shirt, he met the family downstairs. The house smelled of bacon. Sarah was in the kitchen and Alistair was sitting in the living room reading the newspaper. He went into the dining room where Abby was reading and glanced at the cover, 'Where there's a Will', is it a good book?"

"So far. I actually just started it. Did you sleep well?" "Yes, thanks. And you?"

"Quite well."

He sat down. A glass pitcher filled with orange juice was in the middle of the table. The table was set with crystal glasses and white plates.

"Care for some orange juice?" Abby asked. "Please."

She filled his glass.

Frazier, still dressed in his pajamas, finally made his way downstairs. He sat down next to Abby, reached for the glass pitcher, and poured himself a glass. He looked at Clint, who was sitting across from them both.

"Like a refill?" "Sure."

Sarah strode into the dining room carrying a basket of hot sourdough biscuits and set them on the table. She went back and carried out scrambled eggs and a platter of bacon. She set them in the center of the table, wiped her hands on her blue apron and yelled, "Alistair, breakfast is ready!"

Clint enjoyed the family meals together and liked being around them. Back home, when they ate at the same dinner table, the conversation always focused on the ranch, oil business, or Paul's rodeo and hunting adventures. The Browns were a welcome change. He felt like he had a real family.

Minutes later, Alistair joined them. He blessed the food and jabbed his fork into several pieces of bacon.

"Guess who's coming to Africa with us." Frazier looked at Clint.

Abby glanced at him. "You're coming with us! That's wonderful. You're going to love Africa."

Clint nodded calmly, trying not to appear overly excited.

"I'm so pleased to hear that," Sarah said. She grabbed a biscuit and began buttering it.

His mouth full, Alistair said, "You kids better be careful. Africa is not a playground, you know. I've had my share of adventures there, both wanted and not wanted."

"Oh hush, Alistair," said Sarah waving her hand at him. "You'll give the poor boy a fright. I lived in Zambia for 15 years as a girl. It is beautiful and the people are grand. It'll be a good experience."

From the corner of his eye, Clint glanced at Abby. "I can't wait."

Two weeks flew by fast. Wales was more exciting than Clint had anticipated. Abby seemed to know everyone and had friends everywhere they went. Being around her brought Clint joy. Her spirit uplifted him in a way that no one else ever had. Like Frazier, she seemed to have an intimate relationship with God.

Frazier and Clint helped Alistair on the farm in between touring Wales. The weeks at the Browns' house had been the most restful in his life, physically and mentally.

Chapter 17

Saturday, August 15, 1948 had arrived. Frazier, Abby, and Clint were loading their suitcases in the car. He brought only his duffle bag filled with clothes and the white envelope with a little over $4,500 in the zipper.

Sarah hugged Abby goodbye. Teary-eyed, she said, "I can't believe my children are all grown up. I want you both to know I'm proud of you."

She turned to Frazier and in a stern voice and said, "You take care of your little sister."

"Are you kidding, Mum." He smirked. "She'll be taking care of me."

"Did you remember to pack your bible?"

"I wouldn't forget it." He hugged her. "I love you." "I love you too. I'll see you all soon."

She turned to Clint and placed her hands on his shoulder. "You have a wonderful time. I'll be praying for you. God will be with you. You're such a nice young man and I have a feeling this trip is going to change you."

"Thank you and thank you for a wonderful stay. You made me feel very welcomed here."

"You're always welcome." She hugged Clint goodbye.

He'd only known her for a short period of time but she felt like his mother.

They jumped into the car. Alistair drove them to the airport where they would take British Airlines to Madrid Spain. From there, they would take another plane to Angola, Africa, and travel on a train to the town of Kikwit in Democratic Republic of Congo.

When they arrived at the airport, Frazier and Clint grabbed their bags and Alistair took Abby's. Standing next to the plane was Kpassi. Abby darted over to him. She told Clint Kpassi lived in Northeastern Liberia many years ago. That's where Alistair met him. He spoke five different African dialects, including Swahili. He was studying to be a pastor and full-time missionary. Though he had a strong and rugged appearance, his nature was gentle and sweet.

Clint watched in both surprise and jealousy as she hugged him. They seemed so close. He'd never met anyone as accepting as Abby.

He walked up next to Abby and set down his bag. "Clint, you remember Kpassi."

He smiled. "Hello Clint. I'm so happy you are joining us." Clint nodded. "Me too."

Within minutes, a black car pulled up. A nice-looking brunette woman stepped out first followed by a man wearing gold framed glasses. Abby hugged them.

"Clint, this is Jacqueline" "Hi," Clint said.

She had soft brown eyes and delicate cheekbones and looked to be in her late 40's.

"Hello," she said.

"And this is Claude Abney, Jacqueline's husband. He shook Clint's hand, "Hello."

"Hi." *He looks older,* thought Clint. *In his late 50's. She's a knock out. What's she doing with him and where'd all his hair go?*

"Claude is a doctor and Jacqueline a nurse. Dr. Abney has been a doctor for almost twenty years and had traveled to five different countries providing medical care, so he is experienced and prepared. They've been to Africa twice before: Zambia and South Africa," Frazier said. They both speak French fluently and quite a bit of Swahili.

"We understand it perfectly," Jacqueline said.

Abby then approached a young attractive man who looked to be in his mid-twenties and hugged him.

"This is Mark."

Clint clenched his jaw as jealousy took root.

Mark held out his hand and shook Clint's. "Welcome." "Hi," said Clint, cautiously.

Clint studied Mark. He had an aristocratic face and green eyes. He was about six feet tall, had broad shoulders, and clean-cut features. He looked like a quarterback.

Why's he coming? Don't even think about getting near Abby.

"Mark is a student at Wales University. He joined the Church several months ago. He is studying foreign languages," Abby said, enthusiastically.

"He's planning to become a teacher. Oh, and he's also engaged to be married to one of my closest friends."

Relieved, Clint said, "It's good to meet you."

Alistair gave a round of hugs to each of them. "Be careful and write often. Our prayers are with you."

Then he left.

Minutes later, they boarded the 30 seat plane.

Clint took seat 5A. Frazier sat beside him. Abby sat next to Kpassi. Clint could feel the jealousy continuing to rise. Kpassi wasn't a threat but her attention was so fixed on him. She obviously loved being around him. He leaned forward and watched her interact with Kpassi, speaking incessantly, smiling the entire time.

She's so innocent. She's is going to be a challenge, but I'm up for it. I really like this girl . . . I think I love her.

He laid his head back on the seat. He wasn't sure what to expect once they arrived in Africa, but was looking forward to a nice hotel room, preferably with room service. Once the plane left, he dozed off.

They landed in Madrid where they had a twelve-hour layover and traded some of their American dollars for money of the country they were going to. Clint traded only five hundred dollars and kept the rest of his money in his envelope.

They caught a plane to the country of Angola, located north of Namibia, south of Democratic Republic of Congo, and west of Zambia.

Clint had slept most of the way. He loosened his seat belt, propped his chin on his hand, and stared out the window. The plan flew over a canopy of trees and a dark, almost black, muddy river.

The plane veered right towards a highland of rolling hills and deciduous trees. Abby was chattering excitedly, talking to Kpassi and Jacqueline.

The sun was blazing when the planed arrived at two o'clock. After being raised in Texas, Clint was used to the scorching heat.

Two drivers took them to the Luanshya in a cart pulled by mules where they would catch the train. They went through rugged grasslands scattered with livestock. The village was small and town streets, red and dusty. Men, women, and children walked along the crowded streets with many barefoot on the hot road. Some young women wore blankets of ochre and elaborately beaded gorgets. Other women were dressed in colorful wrapped skirts and cloaks with earrings and bracelets. Many of them carried large baskets filled with fruit and vegetables on their heads.

Some of the men were bare-chested and wore colorful cloths draped around them. Several had a broad red thick stripe painted vertically down their chests and held swords. They stood erect looking like they were guarding something. He wondered who they were and what they were protecting.

A market had been set up under a canopy of woven palm leaves stretched over sticks.

Women sat under the shelters and sold dates, nuts, clothing, art, and jewelry.

"We have two hours before the train leaves, so we have time for a bit of shopping," Frazier said.

Claude and Jacqueline went with Kpassi to a vendor selling food and drinks. Abby, Frazier, Clint, and Mark walked towards the market.

Red dust floated in the air with every passing cart. Shrill voices called out bargaining as the hands and eyes of customers rummaged through their items. Clint couldn't understand them, but from their body language and persistency, it was obvious they were trying to make a sale.

He was close behind Abby when she lowered herself under one of the canopies fingering bright silk clothes. A thin frail African woman watched Abby as she examined a silk scarf. She pulled a black wallet from her green and white purse and handed the woman 5/100 of a Rand which was 5 cents in American money.

Frazier was right behind him as he strolled. He studied a wood carving of a rhino, amazed at the fine craftsmanship. The wood carvings included giraffes, hippos, and birds. There were also water pitchers and cups made of clay, decorated with bright colors.

He moved towards a woman with a blue scarf on her head and a plus size cloth draped around her body who was selling jewelry.

She held up a beaded necklace. "Unaweza kununua." "What did she say?" Clint asked, leaning toward Frazier. "She wants you to buy from her."

Clint looked for several minutes until he found a necklace made of cowry shells. He glanced over at Abby who was purchasing fruit. He bought the necklace and gently stuffed it in his pocket. He decided he would wait for the right time to give it to her.

Clint watched Abby stop beside two young children sitting on a street corner. She handed each of them a piece of fruit and patted them on the head. The children devoured it.

He joined her. By this time, she was studying one of the masks made with elaborate designs. They shopped for another half hour before joining Kpassi and the Abneys. A cold glass of water was a commodity and expensive, but worth the price.

Chapter 18

They boarded the train at noon. Clint had paid $20 each to upgrade everyone's tickets to first class. He and Frazier shared a room. Abby was right next door to them.

Clint threw his duffle bag on the bed covered with a fine gold linen blanket. He strolled over to the window, and opened the gold curtains.

"Thanks again for the upgrade Clint," Frazier said. "The room's incredible."

"Glad to do it."

Clint and Frazier changed clothes and went into the club car. Clint sat down next to Abby while Mark and Frazier sat across from them. Kpassi soon joined them.

"Where are the Abneys?" Kpassi asked. "They are resting in their room," Abby said.

Clint stared out the window at the incredible ever-changing scenery flashing past.

The train drifted through the fierce desert land of Angola. He marveled at the spectacular wild beast migrating across the plains.

Clint watched tall antelopes with massive spiraling horns running at the speed of lightening. He wondered why they were running and then saw an immense group of cheetahs dashing behind them; trying to catch their dinner. The antelope were fleeing for their lives.

"Look!" Abby said. She pointed with her out-stretched hand. "Aren't they spectacular?" There were dozens of lions. "The majesty of them is breathtaking. They truly are the kings of the jungle."

"As you can see, the continent of Africa is a rich, vast, diverse land," Kpassi said. "Some of the grandest waterfalls in the world are in this region." "Several hours ago, we passed the grave of Chief Mukungule, chief of the Bisa people who lived in the valley. He was buried under a large sausage tree in a beautiful area of the forest where you can hear the falls in the distance. The people have an annual ceremony where the Bisa elders visit the grave bringing offerings to the chief of food and tobacco.

"What's a sausage tree?" Abby asked.

"It is a tree that has sausage-like fruit hanging down on long, rope-like cords. The fruit is eaten by baboons, elephants, giraffes, and monkeys.

"Many different cultures exist within an individual country. Much of Africa's cultural activity centers on the family.

"People across the continent are remarkably diverse by just about any measure. They speak a vast number of different languages and live in a variety of dwellings."

Clint listened intently to Kpassi. He found himself fascinated by the history.

"Over the centuries, people from other parts of the world have migrated to Africa and settled here. Quite a few Europeans immigrated particularly to South Africa, Zimbabwe, and Algeria.

"You will enjoy Africa, Clint. The village we are going to is small and simple, but the people are warm hearted and extremely welcoming."

"I'm guessing from the last village, the weather will be hot," Clint said. "Actually, because of its high elevation, temperatures are generally moderate, except in October. It will be stiflingly hot, but for now, it's relatively dry and cool."

Clint continued to gaze at the vast open spaces, the wildebeest crossing plains as far as the eye could see.

He had seen the brightly illuminated New York City, the powerful and inspiring landscape of the Grand Canyon, the diverse country of Spain with its bullfights and crowded beaches, and the beautiful landscape of the Riviera, but nothing quite compared to this. He had to admit, Africa was by far the most beautiful place he'd ever seen. It was truly an untamed experience.

They brushed by the Mwaleshi River, surrounded by a mosaic habitat of Cathedral Mopani trees and open plains. The train swept past herds of buffalo, cooksens wildebeest, and impala. They passed through transitional woodland to a riverine forest much higher up. There were big lush trees such as the great ebony trees. Giraffes appeared, moving unhurriedly among the trees, browsing daintily among the upper branches.

That evening, Clint rummaged through the bags in his room until he found the necklace he'd bought for Abby. While Frazier was taking a bath, he dressed in a pair of white pants and a light blue blazer, his hair neatly parted on the side. He left the room and went into the dining car.

Wine bottles with dripping candles sat on the red table cloth. Mr. and Mrs. Abney were seated glancing at the menu. He sat down next to them.

"Hi."

"Hello," Jacqueline said. "Thank you again for upgrading our tickets. The rooms are very nice."

"You're welcome," Clint said, before picking up a menu.

Clint eyed a waiter who passed by carrying two glasses of wine. *It's been weeks since I've had a drink. What I wouldn't give for a shot of whisky.*

Minutes later, Frazier showed up, dressed in black slacks and a cream shirt. "I'm famished, what's for dinner?" He sat down next to Clint.

Clint was reading the menu. He briefly glanced over towards the entrance of the dining room. His stomach tensed. Abby stood, shimmering in a red silk dress. Her hair was swept up on top of her head and red ruby lipstick complimented her flawless pale skin. At that moment, she was the only woman in the room. Silence took over the large group of men sitting two tables over. They stopped mid-conversation to take in the sight of her. She tossed a smile at the gentlemen and made her way to the table.

Clint stood. "You look beautiful." "Thank you." She smiled.

He walked around the other side of the table and pulled out her chair. She sat and glanced up at Clint. "Thank you. Where are Mark and Kpassi?"

They decided to eat in their room. They're tired and wanted to rest," Frazier said.

A waiter wearing a white jacket approached the table. "May I bring you some wine?"

Clint looked at Abby. "No thank you."

"No, just water," Clint said. He was deliberately trying to look sober in front of Abby.

They ate a meal freshly prepared on board by the chef: Doumea, a type of catfish, rice, and corn.

"How long till we arrive in Kikwit?" Clint asked.

"We'll probably arrive in a little less than a day," Frazier said. "From there, we will take a car to a small village of Boende. It should be almost a day's ride. The village is in the Democratic Republic of Congo."

"Kpassi will be our guide," Abby said.

I suppose a nice hotel is out of the question, thought Clint.

"I'm thrilled and excited. My mum says the people are primitive, but warm," Abby said.

Frazier took a drink of water and set his glass down. "Well, don't get too excited. There is much work to be done."

"Work?" Clint asked.

"Yes. We have to help establish medical quarters for Claude and Jacqueline, assist with gardening, and rebuild the school. The last one was destroyed in a storm last year.

"A storm?" Clint said. "Does it rain a lot?"

Yes, but a couple of years ago, it was unusually bad. It hit hard and destroyed some homes. The huts we will be staying in are pretty sturdy though, so no need to worry."

Clint sipped his water again, this time downing the whole glass. *What did I get myself into? Now, I really do need a drink.*

"It's getting late," Jacqueline said. "I'm tired. We should get some sleep." "Yes, it's been an exhausting trip. The couple stood up. "Goodnight everyone," Claude said.

"Goodnight. I'm a bit tired as well." Abby stood.

Frazier went back to the room while Clint walked Abby to hers. He wanted to give her the necklace but didn't feel the timing was right.

"Don't be too overly anxious about the trip." Abby said. Frazier made it sound a bit grim. It's extraordinary and there'll be plenty of time for exploring. I promise it won't be all work."

"Oh, I'm not worried. I've lived on a ranch my whole life." Although he'd barely done a full day's work, he wasn't about to let her know that.

"Thank you for escorting me to my room. You're quite charming, Clint." Her eyes brightened. "I do look forward to knowing you better."

He didn't want the night to end. He had to fight to keep from kissing her.

She kissed him on the cheek. "Good night." He smiled back, "Good night."

It was hard to sleep. Frazier made the trip seem hard and consuming, but none of it mattered. Clint knew he was falling in love.

The trained arrived on Monday. The town was located on the Kwilu River in the southwestern part of the Democratic Republic of Congo.

Clouds sailed over the pale blue and violet sky. The air almost seemed alive over the land, like a burning flame.

The people seemed a bit more primitive then in the other village. Clint watched a tall man, wrapped in a blanket, move by them. His face was daubed with white clay.

The weather was cool and the team was exhausted. An African man came running towards them with his large belly bouncing.

"Kpassi," he said. Kpassi hugged him. "Gatura, furahiya kwa se wewe."

Clint looked at Abby. "What did he say?" "He's glad to see him."

As the man spoke, Abby said, "He says, they've been waiting for us. The cars are over there."

Clint looked at the two jeeps.

"He thanks my parents and church for the money to purchase the cars. We would have had no transportation to the village if it hadn't been for them. Kpassi said you're welcome, they were happy to do it."

The Abneys and Mark rode in one car while Frazier, Abby, Kpassi, and Clint rode in the other.

The car jolted forward. They swept past a foot plateau where herdsmen were hoeing their land. The trees and bushes surrounding them began to thicken.

It was almost a fifteen hour drive up to the narrow mountainous trail. The forest had hundreds of different kinds of trees. They stopped a few times in a couple of remote villages to put fuel into their tanks, eat and rest. Finally, the cars pulled into a small village.

Chapter 19

They climbed out of the jeep. Clint's body ached from the endless bumps and jolts. He moved his head right and left to remove some of the stiffness. The altitude made him dizzy. He remembered Frazier saying it was about three thousand feet. The surrounding trees were thick and green.

They walked onto the wet muddy ground. Clint looked around, examining his environment. Most of the houses were huts made of short wooden poles and grass. Two of buildings he could see looked like they were made of red stone.

Earlier, Kpassi told them the small community was somewhat isolated. Neighboring villages, of similar size, were almost 20 miles away. The largest city was over 150 miles away.

What have I gotten myself in to? He thought again.

He glanced over his shoulder and noticed a stream of dirty water.

Several men dressed in cloths wrapped around their entire bodies stood and watched them. They had strong broad shoulders and stood upright. The women seemed dignified and gentle, dressed in long colorful cloths wrapped around them, some of them heavily decorated in ornaments and accessories.

A short old man with a refined face moved over to them. He shook Kpassi's hand. They spoke in Swahili.

"This is Gamba. The townsmen have appointed him the highest-ranking chief. He is honest, hardworking, and carries great significance among the people," Kpassi said. "He has invited us to join him for dinner."

He appeared to be a crafty man, with a fine manner. Kpassi placed his hand on Abby's back.

"This is Abby."

She smiled, shook his hand, and then spoke in Swahili.

Then he introduced the others. Clint met Gamba's gaze with directness and respect. He shook Clint's hands warmly with his gentle, yet callused hands.

"He will show us to our quarters."

Gamba led them through the village. They passed one of the red stone buildings. A large fig tree and a garden with fresh corn growing were located at the side of the home.

"This is Gamba's home," Kpassi said.

Clint held his bag tight and stayed close to Abby. He found the experience somewhat frightening. Abby, on the other hand, seemed right at home. She smiled at everyone she passed.

Gamba motioned for Jacqueline and Claude to stay in a small hut not far from his home.

They would stay at the clinic once it was built. Abby's sleeping quarters were right next door.

"Frazier, you, Clint, and Mark will sleep here."

The hut was two homes over from were Abby was staying. "I will stay with the driver."

Frazier had to crawl to go in since the doors were low. Clint followed and then Mark. His eyes went straight to a large black bear skin covering the floor. The hut was a single room with no windows. In the middle of the floor was a fireplace. Long thin horizontal beams were used to hold the walls up. At ceiling height, were longer lighter poles for the roof rafters.

In one corner was a pile of wood neatly cut up into billets and in another, a large earthen jar filled with water next to an empty bowl. A small lantern was illuminated and a pile of blankets, folded neatly on one of the cots.

Clint was struck that there was no real bed. He wasn't sure what to expect, but thought at least he'd have a comfortable bed and a pillow to sleep on.

"Where or how do they cook?" Clint asked.

"Cooking is done on a hearth three or four yards away outside the house," Frazier said. He threw his bag on the floor. "When it rains, it's done in the fireplace."

He tossed his bag down next to Frazier's.

I'm guessin' there aren't many nearby banks. Where am I going to stash my money?

He continued to stare at the tiny space. *From a suite in Nice and a villa in Cannes, to a hut in Africa. Who would have thought?*

"The huts are made sturdy and laced in large oval leaves, so don't worry. Not even rain can get in," Frazier said.

Clint nodded, nervously.

"Where do they bathe?"

"In the river. I could use a good bath myself. What do you say we take a dip?"

Frazier grabbed a blanket next to the cot to dry himself, along with a bar of soap and a change of clothes. Clint and Mark both took blankets and extra clothes and followed Frazier to the river. The water was cold but Clint didn't complain. It felt good after the long ride.

Afterwards, they joined Abby right outside her hut. She was dressed in a straw hat and a thin blue dress. "Shall we go do a little exploring?"

Clint stood close to her. Women working in a garden not far from Gamba's home, glanced up as they passed by. They were removing weeds among the rows. Several women passed by, carrying pitchers on their heads. Clint nodded and smiled.

"Where are they going?" he asked.

"I'm not sure," Abby said, fanning herself.

The weather was cool but the long exhausting trip caused her to perspire. "Why are some of the women dressed with so much jewelry?" Mark asked. "The unmarried girls decorate themselves with iron bracelets and anklets, and flowers in their ears," Abby said. "They also wear necklaces made of red berries and white shells. It's rather beautiful. You might say they are ladies in waiting. The material worn by the men is made of bark. The women pound bark against a rock until the fibers get soft and the hard parts break off. Then make small pieces of cloth; pounded and sewn together."

They walked along a narrow path. The woods were filled with trees high enough to shade the windows of a tall apartment building. They wore a crown of luxuriant green.

"The forest is a home to creatures unseen by most humans," Frazier said.

The trees were varied, unlike the spear-shaped leaves or smooth trunks he'd grown up with in Texas.

A herd of elephants grazed in a meadow. Clint smiled, amazed by the gentle beasts. It was intriguing to be so close to them. They ate and strolled onward.

The sunlight was dense and massive heavy-scented lilies were everywhere.

"The people here are mainly farmers and fishermen," Abby said. "You'll get to experience it, Clint. They catch hundreds of fish at a time in the Kwa river."

Clint nodded and kept walking, not overly thrilled.

At seven o'clock, they arrived at Gamba's home.

Gamba opened the door, smiling broadly. He motioned for them to enter. They strolled onto the stone floor and noticed a small Persian carpet with dyes of green, orange, and yellow on the floor. Spears, bows, quivers, and nets hung from pegs on the walls of the living room. Clint looked into the kitchen and noticed a small iron stove.

His wife, a short stout woman with a colorful headdress covering her head, placed a bowl of papaya on the table.

"This is my wife, Fatuma."

She greeted them politely, smiling graciously and motioned for them to sit at the table.

A teenage boy and girl walked into the house. Fatuma snappishly spoke to them, waving her finger. The boy and his sister sat at the table.

"This is my son, Chiamaka. He just turned 16."

He had handsome features and a proud bearing. He was tall, thin, seemed friendly and personable, and he had a bright smile.

"Hello," he said in English.

"And this is my daughter, Mardea. She is 11."

She had high cheek bones and was dressed in an orange cloth wrapped around her slender body, and wore a colorful wrap around her thick short hair. She appeared reserved.

"Hello," she said shyly, also in English.

"Sit down, both of you," Gamba said, in a strong and assertive voice. "You are late."

Fatuma served the food, stacking each tin plate with plenty. They drank from cups made of tin.

Clint started to take a bite. Gamba said, "Let us give pray." "Chiamaka," he said.

They bowed their heads as Chiamaka prayed. "God, we are grateful for the food. We are grateful for our guests. Thank you for your blessings. Amen."

Clint whispered in Abby's ear. "How'd he learn to speak English?" "Missionaries have been coming here for years. They taught him and his sister in school. Gamba and Fatuma speak a little English but seem to understand it okay."

They ate strips of beef, yams, peanuts, and fruit. Kpassi, Abby, and Claude did most of the talking during dinner. They spoke in both English and in Swahili. On occasion, Abby would whisper in Clint's ear to interpret.

Clint smiled and laughed when they laughed. They were simple people and very hospitable. It was evident they were poor, yet appeared content and happy.

After dinner, they gathered in the street with the villagers. They sat in a circle. There were three men sitting separately with several goblet shaped hand drums.

Ten men dressed in brown cloth wrapped around their waists and magnificent lion-shaped head dresses on their heads, carrying clubs, stepped into the center of the circle. Their bodies and faces were painted with an assortment of bright colors.

"They are going to dance a welcoming dance," Kpassi said.

The drums began to beat. They were loud and strong. The drumming became more rhythmic. The men began to dance in perfect unity, covering the entire circle. People smiled and cheered. Eventually, several women clothed in beautiful colorful garments joined them. The earth seemed to tremble with the thunder of the drums as the dancers thrust their cowhide shields forward and waved their clubs. Their legs moved together as if all the dancers were one person.

Abby, with a huge smile on her face, swayed her body back and forth to the sounds of the drums. The townspeople shouted once the dance was complete. Clint stood up next to Abby after she stood and applauded.

When the emotions calmed down and the crowd dissolved, Clint walked Abby to her hut.

"I told you it would be an adventure."

"You weren't kidding. Oh, but a good one." He was trying to appear optimistic.

He wanted to give her the necklace he'd bought her, but the timing still didn't seem right.

"I'll see you in the morning, Clint." "Good night."

The week was spent building the medical center. Once complete, it would consist of three rooms; the largest room being the clinic, a bedroom, and a kitchen.

The men worked night and day on the building. Clint had a bit of experience with assembling buildings. Once, he helped his brother Will build a shed to house farm supplies and a small tree house in back of their mansion. They painted walls, scrubbed floors, and built cabinets to store the medical equipment. There was enough medication to immunize at least 200 people against some of the deadly diseases such as malaria. Claude and Jacqueline planned to begin seeing patients immediately.

The Abneys had mentioned during the train ride that they were planning on traveling to Africa at least twice a year, staying two to three months at a time. They had a heart for the poor and strong faith in God. Clint had grown to like them both.

It was Monday evening. They'd been there a little over a month. There was a luminous haze in the sky. They'd finished building the medical facility a few days earlier and started on the school. Clint handed Mark a nail. He grabbed the nail and knocked it into the wall with a hammer. They were adding shelves to a small school house they'd built for the children in the village. Mark planned to teach the children English and math. Kpassi and Frazier were adding the last touches of paint to the walls.

A large drop of sweat rolled down Clint's nose.

Abby walked up to him carrying a pitcher filled with water and cups. "You thirsty?" she asked.

His throat was dried out. "Yeah."

She poured glasses of water for both him and Frazier. Clint gulped it down with one swallow and then handed her the cup to refilled.

"Abby, where do they get the clean water? I heard water was a scarce commodity in Africa."

"Yes it is. It's a source of prosperity and futurity. With the help of my parents and members of our church, we provided the village with 1,000 gallons of clean water. It's stored in a shed in large plastic containers next to Gamba's house."

He drank the water and climbed back on the ladder to finish working while Abby brought water to Frazier and Kpassi.

They finished adding the final touches to the school that night.

Clint felt battered and bruised, but he looked at the building he helped to make with a sense of accomplishment. For the first time in his life, he felt like he made an important contribution.

Chapter 20

Frazier, Mark, Abby, Clint, Chiamaka, Gamba's son, and four men from the village climbed a steep mountain. The long splendid waterfall before them was breathtaking. They watched as it tumbled in multiple stages, shrouded in mist, and thundered as it crashed into the rocks below a jagged cliff.

Clint felt a visceral response deep inside his chest as he stood and gazed at it.

"I've never seen anything like it," Abby said. "It's magnificent," Frazier said.

Two months seemed to fly by. They'd taken a canoe down the river to the opposite side of the forest. The narrow boats made from a wood frame and covered with discolored birch bark were large enough to hold six people.

Chiamaka was their guide as they hiked and explored the thick, wet woods. Gamba insisted the other men travel with them for protection.

The day before, they'd gone fishing on the Kwa river, which branched off from the Congo River. Thousands of different fish filled the river, some of them weighing three hundred pounds.

They had caught hundreds of fish by setting nets ten feet wide at the mouth and fifteen feet long. Clint, Frazier, and Mark helped some of the young boys clean them.

They moved past a small mountain. A magnificent rainbow appeared on the horizon. They sat down under a baobab tree, rested, and ate. Gamba's wife had packed a hearty lunch of baked fish, papaya, mangos, and yams.

Abby sat across from Clint, staring endlessly at the magnificent view: thickets of wild flowers, shrubs and young trees. She seemed right at home. Clint wondered what attracted him to her. He liked his women gorgeous and wild. She was beautiful, but simple, raised with strong values and innocent. She had a rare ability to be what people needed, when they needed it.

Part of his fascination, even though he wouldn't admit it, was her lack of romantic interest in him. He was rich, handsome, everything a woman could want, yet she seemed disinterested.

He was sitting in the midst of one of the most spectacular views in the world and all he desired to do was look at her.

Frazier, who was sitting only a few feet from Clint, took a gulp of water from a canteen and leapt up.

"Shall we get moving? There is a great deal of unexplored country."

Chiamaka led them two more miles. They encountered a herd of elephants. The elephants were feeding, drinking and seemed to be socializing. Clint thought to himself, this is really real. There are no fences, no zoo to protect you.

They walked paths made by the animals through the forest, brushing their way past thick trees and bushes as the leaves slapped them in the face.

"Look, there," Abby said, a rise of excitement in her voice.

A gorilla stood leaning on its knuckles on a jagged cliff. It looked fierce. The dark, thick-haired animal stood still for several seconds before knuckle-walking in the opposite direction. There were at least two dozen gorillas lying on the thick lush grass. One lay on his back, looking perfectly relaxed. Another was chewing on some leaves.

Clint took a few more steps to get a closer look. Suddenly, a big black gorilla with strands of silver and gray ran towards him with great speed. The animal stopped only a few yards in front of him. It stood upright, slapped its hands against its chest, and made a horrific roaring sound.

Clint could feel blood rush to his face. His lips tightened as he tried to stay calm; he was terrified. There were three other gorillas not far behind.

He felt Abby take a step back. "What should we do?" she asked in a whisper, her voice shuddering. She clutched Clint's arm.

"Be very still," Chiamaka said. "If you run, it will chase you."

Clint glanced at Frazier who looked scared. The natives, however, appeared unafraid. They simply held their spears close as if ready to attack in a moment. The gorilla let out another roar, turned, around and walked away.

The natives had a sense of risks in life. In a moment of extreme tension, they seemed ready to give their lives. Clint found the encounter both terrifying and fascinating.

They spent the next few hours exploring the forest. The trees shaded them.

"Look," Abby said, pointing upward. There were two chimpanzees. She laughed. "They're playing."

The chimpanzees were wrestling and chasing one another. On occasion they would blurt out laughter like vocalization.

They walked under a huge canopy of trees entangled with monkey vines and past a gorge with a large pool at the bottom, where they could see huge pods of hippos.

"Thousands of creatures live in the forest," Chiamaka said. "Look, over there," Frazier said.

"Where? Abby asked.

"Over there. It looks like some sort of deer."

A reddish-brown coated creature with white-yellow stripes was standing on the opposite side of the forest.

"What is it?" Mark asked.

"It's a Bongo," Chiamaka said.

Abby took a few steps forward. "What's that?" "An antelope."

"It's beautiful," she said.

They made their way back to the canoes. The villagers used jagged edge paddles with the shape of a large spear for their canoes. The boats glided on the river, surrounded by a mass of trees and shrubs.

The sun was overhead hovering over the river. The color was so intense, almost black and the sky was gradually turning gray. Flamingos moved with grace across the deep green grass of the riverbanks.

They were almost back at the village when they stumbled upon dozens of rhinos basking in the river.

"Everyone be very quiet and still," Chiamaka said. "The animals are usually harmless, but very territorial." Clint froze instantly, taking deep breaths. He glanced back at Abby who was sitting directly behind him. Her face was a mask of concentration; so intense.

A rhinoceroses moved only yards from them. Clint thought it was planning to attack. The boat began to sway side to side. The rhinoceros was guiding her baby towards the shore.

Once they hit the shoreline only a few miles from the village, Clint was relieved and exhausted. It had been the scariest and most exciting experience of his life.

The next afternoon, Abby and Clint were working in the back room of the medical clinic. They had seen at least nine villagers enter for care.

Dr. Abney treated people for many illnesses: hypertension, guinea-worm, broken bones, hepatitis. Days earlier, he'd taken several splinters out of Clint's hands and bandaged Mark's ankle, which he had sprained when he fell from a ladder.

After lunch, Dr. Abney and Jacqueline left to make a house visit to a sick young child.

Abby watched Clint as he marked the measurement on a board with a pencil line. Using c-clamps, he attached the board to a sturdy table, positioned the pencil line just off the edge. He double-checked his measurements and carefully cut the wood using a handsaw. Once he was done, he and Abby sanded the rough-cut edges with sandpaper. They were building some storage shelves for the clinic to store more medication.

"Why don't we take a break, Clint? I'm getting tired and it's so hot."

She poured the both of them a glass of water from a wooden pitcher that was sitting on the table right next to them. Clint gulped it down.

"You know you're really quite the craftsman. Where did you learn to build?"

"I built a tree house with my brother and did some work around the ranch when I was younger. I guess I have knack for this sort of thing."

Clint looked directly in her eyes. "I'm glad I came here." "I'm thrilled you're here."

Clint smiled. "I like the people and you. You're unlike any other woman I've ever met. You don't care about wealth and position, only helping others. "I always try and focus on God's heart for the people on mission trips and in my everyday life. Helping people is what is important, not materialist things.

His feelings for here deepened every time he was around her. Her gentle nature and caring heart drew him closer and closer to her. Not knowing how she felt was unsettling. He thought to himself, now or never.

I care for you, Abby."

She gazed directly into his eyes. He sensed a change in her demeanor. She seemed almost nervous. She smiled, "Well, I . . ." Before she couldn't finish her sentence, Chiamaka dashed through the door with a look of fear on his face.

"Abby, can you help us?" He was breathing heavily. She stood. What is it, Chiamaka?"

Taking deep breaths he said, "Dr. Abney needs your help."

Clint and Abby followed him down the road. They stopped at a small hut and peeked in. A little girl who looked to be around eight was lying in a bed, sweating. She had streaks of yellow in her eyes. A thin frail elderly woman, wrapped in a brown blanket, sat still and quiet next to her on the floor.

Dr. Abney was kneeling next to the girl while Jacqueline stood on the other side, blotting the child's head with a wet cloth. Dr. Abney came outside to talk to them.

"What is it?" Abby asked. "What's wrong?"

"The girl suffers from jaundice. She desperately needs treatment. I have the medicine and equipment back in the clinic, but her grandmother refuses to allow her to be treated. Without help, the child may die. I thought perhaps you could speak to her, Abby."

"I'll try." She crawled into the hut, Dr. Abney right behind her. Clint dropped to his knees to listen, although he couldn't understand them. Abby knelt by the child's bedside and began to speak to the grandmother in Swahili. They spoke for almost five minutes. She stood and motioned for the doctor to go outside. This time, Jacqueline followed them out.

"She fears for the child's life. Her son was seen by a doctor and then died. She doesn't want to lose her granddaughter the same way. I explained to her that things were different. You had medication that could help her. She has agreed that you may take her little girl to the clinic."

"Wonderful Abby, I knew you could convince her. Clint, help me carry her."

Clint crawled inside, lifted the girl from the bed, and held her tightly, smiling. Once they entered the medical clinic, he gently laid her down on the examining table.

Jacqueline created a bed for her towards the back of the building and placed an IV in her arm. They planned to monitor her progress and continue administering the medication for a few days.

A harsh wind blew as the sun slipped away. Around 30 people gathered that Sunday evening in the other stone building which was the church, to attend the service.

After a round of singing and prayer in their native language, Kpassi stood up at a wooden pulpit. In Swahili, he said, "I am going to talk from the Book of John in the Bible." Mark who was standing next to him translated to English. A few people, including Gamba and his family, had bibles and turned to the Book of John. Clint shared with Abby.

Kpassi said, "John 3:16 states, "For God so loved the word that he gave his only begotten Son, that whosoever believeth in him should not perish, but have everlasting life." He laid down the bible on an empty chair and cleared his throat.

"All men have sinned. None are perfect, but we have a God who is perfect and his grace for us is never ending. So much that he would give up his only son to save us. God's love for us is overwhelming. No matter what we do or say, we can never change that. He loves you and desires a relationship with you."

Clint's attention was on Abby. Her eyes were set on Kpassi. Clint watched her as she nodded in agreement.

Clint said a small prayer. God, help Abby fall in love with me. We'd be great together. I'd even be willing to go to church, at least once a month . . . . okay, okay regularly, Amen.

Kpassi said, "No matter what you have done, God will forgive you."

Kpassi walked to the center of the room. Mark followed, still translating.

"Each of you, bow your heads and repeat this prayer. God, forgive me for all of my sins.

I want to receive you as my savior. I believe you sent your Son to die for me and I want to live my life for you. Amen."

They stood and sang one more song, then gathered in a kitchen for rice pudding.

That evening in his hut, Clint slid out of his shoes, pulled off his shirt and jeans, and laid it on the floor. He felt tension in his back from working all day. He stretched his arms above his head several times to relieve the stiffness, then rolled up in his blanket and settled on the uncomfortable cot.

It was hot, making it hard to sleep.

After staring at the ceiling for ten minutes, he sat up and rested his hands on his chin. The service had brought back memories of his father. He leaned over and pulled the bible from his bag. He studied the book for a few minutes. A feeling of despair swept over him. Thoughts of the gentle kind man he'd left behind began to resonate through his mind.

He must be worried, he thought. *I should have stayed in touch. I think he would actually be proud of me if he knew what I was doing.*

Kpassi and Frazier were planning to drive to a city about 150 miles away, in a couple of weeks to get more medical supplies. I'll go with them and try calling him then. If I can't reach him by phone, I'll write.

Clint unexpectedly realized how much he missed his father.

Chapter 21

James stood in the waiting room of Baylor University Medical Center watching Paul incessantly pace back and forth as they listened to the arduous groans coming for Aiko's room. Hiro was sitting by the window nervously awaiting the birth of his first grandchild. Kameko, Aiko's mother, was in the room with her.

"Calm down Paul," James said. "You're going to wear yourself out with worry. Aiko is fine, and soon, you will be the proud father of a baby boy or girl."

"I can't help it," Paul said, fidgeting. A drop of sweat fell from his forehead.

Aiko had a difficult pregnancy, aside from her invariable cramping, nausea, and extreme back pains. The doctor had confined her to a bed one month prior.

After twelve long hours, the sound of an infant crying echoed down the hallway. Paul froze in his steps. The doctor walked out of the room and down the hallway towards them, with his blue surgical gown still covered in blood.

"Congratulations . . . you have a son."

Paul clutched both his father's shoulders. "It's a boy a boy!" Excited, his nervousness turned to joy.

James hugged him. "Congratulations son."

Hiro hugged Paul and then James. "It is good feeling to be grandfather. I am very proud."

"Yes it is," James said, exhilarated.

Paul asked the doctor, "Can I see them?" "Of course."

Paul dashed quickly down the hallway and opened the door. James followed him trying to take a look at his grandson. Aiko lay, holding the tiny infant. Paul knelt beside her.

"Come in, come in," Kameko said waving her hand at James.

James walked over to the bed, Hiro right behind him. His heart melted when he saw the little black haired baby with slanted eyes.

Paul touched Aiko's hand. "Are you okay?"

"I've never been better. This is the happiest day of my life." Paul kissed her gently on the lips.

"What is his name?" James asked, softly.

"We decided to call him William Hiro Edison," Paul said. He stroked the baby's head, tenderly.

"That is a fine name," James said. Tears came to his eyes. "A very fine name; he is truly a beautiful baby."

"He is, isn't he?" Paul said.

James, Hiro, and Kameko stayed for an hour. Paul stayed the night with Aiko.

<hr>

One week flew by. The blazing sun was shining bright at eight in the morning. A cool breeze gave some relief while James and Paul sat on wicker chairs on the balcony of Paul's house, drinking coffee.

James felt his forehead, he was sweating profusely. "You okay, Dad?" Paul asked.

"Yes, just a slight headache. I didn't sleep much last night."

One of the ranch hands, a young slender blonde-haired man, approached Paul.

"Mornin' gentlemen."

"Good morning Sam," James said.

Paul, who was dressed in dusty pants, a plaid shirt, and a brown cowboy hat stood up. "Mornin', ready to roll?"

"Yep. The cattle are loaded. We'll leave whenever you're ready." "Give me five minutes."

"How many are you planning to auction off?" James asked.

"About 200. They'll probably go in a couple of hours since we got some of the best bred cattle in the state. The number keeps multiplying. I need to hire a couple more ranch hands. I'm interviewin' a couple of men later this evening."

Aiko, dressed in a simple light green summer dress, stepped out on the balcony with the one week old infant strapped to her chest. Paul kissed his baby on the head.

"I thought we'd go for a little walk before it got too hot," Aiko said.

"Sounds good. I'll be back sometime this afternoon," Paul said.

"All right. Have fun at the auction." She kissed Paul and then walked down the stairs.

James grinned, "Have a nice walk." "I will."

Paul went into the house.

James leaned back in his chair and gazed at the sky. A wave of tension swept over him. Two years had flown by and still no word from Clint. Not a day went by when he didn't worry. *Was he okay? Was his lonely? Why hadn't he written?*

James feared for his life. Clint loved living life on the edge and it often meant destruction. If he met the wrong friends, which was usually the case, there was no telling what might happen.

In the midst of his worry, he felt God's hand of protection on Clint's life. He had to believe God would watch over him and someday and he would come home.

James took one large drink of coffee, lifted himself out of the chair, and climbed down the stairs. He moved to the white fence next to a large brown barn and untied a black stallion. "Let's go home, Revelation. We have a lot to do today. He rubbed the horse's flank.

He planned to spend most of the day in the office meeting a few of the board members to discuss international distribution of oil. He hired Hiro Yoshi to be Production Operations Manager. Hiro knew very little about the oil company, so he studied endlessly and soon became one of James top managers. Paul was given complete charge of the ranch.

He put his feet in his stirrups then moaned as he lifted himself into the saddle. He felt numbness in his left hand. He shook it several times. Feeling dizzy, he shook his head. Paul came back out, holding the keys to his truck.

"Dad, you leavin'?"

"Yes. I have to go into the office for a few hours. Why don't you and Aiko have dinner with me tonight?"

"What time?" "Six o'clock." "We'll be there."

James said, "Let's go boy."

He rode a few feet. Dizzy, he shook his head again, hoping the feeling would go away. He was having problems staying balanced on the horse and began having trouble seeing. Within seconds, James felt his face go weak and his mouth turn down. It became hard for him to see. He felt like he was going to pass out.

James rode only a few more yards before falling off the horse. He could hear Paul scream, "Dad!"

James felt Paul kneeling beside him with his face over his mouth. Sam and a few other workers ran over.

"Get some help!" Paul yelled.

Sam ran into the house and returned minutes later. "An ambulance is on the way."

"Dad, help is on the way, don't worry. You'll be okay." That was the last thing James could remember.

James woke up in the hospital. He couldn't feel his left side. He tried to speak but was unable to form the words.

Aiko was standing near the bed holding the baby. "Paul," she said.

Paul approached the bed. "Dad." He grabbed his right hand. "Dad . . . you've had a stroke."

The doctor walked in.

Paul stood up. "Is he going to be okay?"

"I've put him on several medications that will help to thin the blood, break up clots, and repair any broken blood vessels. He's going to need a lot of therapy; speech and physical therapy to begin with. It won't be easy, but he should recover. It was not as serious as it could have been."

"Thank you Doctor. Just do whatever it takes," Paul said.

James felt helpless. He'd been a strong and robust man his whole life and now, felt as though the life had been stripped from him. He closed his eyes hoping this nightmare would end.

James spent the next few months in extensive therapy. He was tenacious and forbade himself to give up easily. He was determined to fight and become the strong, confident man he'd always been. It was frustrating; the speech was the worse. Unable to form his words, he felt a loss of control. It was hard to swallow and urination was equally difficult. Still, he didn't give up easy. He put one hundred percent into his therapy, trusted God with his health, and believed he'd completely recover.

One night, Hiro was sitting by James bedside. Paul was standing right beside him.

Don't worry about work. I work double time to make sure everything runs smoothly. You just get better." Hiro kindly said.

His words slurred, he said, "Thank you. You . . . best friend I have." Hiro smiled and left the room.

Paul sat down next to James. "Paul."

"Yes Dad."

A tear ran down his face. "Clint . . . . I mus . . . see . . . . Clint." "What Dad . . . I don't understand."

"Find Clint . . . . Please." he gripped Paul's arm with what bit of strength he had. "I must see him."

"I'll do everything I can, Dad. I'll contact the American Embassy in France. I'll check every hotel. I'll do what I have to and bring him home."

James nodded and closed his eyes.

Chapter 22

Clint got up early, grabbed a blanket, and walked to the river. He slowly dipped himself into the water. The cold water shocked his senses at first. He sunk down slowly. Gradually his body adjusted to the temperature. The cool water felt good. The village was a welcome change. There was never a dull moment. Clint felt alive, important, and he was falling in love. He lowered his head under the water then emerged. Abby was standing near the banks. She straightened her light grey shirt before sitting down. She shaded her eyes from the sun. "You're up early".

His heart began to beat violently. He raised his body up. "Yeah, I thought I'd get an early start. You look gorgeous." She smiled, "thank you." She sat down on the grass right next to the river. He lifted himself up and eased his body down right next to her. She scratched his scruffy beard. "You look handsome. The beard compliments you're soft brown eyes." A hard knot formed his throat, "Thank you." He studied her eyes. He could tell by the way she gazed at him there was an attraction. Could she be falling in love. He leaned slightly back; her eyes followed him. "I never realized just how handsome you really are Clint." "I noticed how beautiful you are," he said. There was an intensity in her eyes. The corners of her mouth went upwards. She leaned backwards, her eye brows raised. "What will you do when we return to Wales? Will you stay longer?" "That depends. Will you be there?" Her voice softened, "Of course." *Finally, this girl is starting to fall for me.* He leaned in to kiss her when he heard Frazier's voice. "There you two are. Let's go, there's much to be done. Clint we need your help, one of the windows needs to be fixed and from the looks of the sky, a storm might be coming. And Doc is looking for you Abby. Clint was mildly disappointed. "We're on our way." He lifted himself up and then grabbed Abby's hand. She walked closely beside him. He felt her eyes on him the entire time. They stopped next to the clinic. "I guess I'll see you later," Clint asked, though it was more like a statement.

Her eyes fixed on him. "I'm looking forward to it." He watched her walk into the clinic. Finally he thought to himself. Clint knew he'd found the love of his life and a new beginning.

That afternoon, Clint stood on a ladder outside of the medical facility drenched in his own perspiration. October was hot and humid.

He dug a screw out of his pocket, placed it on the window, and twisted it into the hinge. A gushing wind had blown through the village the day before, causing three of the window hinges to loosen.

He climbed down the ladder. Clint rubbed the palms of his callused hands, wiped them on his trousers, and scratched his chin. He turned around and gazed at the small isolated village. His mind drifted as he leaned back against the wall.

Clint felt a sense of freedom he'd never known. He was at peace here and had grown to like the people. Many of them had become his friends. They were simple, undemanding, and hardworking. They were poor, yet giving.

Two women passed by him, smiling broadly. He held up the palm of his hand and said hello. Abby was walking towards him carrying a pitcher of water and glasses on a tray.

He smiled as he saw her approach. She was dressed simply in a pair of blue pants and a grey shirt and wore no make-up. She had such a lack of vanity. Clint thought she looked gorgeous.

He pointed farther up the road. She was almost to him when she turned around. At least twelve young African warriors who sprang out from behind the thick trees and brushes walked towards the center of the road. Their bodies were adorned with more jewelry than the eye could see and they were carrying spears.

The villagers began to gather in the street. The Abneys, Chiamaka and Kpassi were among them.

Clint and Abby walked down the road. Clint stood with his arms crossed, eyeing the fierce looking warriors. The atmosphere was tense.

One of the men, dressed in leopard skins, looked at Clint. His eyes bore right through him.

We should have weapons, guns, something. They could start attacking at anytime, thought Clint.

"You think they're dangerous? he whispered to Abby.

"I don't know," she said. "Kpassi doesn't appear to be afraid."

Kpassi approached the men. He spoke in an African dialect, different than what Clint had heard. He turned around and motioned for one of the townsmen to approach him. The man walked up to Kpassi. After an exchange of words, the man ran towards one of the huts.

By this time, more townspeople including Mark and Frazier had congregated.

Kpassi walked over to them.

Frazier looked at Kpassi. "Who are they?"

"The men are from the Lulua tribe. They are not usually violent people."

"Well, what is it they want?" asked Jacqueline, who sounded scared. "Food, supplies. Another tribe invaded their village and stole their food, clothing, and many of their weapons."

"I've never seen so much jewelry in my life," Abby said.

"Their body decorations symbolize many things, like the relationship between mother and child," Kpassi said.

"Who is the one in the middle, dressed in leopard clothing?" Clint asked.

"He is the chief."

A few men appeared carrying baskets of food; mostly fruit and a few spears and knives. They handed the baskets to the warriors. One of them spoke to Kpassi. They left the village.

Clint sat on a chair in the school house where about 20 people had gathered for a meal to celebrate Gamba's birthday. His back turned to Abby. She was playing with a four year old boy named Freeborn. His mother had been ill with pneumonia so she and a few other women in the village took turns caring for him. He had a bright smile, good temperament, and seemed to have bonded with Abby.

Chiamaka, who was right next to Clint, lightly smacked Clint in his belly. Clint laughed and grabbed Chiamaka's hands, playfully forcing them behind his back. He laughed trying to free himself from Clint's strong grip. From the corner of his eyes, Clint felt Abby's eyes on him.

Chiamaka and Clint had become friends. Chiamaka was smart and had a gentle nature. Clint had developed a sincere affection for him.

He turned his chair toward Abby.

"Would you like to go for a walk?" "I would love to."

He patted Chiamaka on the back. "I'll deal with you later."

The boy laughed before punching Clint in his stomach one last time. Abby handed Freeborn to a village woman sitting two seats over.

Clint grabbed Abby's hand and led her outside. Looking up, he saw a billowing of black clouds hovering over the village.

"It looks like Frazier is right, rain is coming," Clint said.

She glanced up. "Yes, I think it might be a bad one. Storm, that is." "Chiamaka has taken quite a liking to you."

"He's a great kid or should I say, young man. Like the younger brother I never had. I'm gonna' miss him when we leave. He says he wants to go to college. How can that be?"

"It would be hard. He'd have to travel abroad and they don't have much money."

He led her a little farther, close to the river.

"I can tell you're getting attached to Freeborn."

"Yes, I've grown quite fond of him. He's bright and has exquisite eyes. He's one of the most gorgeous children I've ever seen. I hope to have a child just like him someday."

"You'll make a great mother." "Thank you."

"I think this trip is changing me, and you . . . I've never met anyone like you. You're kind and caring, you have a big heart."

"And you too, have a big heart." Clint laughed.

"What's so funny?"

"I was visualizing my brother's face if he'd heard you say that. Trust me Abby, I don't have a good heart. I've made more mistakes than I can count." "Haven't we all. You said this trip is changing you; I'm assuming for the better."

"Yes, but I've only touched the surface. My father did tell me once that if you hang out with wise people, you will become wise yourself. I've been around you for months, so maybe it's rubbin' off."

She smiled. "You're father seems like a wise man."

He studied her more closely. This was the first time in his life he'd sought approval from anyone. She walked closely by him; she appeared nervous.

He looked at her for a long moment and they locked eyes. He said, slowly. "I have something for you, Abby." He handed her a small box.

"Was is it?" she asked. "Open it."

He watched her eyes glisten with joy as she opened the box. She pulled out the necklace made of cowry shells. "It's beautiful. Will you put it on me?"

She turned around and he fastened the clasp. She spun back to face him. His hands lingered for a moment on her shoulders. Clint didn't want to let her go. He was getting ready to speak; he'd actually rehearsed his words. They both spoke simultaneously, "Abby." "Clint."

They laughed. "You first," Abby said. "No, you first," Clint said.

"I truly am happy you're here. We could have never gotten this much done without you. I do enjoy being around you. I find you rather charming."

She touched his face. "You're different than any man I've ever met. You have strength and confidence."

"I've never met anyone like you. You're kind, generous, beautiful inside and out. I've been to some of the most beautiful places in the world and dined at the most expensive restaurants. But these past few months have been some of the best in my life. I feel a transformation taking place in me and I can't explain it. It's like I'm becoming a better person."

He looked at her with such intensity of emotion. "You make me want to be a better man. For the first time in my life, something other than me is important."

He rested his hands on her shoulders. She leaned into him.

"I have feelings for you that I can't explain." He kissed her. "I've wanted to do that from the moment I first saw you," he murmured quietly before his lips touched hers again.

They held one another for a long time before he felt drops of rain on his back.

"We should get back. It looks like a bad storm might be coming in," she said.

The rain began to fall harder. They finally approached Abby's hut. Before entering, she kissed him. "I'll see you tomorrow."

"I can't wait," Clint said. He kissed her lightly then ran back to his hut. His clothes were drenched. He grabbed a blanket to dry his hair and threw it down on the floor. He lay back on his bed. He smiled thinking of Abby.

I've never felt this way about a girl. I can't imagine life without her.

About twenty minutes later, Frazier and Mark came in. Clint was jotting down some words on a paper.

"What are you doing?" Frazier asked.

"Writing my father a long overdue letter. I was planning to call him from Brazzaville, but since we never made it, I thought I'd write. I'm not sure if there'll be a phone there anyway."

"I doubt it very seriously. We do intend to go in a couple of days though, you can ride along. I've been known to be wrong a time or two," Frazier said.

The sound of thunder reverberated through the sky. "Wow, that's some storm," Mark said.

Again lightening struck, and this time they could hear a tree crashing to the ground.

"Are the homes strong enough to withstand this?" Clint asked.

"I can't be certain," Frazier said. "A couple of years ago, they had about five days of heavy rain and dozens of homes were lost. Let's hope this storm doesn't last that long."

Mark pulled out a deck of cards. Lightning flashed and thunder sounded with the voice of a cannon. They sat on Clint's cot and played cards. After about an hour, they heard a woman screaming. They threw on their coats and ran outside. Gamba's wife was yelling, hysterically, in the middle of the road.

She cried out, "Mardea, Mardea!"

Kpassi was obviously trying to comfort her. They ran up to them. "What's wrong? What is it?" Frazier asked.

Chiamaka was next to her.

"She says Gamba took their daughter hunting. He usually took Chiamaka, but she begged him to go. They were supposed to have returned over two hours ago. She fears something bad has happened."

Kpassi spoke to her and turned to the others. "We must search for them. We have to find them before it gets any darker. I'll get the lanterns."

"Won't it be difficult in this storm?" Mark asked.

"If we don't go now, they may not survive. They shouldn't be too far."

"I'll go with you. I know the forest and the direction they headed," Chiamaka said. "I'll go get some supplies." He ran towards his house.

Frazier, Clint, Kpassi, Dr. Abney, Mark, and Chiamaka set off on foot in search of them. They were covered with tarps, each carrying a lantern. They tried to maneuver through the heavy rain, but the strong gusts of rain made it hard to walk and see. A tree branch swiped Clint across the face, ripping through his skin.

More than half an hour later, they reached the river. The waters rose rapidly. Clint, who was right behind Frazier, saw a large tree swaying back and forth.

"Look out!" he yelled.

A branch fell traveling at a massive speed. Clint ducked. He heard the sound of someone moaning, looked back, and saw Mark kneeling on the dirt.

"Mark's been hurt," he said.

"Are you all right?" Frazier asked.

Mark sat up and stroked the side of his head. There was blood on his hand.

"Can you get up?" Clint asked.

"I think so," Mark said, still rubbing his head. Clint knelt beside him. Mark wrapped his arm around Clint's neck and struggled to his feet.

Mark's voice was quivery and weak. He lowered his head, rubbing it several times. "I'm all right."

"Are you sure, son?" Dr. Abney asked. "Yes."

"Come on, let's keep going," Kpassi said, loudly so the others could hear him over the sounds of thunderous rain. They walked on.

"I think I hear something," Frazier said. Everyone stopped.

"Down there," Chiamaka said.

It was Mardea. She was holding onto a rock by the river to keep from falling in.

"I'll get her," Chiamaka said. "No, I'll go!" Clint shouted.

He slid down the wet, slippery hill. His feet were covered with mud, so it was hard to stand. He lost his balance, slipped and fell, bumping into rocks and broken trees. He grabbed the branch of a fallen tree. He was only inches from falling. The water was high and racing downstream at an extremely dangerous pace.

A voice yelled out, "Are you all right?"

"Yeah!" He rose to his feet. His heart was pounding. "Mardea, I'm on my way. Hang on."

He steadily made his way along the bank, took two giant steps, and finally reached her. "Can you hold on to me!" he yelled.

"I think so."

She held him tightly as he wrapped his right hand around her waist. They climbed the hill, taking slow and steady steps. A strong arm grabbed him.

"Let me help." It was Frazier. Frazier stepped around the girl and held her from the other side. She clung to them both, sobbing the entire time.

Once they reached the ground, Chiamaka hugged her. Kpassi asked, "Where is your father?"

She pointed upstream. "My father was hurt. He sent me to get help but I slipped and fell."

"Doctor, take her back to town. We will find her father," Kpassi said.

"I need to go back with him," Mark said, his voice was hoarse. "It's hard to see and my head is hurting, badly."

"Yes," Dr. Abney said. "I'll examine you in the clinic."

Claude grabbed Mardea's hand, and he and Mark started back to town. They found Gamba only ten minutes away. He was lying under a tree. "Are you okay? Can you walk?" Kpassi yelled.

"I think my leg is broken," he said.

Frazier and Kpassi picked him up and carried him home.

When they arrived at the village, they noticed that one of the huts had been blown away like cotton. Many of the townspeople had gathered in the church.

Clint and Frazier stayed with Gamba and Kpassi went into the church. Clint was worried wondering if Abby was okay, but Gamba's wife assured him she was fine. She was in the clinic with the Abneys.

Fatuma wrapped Gamba's foot in a bandage until the doctor could examine it in the morning. He was lying down in the bedroom. Clint slumped to the floor and sat next to Frazier by the fireplace.

It had been raining for over ten hours. He could hear the tiles falling from the roof of the house next door, littering the ground. The winds were forceful and strong as though any minute, the house could fly off, carrying them in it.

"Thank you Clint. You saved my sister's life," Chiamaka said, who was sitting on a chair. His sister was lying on the couch, sleeping.

"Yes," Fatuma said in her deep accent. "We are very grateful."

She was weaving a beautiful cloth with bright silk threads, sipping on a cup of tea. She took frequent breaks to check in on Gamba.

Clint felt humbled and emboldened. He didn't know what to say. He smiled. "You're welcome."

Frazier hung his head, drifting off to sleep. At one point, his head rested on Clint's shoulder. He jerked up as the rain slammed against the door with staggering force.

"Sorry," he said, looking at Clint. "No, it's okay."

Clint sat, thinking as he stared in a distance.

Frazier rubbed his eyes. "What are you thinking about so hard?"

Clint slightly leaned forward. "I'm just glad to be alive. I could have been killed tonight. That tree branch could have crushed me. I almost slipped and fell into the river." He slightly shook his head. "I've never been so scared."

Frazier chuckled. "Perhaps God sent an angel protect you." "Doubt that. I think in my case, it was just luck."

"I have a feeling God's protected you in your life more than you know. Besides, no sin is too great that He wouldn't forgive. He's protected me a time or two and forgiven me more than I can count. He loves us, regardless of our mistakes. It's called grace. Grace is receiving God's goodness even though we don't deserve it."

Frazier patted him on the back. He smiled and stood. "I'm going to get a tad of tea. Anyone want one?"

"I would," Chiamaka said.

"Clint?" Frazier asked, staring down at him. "No thanks."

He pondered Frazier's words for a moment. Could God actually be looking out for me? Why would He care?

He leaned his head against the wall and closed his eyes.

Chapter 23

Clint, Frazier, and Kpassi walked outside and surveyed the village. The sky was gray and dim. A portion of the village lay in ruins. Tree branches and debris from some of the huts that had been blown or washed away, were scattered on the streets. The effects of the storm had also caused the river to crest several feet far above its normal level which caused severe flooding. The crops had been destroyed. Clint approached what had once been a garden covered with glossy blades of young rice and Guinea corn. The thick mud stuck to his shoes, making it hard to walk. He shook his head. Frazier moved to him, the bottoms of his pants swamped in mud. "All that work and in one day, it's gone," Clint said, solemnly.

"Don't worry. We can replant. It could have been worse. Like I mentioned before, a few years back, it rained so hard the entire village was destroyed."

"How can you always manage to remain so calm? I don't get it," Clint said, baffled.

Kpassi approached. "Our biggest concern is malaria because of the mosquitoes growing in the water. We've stored a few malaria nets in the clinic, but not enough for all of the villagers."

"We still have 50 gallons of water to get us through a few weeks. But don't worry, we can get more. At least the medical clinic still looks intact," Frazier said.

Clint eyed the clinic. There was a broken window and it looked like a couple of hinges on the door were missing. He walked into the building with Frazier and Kpassi right behind. Claude strode into the room holding a cup of tea.

Claude stuck his head out the door and impassively surveyed the village. He closed it again. "Rather large storm, wasn't it?" He took a sip of his tea.

Frazier said, "That's putting it mildly." "Let's hope no one was hurt," Claude said. "Where's Abby?" Clint asked.

"She went out early to make sure all the villagers were okay." "How's Mark?" Frazier asked.

"He's resting. He has a reasonably large bump on his head."

Jacqueline entered the room from the kitchen. "I just made a fresh pot of tea. Would anyone like a cup? I'm sure none of us got much sleep last night."

Abby swung the door open. Her face was pale and she was out of breath.

Clint was relieved to see her. "Come quickly!"

"What's wrong?" Frazier asked.

"I can't find Freeborn or his mother. Their home was destroyed by the storm. "I'm . . . afraid."

They dashed towards the east side of the village. A tree had crashed down, punching a large hole in the roof, flattening it. They began removing debris. The furniture, beddings, and clothes were everywhere.

They'd been working for about ten minutes when Kpassi said, "Frazier." Frazier went to him and Clint followed. Freeborn's mother was found lying under the buried tree. Clint saw terror on Abby's face. Claude knelt down to feel her pulse. Jacqueline grabbed Abby's hand.

Claude slowly stood up. "She's dead."

Sadness and fear were etched on her face. Jacqueline hugged her. "Let's keep looking for the child," Kpassi said.

Jacqueline led the grieving Abby away from the house.

Finally, Clint pulled the debris off a sturdy wooden table. He knelt down and looked under it. The little boy was lying there, motionless. He picked the child up. The boy wasn't' moving. Clint thought for sure he was dead.

"Doc," he said.

Claude rushed to see the child followed by Kpassi and Frazier. He positioned his ear next to the child's mouth to feel for breaths and felt his pulse.

He turned, smiling. "It's a miracle. The child is still alive." Abby ran to them.

"His mother must have slipped him under the table, hoping it wouldn't cave in," Kpassi said. "She was wise. She saved her son's life."

Abby kissed the boy on the forehead. Claude carried him to the medical center to examine him.

"What a miracle," Clint said.

Clint felt Frazier's hand rest on his back. "Perhaps the same angel looking after you was looking after him as well." Frazier darted to catch up to Kpassi.

Frazier, Kpassi, Clint, and many men in the village inspected the town and assessed the damage. Five huts had been completely destroyed, seven other huts needed repairs. Abby, Clint and Frazier' huts were still intact. He eyed the once beautiful tree that had stood in front of his living quarters. It was desolate. The limbs were completely bare.

The medical center and school needed minor repairs. It would take weeks to repair the wreckage from the streets and rebuild the homes.

The Abneys treated a number of patients for broken bones, cuts and bruises. One little girl had been struck in the head by a pole crashing down from the roof. She had a mild concussion. An elderly man suffered a broken hip from a fall he took trying to make his way to the church.

⁓⤳⤳�⤳⁓

That night, Clint, Frazier, Kpassi, and Abby joined Gamba and his family for dinner. Freeborn was nestled close to Abby; she and Jacqueline took turns caring for him. They'd just finished eating when there was a knock on the door.

"Come in," Fatuma said. Claude walked in looking tense.

Gamba grabbed his cane and stood. "Can we get you something to eat?"

"No, thank you."

"Is there something the matter?" Abby asked.

He cleared his throat. "I'm afraid Mark isn't doing well. He's burning up with the fever."

"How serious is it?" Frazier asked.

"It doesn't look good. I think the bump to his head caused severe brain damage. We've got to get him to a hospital. There isn't much I can do for him here."

"Where's the nearest hospital?" Clint asked. "I'm afraid it's about over 150 miles away."

"Frazier and I will take him," Kpassi said. "We may have to take a detour. The storm may have washed out several of the roads."

"We'll need to begin packing right away," Frazier said.

"You'll need your rest," Claude said, in a stern voice. "We've all had a terrible night and we're exhausted. Get some sleep."

"He's right," Kpassi said. "It might be dangerous to travel at night. We can't chance the roads being flooded. We will leave early."

Abby's looked scared.

After they finished eating, Clint walked her to her hut. She was holding Freeborn's hand.

"Will you both be okay, alone? You could always stay at the clinic."

"We'll be fine. I'll see you in the morning."

She kissed him on the cheek and went inside.

Clint went into his hut. He slipped into a clean pair of cotton pants and plopped himself down on his cot, leaning against the wall. He was beyond fatigued. The room was hot and humid.

He was scared for Mark. They'd become so close; almost like brothers. He closed his eyes and said out loud, "God help him. He's a good guy . . . never done anything to hurt anyone." It was hard for him to fight back the tears.

Frazier walked in. Clint jumped up and wiped his eyes. "You okay?" Frazier asked.

"Yeah, I think I got some dust in my eye."

"We should get some sleep. We've got an early start." "Yeah." He laid down.

Frazier took off his wet shirt and changed his pants, then plopped himself down on his wool blanket and rested his head on his pillow.

"Clint?"

Clint rolled around. "Yeah?"

"Take care of my sister while I'm gone. She's a bit stubborn sometimes and does too much. Someday, she'll realize she can't save the world."

"I will."

They were silent for several seconds. "Do you love her?" Clint took a deep breath. "Yeah . . . I do."

"Good. You two are good together. I couldn't have asked for anyone better for her. You just promise you'll protect her."

"I promise."

Frazier turned around. Clint gazed up at the ceiling. A deep love had grown in his heart for Frazier. There was only one person he had more respect for; Will. In a small way, he felt that God gave him a brother in place of Will.

"Frazier. Are you asleep?" "No. Not yet."

"Thanks for letting me come here and for being a friend. It's strange, but I'm happy to be here in spite of everything that's happened.

"I've always felt isolated. Alone at home . . . France . . . nothing seemed to help. I've been so bitter and angry these past few years . . . actually, most of my life. I think it started when I lost my mom. I hated her for dying. I never got along with my father, even though he's a good man. I hated my brother Paul. The only person I loved was my bother Will, and he died. I guess you could say I rejected everyone around me. I was rich and had it all, but I hated my life. But this trip is changing me. I'm not angry or resentful anymore. I actually feel like my life has meaning and I've learned to appreciate things.

"I'm sorry to keep going on like this. It's just, for the first time in my life, I'm actually grateful. And I owe that to you and Abby. Watching the two of you, the way you live. It's a true testament that there is a God."

"Clint, it's been a pleasure getting to know you. You've become the brother I never had. And we couldn't have done all we have without you. You've been a Godsend. I genuinely think you're a grand person."

"I wish I were more like you and Abby."

Frazier propped himself up on his elbows. "You are who God created you to be and someday you'll understand. God has a good plan for you. Regardless of your past, your future is what counts. We should probably get some shut eye, don't you think? I've got a long day ahead and you have much work to do."

"Good night, Frazier." "Good night, Clint."

Clint felt renewed physically and emotionally; like life now had purpose. For the first time in his life, he felt compassion for someone and something other than himself. He would give his life for Frazier and Abby. He knew one thing for sure. He planned to live the rest of his life with Abby.

He closed his eyes and within minutes, he fell asleep.

When they woke the next morning, Frazier and Kpassi packed a few clothes and loaded the car with blankets, water, and food Fatuma had prepared. It was enough to last for two days. Mark was bundled up tightly in blankets in the back seat. His eyes were closed but his body was shivering. Clint bent down and laid his hand on his pale, moist forehead.

"You'll be okay. I know you'll make it. Just be strong."

Abby bent down and kissed him on the cheek. "I'll pray for you. Remember, we love you."

Frazier came from the clinic carrying medication that Claude had given to Mark for severe headaches and nausea.

Abby grabbed Frazier's hand. "Please be careful." "I will, love." He hugged her.

She hugged Kpassi. "Be safe." He nodded, "We will."

"Have a safe trip. We'll see you soon," Clint said.

Clint grabbed Abby's hand as they watched the car drive off. "Let's have some breakfast," Claude said. "We have much to do."

Chapter 24

That week, they repaired huts, the clinic, and mended the windows and hinges in the classroom where Mark taught the children. They gathered for prayer, nightly. They prayed for Mark's health, other sick people in the village, and a safe return for Kpassi and Frazier.

While Clint's days were spent working, his evenings were spent with Abby. He was falling deeper in love with her every moment they were together.

Monday night, Abby and Clint went for a stroll along a narrow path a few feet outside of the village. Abby was dressed in a kanga. The brilliantly colored dress was wrapped around her figure, accessorized by the seashell necklace Clint had given her. She wore the necklace every day. Her deep brown hair gleamed in the light shed by the setting sun.

"How is Freeborn?" Clint asked.

"Physically, he is fine, but still asks for his mother." "What do you tell him?"

"That his mother is with God in heaven. That she loves him and is watching over him. I assure him he will be fine."

"What will happen to him? His mother was his only family wasn't she?" "He will be taken to an orphanage. The nearest one is over 200 miles away. The nuns at the orphanage are good women. I met them when I was twelve when my father and I went to visit. They will give him all the love he needs."

"You really care about him, don't you?"

"Considerably. I've grown to love him. It will be hard to say goodbye."

She stopped by the river and sat on the grass. Clint sat down next to her and wrapped his arm around her.

"I decided to donate the funds I saved to attend the university, to the villagers. They need it far worse than I."

His eyebrows arched. "But Abby . . . college . . . . it's so important to you. It's all you talked about."

"I know, but school can wait. I'm young you know. There's plenty of time for that. I can always raise the money again. The townspeople need it more. They need more clean water, material for clothes, and seed for food."

The money stashed in his room flashed in Clint's mind. He had a little over $4,000. It was like $400,000 to the villagers. "That won't be necessary . . . I'll give them the money. I have enough."

Abby looked shocked.

"I've lived a privileged life, Abby. For the first time, I have a chance to do something for someone else. These people have become like family to me."

"That's so kind of you."

His gazed drifted downward. "I'm not as kind as you think. I've done a lot of things I regret."

She touched his arm. "Haven't we all."

His heart pounded with anticipation. *I have to be honest and get this off my chest.* He hesitated at first.

"Do you remember when I told you about my friend, Ted?" "Yes."

"I wasn't completely honest. The men chasing him said he had to come up with some money or else they'd kill him. He asked me . . . he begged me to lend him money. I told him no."

"Clint, you . . ."

"No . . . please, let me finish." his voice was calm and his face was somber.

"I had thousands and thousands of dollars. My Dad gave me a fortune. It would have been easy to give it to him, but I was too greedy. I didn't care. I was selfish. That day, he killed himself."

Abby tilted her head. "You can't blame yourself for that."

"If I would have given him the money, he'd still be alive. I could have saved his life. Instead, I gambled almost every dime away. I've really come to grips with what I did. I hate it. I'd change it if I could."

"No one's past is irrelevant. We've all made mistakes, but we should learn from them rather than live a life of regret. You focus on your failure and that's who you become. You need only focus on the future, what you can change, and the difference you can make."

Clint was struck by her words. She was more mature than anyone he'd ever met and so nonjudgmental.

Clint said, "My father once told me no one is in control of your happiness but you. You have the power to change anything about yourself or your life that you want to change. I didn't understand him at the time. But now, I do."

He pulled her forward and touched his forehead to hers. "I'm a better person when I'm with you. I've never felt this way about anyone. I can't imagine my life without you."

"I feel the same way," she said. "I love you."

"I love you too, Clint."

He kissed her. They sat and held one another for a while before he took her home. He kissed her goodnight and went back to his hut.

He changed clothes and lay down in bed. He was living in a hut, working ten hour days in exhausting heat, bathing once a week in the river, and being eaten alive by the bugs. But being in Africa with Abby was the happiest time of his life. He knew he was becoming someone his father would be proud of. Once he got the chance, he planned to call him and tell him he loved him.

~~~∞~~~

Tuesday morning, the sky was still light, and the weather was cool. Many of the townspeople gathered in the church building for a community meal and afterwards, bible study. Clint finished getting dressed after bathing in the river, grabbed the bible from his duffle bag, and shoved it in the pocket inside his jacket. He stopped by Abby's hut. As she stepped out, she straightened the pretty white cotton dress she was wearing and moved a stand of hair from her forehead.

"You're gorgeous," Clint said.

"Why, thank you sir," she said as she linked arms with him. "Where is Freeborn?"

"Fatuma's helper, Babatoura, has him." They walked towards the church.

They ate bread, yams, and fresh fruit for breakfast. Clint was famished and went back for seconds.

Gamba read from the book of Psalms. "Psalms 23. The Lord is my shepherd; I shall not want. He maketh me to lie down in green pastures: he leadeth me beside still waters. He restoreth my soul: he leadeth me in the paths of righteousness for his name's sake. Yea though I walk through the valley of the shadow of death, I will fear no evil: for thou are with me; thy rod and thy staff they comfort me."

It was a similar message of that he'd heard at his father's church, only now, he actually listened. After the sermon, he felt his spirit was renewed.

Mid-afternoon, Clint and Abby were lying on the grass, not far from the village. Abby laid on her stomach and Clint was beside her on his back. "I hope we make it to the big city soon. I have a large hole in my right shoe."

She looked. "Ah yes, that is a fairly large hole. Don't you have another pair?"

"Yeah, but I left it at your house. I didn't think I'd need two pair and wasn't planning on doing this much . . . although I don't mind."

"We'll have to fix that. I'll personally see that you get a grand pair. Hopefully we can drive into town in a couple of days. The Abneys are short on supplies as well, so I'm sure they'll want to go."

He planted his head down on the grass to relax. "So, when will Freeborn go to the orphanage?"

"Tomorrow. The driver who brought us here was planning to take the child, but since Frazier and Kpassi took the only running car, they will have to travel by boat. I plan to go with them."

"I'll go too."

"We'll take him together." She smiled. "It will give you a chance to see more of Africa. It truly is the most beautiful continent in the world."

"I can't seem to keep my eyes off of you long enough to notice." She grinned.

He started to kiss her when all of the sudden, they heard the sound of gunshots. Abby grabbed Clint's jacket. "What's that," she said, her voice shaking.

"I don't know."

They darted behind one of the huts. A bullet went off, sending the glass window at the clinic, shattering. They hit the ground. A loud panic filled the town. In seconds, the whole village was a mass of running people. There was much confusion, men and women were scrambling to find safety.

At least six black men were holding riffles, some crawling in and out of huts. Most of them were wearing trousers. A tall muscular man wearing filthy brown pants and a dirty shirt was pointing a gun at one of the village men. He shot him point blank, sending him plunging backwards.

Clint tried to comprehend what was happening. There was the sound of blows of bodies falling to the ground and over his head, an undulating spear. Bullets spiraled through the air. Clint and Abby stayed hidden behind the hut. Abby held her hands against her ears to shut out the screams of the women and children.

The bodies of three men and two women lay on the ground. He felt a hand grab his shoulder. He jerked forward. It was Gamba.

"Are you both all right?"

In a whisper, Clint said, "We're fine. Where is your family?"

"My wife and daughter are hiding in the woods as are most of the woman and men. They are safe for now. We must protect the women from these men. They rape them."

"What about the Abneys?" Abby asked, as her voice trembled.

"I believe they are hiding somewhere near the medical center. Come, follow me."

He led them behind a clump of bushes, not far from the hut. They crouched down low.

"We should be safe here."

"Who are these men?" Clint asked.

"They are rebels led by the Tutsi ethnic group who are a tribe of fierce and shrewd traders and cattle-dealers. They consider themselves to be superior to everyone."

"What do they want?" Abby asked. She tightened her grip on Clint's arm.

"They come to seek food, money, and anything of value. They will go from home to home until they find what they are looking for."

Just then, Clint had a vision of the envelope filled with money by his cot.

"The rebels are disciplined and better trained than the Congolese army. They control much of the regional capital of Goma. We've dealt with them only one other time. Once they have what they want, they will leave. We hide our children in the woods because they have been known to trade children for money or cattle."

"Why, what good would a child do?" Abby asked.

"They're used as workers in the villages; slaves. Some are as young as four years old."

"Shouldn't we fight back?" Clint asked.

"No. It will only lead to more bloodshed. We must stay put."

It was evident Abby was trying not to cry. Clint grabbed her hand and moved her close to him.

Two of the rebels stood guard while the others searched the homes. One of the men began to yell, "Fedha, fedha."

"What's he saying?" Clint asked. "Apparently they've found money." Clint tried to get a glimpse.

The man, who appeared to be the leader, spoke. "What's he saying?" Clint asked.

He told his men to find the owner of the white envelope," Gamba said.

Clint looked at the stocky filthy man carrying his envelope. Nerves shot though his spine.

Suddenly Gamba said, "Chiamaka."

A scrawny man was pointing a gun at Chiamaka's head, leading him to the center of the street.

Gamba started to go after his son.

Wait, Clint's voice froze as Gamba was in mid-step. He felt Abby's body tense. "I'll go."

He looked at Abby. She whispered, alarmingly, "What are you doing?" "Just stay."

She moved towards him. He sensed she wanted to help. He grabbed her wrist and squeezed it firmly. "Abby, stay here."

"Clint, you could get hurt."

He stood slowly and unsteadily. His legs were numb from kneeling so long. He swallowed hard, raised his hands and made his way to the center of the road where the men were standing. Trying not to show his fear, he could feel his legs shaking with every step; like any minute they would give out. He tried to control his emotions, meeting their gaze directly.

"The money is mine."

The man gave Clint a stony look, eyeing him from top to bottom. Clint felt his heart cave inside his chest. His eyes darted from one man to the other. They looked mean and were all armed with guns. The man standing directly in front of Chiamaka appeared to be the leader. His face was marked with several deep scars. He was wearing trousers and no shirt.

The large man gripping Chiamaka looked as though he'd been in a fight and his right eye was swollen. There were scars all over his body from his face to his chest and down his arms.

"Let him go. I'm the one you want," Clint said.

The man circled Clint before stopping directly in front of him. He looked at Clint with his piercing brown eyes depicting anger and hatred. He had a muscular build and a horrific stench. He spoke to the man pointing the gun at Chiamaka in Swahili. The man lowered his gun.

"Is this your money?" he asked in English.

"Yes". Clint wondered how the man learned to speak English but wasn't about to ask.

He was silent for a few seconds. "Where did you get it?"

"From home . . . America. My father gave it to me to give to the villagers."

"There must be more where this came from."

"No," Clint said. His legs were shaking. He'd never been more scared in his life. "It was all we could afford." *God let him believe me.*

The man laughed. "A good-looking boy like you should not lie." The man punched Clint in the stomach. Clint fell down on his knees, clutching his stomach.

"Tell me where you got the money or I will kill the boy." "I told you, from America."

Another man walking towards them yelled out in Swahili. He was holding a gun at four young women and three children, one of them was Freeborn. He edged them towards the street.

Clint hoped Abby couldn't see. The leader waved his hands and yelled. The man then screamed at the women and shoved them against one of the huts. He grabbed Freeborn. Babtoura put up a fight. He slapped her knocking her to the ground. He walked several yards and started to put him in the back seat of the car. Abby ran out to the street towards the car and yelled, "No!"

Clint yelled, "Abby, stay back!"

"I can't let them take him!" She yelled, "No, leave him, please!"

The man who pointed the gun at Chiamaka turned the gun towards Abby.

Once again, Clint yelled. "Abby, no, stay back!"

The man shot her in the chest and she fell backwards. "Abby!" Clint screamed.

He punched one of the men in the stomach and slammed his fist into another. He was running toward her when suddenly he felt a large object crash into the back of his neck. He fell to the ground and that was the last thing he remembered.

Chapter 25

Clint sat with his knees cramped and back pressing hard against the stone wall. Knots of pain shot through his entire body. He'd been locked up in the grungy small room for at least six days. Bands of fear gripped his mind. It was torture not knowing where he was or if he'd make it out alive. Once a day, he was given dirty water to drink. He felt like he was suffocating and would die any minute. He felt drained, tired, and hungry.

Clint's stomach knotted every waking moment he thought of Abby; a feeling of overwhelming sorrow griped him. Visions of her being shot played over and over in his mind like a phonograph. A multitude of emotions paraded through him; fear, anger, anxiety. *How could everything go so bad? Why did this happen? Would God let him die? Worse, did God let Abby die?*

He had gone from extreme feelings of detachment to depression and panic; his body trembled and it was hard to breath. He'd never been so scared.

The hard floor caused his back to stiffen so he leaned back in hopes to get some relief. His mind drifted in and out of confusion. Silence whirled all around him until the sound of muffled voices broke through from outside the window. He used all his strength to thrust himself toward the window and knelt down to get a look. The window was covered with dirt but he could see what was going on.

In the center of the road, a black man was knelt with his hands tied behind his back. The leader was standing in front of him, three men not far behind.

The leader circled the man once, moving with stiff arrogance. The man appeared to be crying.

When he spoke, it looked like he was pleading for his life.

The leader grabbed a gun from one of the men and shot the man in the head, sending him flying backwards. Blood gushed from his wound.

Clint sat back down on his heels, bent his head, and closed his eyes. His heart felt as though it would leap right out of his chest. His breathing was shallow, as though he'd just run a race.

"Oh God, I'm begging you . . . help me," he cried out loud. "I don't want to die . . . not like this."

He flashed back on the sermon he'd heard Gamba preach. He'd heard the scripture so many times he had it memorized. In a weak voice, he spoke. "The Lord is my shepherd, I shall not want. He makes me to lie down in green pastures. He leads me beside the still waters . . . He restores me." Clint started to cry. "I walk through the valley of the shadow of death . . . I will fear no evil. You're with me. God . . . . please help me." He buried his chin in his chest.

He sat in misery. Minutes seemed like hours and hours like days. Suddenly, he heard the lock on his door click. When the door flew open, fear exploded through his body and a sharp pain pierced his stomach. It was the same black man who had led him outside the first time. He was holding a glass of filthy water.

He slowly moved towards Clint, looking angry as always. Every other time, he dumped the water down Clint's throat and left without a word. This time he spoke.

"You scared boy?" His voice was deep and harsh. Clint didn't speak.

"You should be," he said, snickering.

He pulled a large rusty knife out of a sheath that looked as though it were made from animal skin. Clint froze instantly, fearing that any minute he would see death. The man gripped the knife tightly and moved behind Clint. Clint thought for sure this was it; he would die. He closed his eyes and clenched his jaw. Clint tensed up as the man set the cup down and grabbed his arms. He cut the ropes binding his hands. Relief struck through Clint's bones.

"Here!" he said, when he moved in front of Clint.

He started to give him the glass when he dropped it, sending it shattering into pieces. Clint shielded his face to protect it from glass.

"Sorry boy, it slipped."

He started to walk away but turned and said, "We may take you to the city to get us more money. We may let you live or we may kill you. Either way, we will get what we want. Say a prayer, boy. Today may be your last."

The man walked out, slamming the door. Clint exhaled loudly. He had survived for now, but knew in his heart, they planned to kill him.

The man had forgotten to tie his hands back. Clint gently massaged his wrists. The ropes had cut off the circulation.

Clint wrestled with the thick ropes wrapped around his feet. His ankles were tied tightly and he felt weak. He leaned back against the wall in exhaustion.

Thoughts from watching that man die sent a wave of terror through him. His body began to shake and he thought he would vomit.

Hold yourself together, he thought.

Just then, a vision of Abby being shot drifted through his mind.

"No!" he said out loud. "I won't die. Not now, I can't, Abby needs me." There was a large piece of glass on the floor nearby to the right of him.

He reached over and grabbed it and began sawing the rope. After an hour passed, he'd managed to cut through half the rope, then took a break to rest. The sun was descending but the sky was still bright. Clint heard the sound of a car starting. Clint peeked out the window and saw the leader leaving with several other men.

Wonder where they're going? He thought. *And where are the others, the place looks deserted.*

Clint grabbed the glass and continued to cut through the rope to free himself with every ounce of strength he had left until it broke.

After stretching out his legs to remove the stiffness, Cling rolled onto his knees. Then he stood slowly and unsteadily, his legs shaking.

He pulled off his shirt, wrapped it around his elbow, and pounded the window, making the hole large enough for him to crawl out of. He could only pray that no one heard him.

He grabbed the window frame and fell out.

After peeking around back to search the grounds, no one was there. There was only one guard, some distance away to the west. *The others must be eating or something*, he thought.

Clint ran in the opposite direction, making his way past the huts, and came up behind a man who was eating something. A canteen hung around his neck. Clint ducked behind a large tree.

A tree limb lay on the ground near his feet. He bent down to pick it up and began to edge towards the man. The man turned around, and Clint knocked him unconscious before he could speak. Clint grabbed the man's canteen, bread, and beef jerky.

His adrenalin set in as he ran to the forest. His legs moved so quickly as though he had the strength of seven men. Tree branches smacked him in the face as he fled for his life.

When he could run no more, he stopped and dropped to his knees. Once he caught his breath, he devoured the food and drank every drop of the water.

His shoes were thickly covered in dirt. He leaned against the tree. The volume of his voice low, "What now? Where do I go?"

I can't be more than a day away from the village.

He clenched his teeth. *How do I get back? I've got to get back to Abby.*

Suddenly, he heard a gunshot. *They must know I'm gone.* He jumped up and ran as fast as he could through the forest, not stopping to look back. He dashed through the tangled undergrowth of shrubs and hanging vines. The bushes and tree limbs slapping against his face made it hard to see. Although Clint was in the best shape of his life, this was the hardest thing he'd ever had to endure. He was weak, but ran for his life.

It was difficult to navigate through the forest. At times, he was blinded by the streaming bands of sun light. As he staggered forward, he felt needles through his shoes. It was as if the forest floor was hard as a carpet of pinecones.

Panting and sore, he stopped and rested for a short time on a hill under a baobab tree.

Then he slowly and painfully forced himself to his feet.

Hours later, the forest had thinned and the land was becoming more flat. He came upon a small stream, stumbled to its bank, knelt, and cupped his hands in the stream and drank. He washed the sweat from his face and then filled the canteen.

Emptiness filled his spirit, but he knew if he had any hope of ever finding Abby, he had to move on. Bugs began to stream around the water like waves of dust. He ran just to escape them.

He walked for several more hours until dark. His heart began to thud, alarmingly. The night was filled with frightening noises, howls, and grunts from wild animals. He felt vulnerable and unprotected in a place surrounded by dangerous beasts. He flinched every time he heard a sound, expecting any moment to be overtaken by powerful claws or jagged fangs.

He wondered if he would make it out alive.

Chapter 26

It dawn, Clint could feel the morning sun begin to burn his skin. His body was stiff and sore. Dozens of ants and dragonflies bites covered his body. The skin on his arms and legs was red, swollen, and began to blister from the bites. He scratched so hard, parts of his skin began to peel off. He stretched his legs to remove some of the stiffness and slowly lifted himself off the ground.

He turned his head left and right to loosen his neck muscles. Suddenly startled by an odd noise, he looked behind the tree and saw a Cape buffalo. This massive creature had thick horns and a stocky built, almost like a cow. Clint remembered Kpassi talking about the dangerous beast. He said they are among one of the animals that will stalk the hunter and gore him with its sharp horns.

Clint stood motionless. His heart pounded like a hammer; terrified that any minute the animal would attack. He slowly moved around the tree to avoid being seen or heard. When the animal moved, he flinched; his heart beating rapidly.

How do I get out of this one?

He knew the buffalo would pursue him if he started to run. He stood still, watching for almost ten minutes. To the east, more buffalo stood about a hundred yards away. The animal eventually made its way to the others. Clint walked cautiously at first, then quickening his steps, not stopping until they were out of sight.

He was exhausted after struggling with more bugs and weathering an occasional thunder storm. He was sweating profusely in spite of the steady rain. Every muscle in his body was strained. He slipped and fell on a large rock. Pain shot through his calf. Ignoring it, he got up and continued to walk. There was a sound of water rushing that got louder as he approached. He ran to the river, drank from his cupped hands, washed his face, and splashed the coolness of the water on his body. As he turned to walk away, he slipped on a bed of leaves and fell into the water. It gently whisked him away downstream until he was able to grab hold of a tree stump and climb out of the river. With little strength, he knelt down on the rough ground.

His lips felt chapped and eyes, swollen. Staring up at the sky, he was almost completely blinded by the sun. As he took a deep breath, despair began to overwhelm him. How long would he wander until he could get to civilization?

"I have no money. I'm stranded in Africa. What am I going to do?"

I have to keep going, he thought, lifting himself off the ground.

After a few more hours of walking, his pulse began beating at a rapid rate, and his breathing was fast and shallow. He felt the cold sweat on his skin as he wiped it away from his forehead. Confused, he stumbled along moving one foot in front of the other. His mind started to wander. He saw shimmering objects quickly became sharp jagged teeth. He approached what looked like a village, but it was hard to see. He took a few steps closer and collapsed.

Clint woke, wrapped in a thin blanket, with a wet towel across his forehead. The sun was shining bright through the window.

A woman with strands of gray mixed in her auburn hair looked at him. She smiled, dimpling her pudgy cheeks.

"Well, it's about time you woke up. We were worried about you." She spoke with a strong Irish accent.

Something pulled at the crook of his elbow. He looked and saw that he was hooked up to an IV.

"I used to be a nurse. I carry medical supplies everywhere I go. You were dehydrated so I inserted the IV."

She poured a glass of water from a pitcher on the dresser near the bed and brought it to him. She slid her right arm around his back and gently leaned him forward.

"Here, drink this." He took a few gulps. "Just a little more."

He drank half the glass. She refilled it and set it on the table right next to him.

"You take a drink whenever you get thirsty."

Her gentle demeanor and kind spirit quieted the fear rising within him.

"Who are you?" he said, still disorientated. "My name is Emma Watts."

"Where am I?" His words were slightly slurred.

"You're in the village of Quicange. You collapsed a few yards away from our farm. We thought you were dead. My son, Albert, found you just in time. You were worn out. But don't fret, we'll get you better."

"How long have I been sleep?" "Almost 24 hours."

His chest felt tight. "I'm so tired."

"You had a severe fever. Like I said, we were worried." He tried to get up.

"No, no, no. Don't think about it, mister. You'll be needin' your rest."

She was getting ready to leave. "There are some clothes on the chair next to the window. Might be too large for you, but you're welcome to wear them."

Clint saw a pair of brown pants and a black shirt. "Try and get some more sleep." She left the room.

Clint slept for seven more hours. He slowly crawled out of the bed. Dizzy and light headed, he stumbled over to the old dresser and looked at himself in the mirror.

His face was beet red and peeling from sunburn. His lips were chapped and his arms and legs were swollen from the bug bites. The beard he had grown had lightened. His shoulders had broadened from all the physical work he'd done on the village, but he was thin. He looked 15 pounds lighter.

There was a silver bowl filled with water on the dresser, a brown towel, and a bar of soap. He dipped the towel in the water and lathered his face, arms, and chest with soap. After bathing, he opened the window, dumped the dirty water out of the bowl, and set it back on the dresser.

He changed clothes and went into the living area. The house smelled of duck. The tiny living room had a scarred wooden table in the center, surrounded by four wooden chairs. Two rocking chairs were next to a fireplace. From what he could see, there was another small bedroom and a tiny kitchen.

Emma stepped out of the kitchen carrying a bowl of boiled potatoes and a plate of papaya.

"Hello," he greeted her politely.

"Well, it's about time you graced us with your presence. How are ya feelin'?"

"Still dizzy, but better."

"You poor dear; you must be starvin'. Let's get you somethin' to eat. Have a seat at the table."

"Is there a telephone I could use?"

"Oh my, no. There isn't a phone almost 125 miles of here. You'd have to go to the big city."

He sat down at the table, still woozy. "The food smells good."

"Why thank you."

Just then a man with bushy black hair and a beard came into the house. He was covered in dirt. His cheeks were chipped by acne scars.

"Hello," he said, eyeing Clint.

He held his hand out to shake the man's hand. "Hi. I'm Clint." The man's grip was firm, his hands were callused.

"I'm Albert. It's good to meet you. You gave us quite a scare. Me and one of the villagers found you. What in the world are you doing wandering around the forest, alone?"

"It's a long story."

"We can talk at dinner. Let me get washed up."

He walked into the room Clint had occupied and appeared ten minutes later, dressed in a pair of faded but clean black pants and a white shirt. He sat at the head of the table. Emma sat next to him.

"Let's pray. Thank you heavenly Father for the bountiful blessing and thank you for the safety of our visitor. May your hand be on his life, in Jesus name. Amen."

"Amen," said Emma and Clint.

Emma put a slab of roasted duck on Clint's plate, followed by boiled potatoes.

"Nothin' like a good hearty meal," she said.

Clint was famished. He took a bite of the potatoes, bit into the duck, and began devouring the food.

"Where are you from?" Clint asked.

"We're originally from Dublin, Ireland," Emma said. "I guess you could tell from the accent. Have you ever been, Clint?"

"No, I haven't."

"There's a saying, have you ever been to Ireland, where the rolling hills are green? It truly is the grandest land that you ever will see. And though those hills of Ireland may be very far away, they're close to my dear heart, no matter what the day."

"My mother the poet."

"And a grand land it is. You've never seen anything more beautiful." She looked at Clint. "You'll have to go."

My husband and I moved to America when I was 29; Flagstaff, Arizona. Albert was only two years old. My husband became a Christian and received a callin' to be a missionary. We traveled to Siam, twice. We didn't start travelin' to Africa until a few years back. My husband died—heart attack. He lived a good, but hard life and God called him home early."

"I was raised my whole life in Flagstaff," Albert said, while chewing on a slice of papaya. "I went to medical school for a couple of years and then dropped out. It wasn't for me. I felt my true calling in life was to be a missionary, just like the folks. I attended seminary school for a couple of years. That's when I met my wife. I was 30 years old when we married. We've been to Africa six times and learned to speak the Swahili language years ago. My wife died of breast cancer when she was 42."

"I'm sorry," Clint said.

Albert nodded. "She was the love of my life." Albert asked, "How'd you end up here in Africa?"

Clint shared the events of the past three months. When he spoke of the rebels attacking the village, he saw fear penetrate Mrs. Watts, forcing the once cheerful grin off her face. Her mouth flew open when he shared how Abby was shot and he'd been taken captive by the rebels.

"It's a wonder you're still alive," Emma said, her voice shivering. "Thank the Lord we've never had a run in with them."

Albert set his fork down. He shrugged and narrowed his eyes. "We've heard of troubles with rebels in these parts many years ago but thought that was history. It's hard to believe they're back and this close to home. Do you know how far away we are from the village you were in?"

"I have no idea. They knocked me out and I wandered in the forest for almost two days."

Albert asked, "What's the name of your village?"

"Boende. Have you heard of it?" There was a touch of hope in Clint's voice.

"Unfortunately, no. I doubt anyone here would know where the village is either."

"I don't know if Abby is dead or alive, but I have to find her."

"If she is alive, it might be hard for you to find her. How long ago did it happen?"

"I think it's been about seven or eight days. I can't be sure. I was locked up for so long, I lost count. I plan to start searching for her right away."

Albert set his fork down and wiped his mouth with a napkin. "Well if she is in fact alive, you don't know where she is."

"I hope she's alive and okay in the village. We had a good doctor, Claude Abney. I'm praying he could have saved her."

"Does he have the medical supplies to heal a bullet wound," Albert asked.

"I don't know. Her brother Frazier and a friend, Kpassi, took another friend to the hospital in the only running car. They were due back any day. They probably would have driven her to a hospital."

"First of all, they might have taken her to a hospital in Kasongo which is about 175 miles from here. Or depending on the roads, they might have gone to a hospital in Kinshasa, which is even farther. Second, it would take almost two weeks to make it by foot and you'd never survive. Every ferocious animal lives in this land. I can't believe you made it as far as you did. Third, if she's not in one place, you'd have to travel another week to make it to the next. Truth is, you don't know where she is. How would you survive? I don't imagine ya' got much money."

"I could travel by boat," Clint said, with a bout of hope.

Albert cleared his throat and took a drink of water. "And go where? To what hospital? If you're going to Kinshasa, then you'd travel west toward Bandundu on the Kasai River. That could take over a week. Of course, you'd need a guide and lots of money and a boat large enough to protect you from the animals."

Clint was disappointed.

"My mom and I will be travelin' on a boat along the Kwango River to Luanda, where we'll go to catch a ship to America. You should consider comin' with us."

Clint bent his head and didn't respond.

"What about her parents?" Emma asked. "Surely they must know by now. Where do they live?"

"In Wales, Frazier and her brother would have called them. They're probably on their way here if they haven't already arrived. They might have taken her home. I can't be sure."

"Like Albert said. We're leaving for America in a few weeks. You're welcome to come with us."

Clint remained silent. A feeling of hopelessness engulfed his soul. Again, he lowered his head, his mind searching for an answer.

What if Abby's still here? Or what if he's right, and she's alive, and her parents have taken her home. I've got to find her. There's nothing in America for me.

"I'll think about it."

Clint felt she had an empathic ear and a compassionate heart. "Meanwhile, we could use your help on the farm."

"Now Albert. The poor boy is exhausted. Don't go workin' him to death."

"No really," Clint said, readily. "I'd love to help. What type of produce do you grow?"

Albert laughed. "Goats. This is a goat farm." "We also grow coffee and rice," Emma said.

After dinner, Clint followed Albert outside. An acrid order filled his nose. Clint noticed the peeling paint and broken fence on the opposite side of the house. A man dressed in a brown cloth wrapped around his body was feeding some goats.

Albert and Emma's house was homey and warm. It had the appearance of a farmhouse. Pale smoke was coming from the chimney and a laundry line with clothing flapping in the gentle breeze.

Albert led Clint to the goats behind the broken fence.

"This is a small farm, about 10 acres. We produce full-blooded African Boer goats."

Clint rubbed the back of one of the goats; its hair was strong and soft. After a quick tour, Clint was exhausted. He went to bed early.

As he lay down, visions of Abby consumed him. His heart was filled with an unspeakable sorrow. It was like living in the midst of a nightmare. The fear and loss has transformed into depression. He rolled over on one side.

How did everything good become so bad? he thought. *My life has become a nightmare.*

Chapter 27

It dawn, Clint walked into the kitchen. Emma was making foufou. He watched her pound boiled white yams with a long thick stick. A steel pan filled with scrambled eggs sat on one burner beside a smaller pan filled with rice. There was hot coffee was brewing on the stove.

"Can I help?" he asked.

"Be a dear and grab that towel and take the bread out of the oven."

Clint grabbed the towel that was hanging from a nail next to a wooden cabinet, opened the oven, and set the bread on the table in the living room.

"Pour yourself some coffee if you like," Emma said. "There's a cup on the table."

Clint grabbed a cup and filled it with hot steaming coffee. He took a sip. The coffee tasted good. He hadn't had a cup in months because there wasn't coffee in the village where he'd been staying.

Albert walked in, dressed in overalls. "Hope you made a hardy breakfast. Clint and I got a lot of work to do on the farm. We'll need plenty of energy."

She waved her finger. "Now like I told you, don't go workin' him to hard. Maybe I should help myself."

Albert smirked. "You wouldn't last a half hour, Mother." His voice was cynical.

"Oh hush. I'm capable of hard work. Do you think cookin' and cleanin' is easy? Besides, I'm only 73 years old. Don't be underestimating me. I'm a strong one ya know.

"One time, Clint, my husband and I were in Siam when a big storm hit. We were scared for our lives. Me and my husband managed to move all the villagers to higher ground for safety. The wind felt like a tornado. Took every bit of strength we had . . . but we did."

"My mother the heroine," Albert said, before sitting down.

"Oh hush. Don't be makin' me out to be somethin' I'm not. The good Lord led the way. We just followed. Enough about me, let's eat."

After breakfast, Clint felt stronger. He followed Albert outside. There was much to do; feeding the goats, mending a fence that held the goats. Clint didn't mind, he tackled one task at a time.

Mid evening, Clint knelt down and added the finishing touch of white paint to the fence surrounding Albert and Emma's house.

Albert sauntered over to him. "Fine work."

Clint finished the last stroke and said, "Thanks." He took a step back to eye his work.

A young African man, wearing a colorful shift and bare chest ran over to them. He spoke in an African dialect.

Albert spoke back. The man walked away.

"A few of the goats got out. They've probably wandered into the field heading east. The grass is higher there. I'll have to hunt em' down before it gets dark. Why don't you come with me?"

Clint dropped the paint brush into the can of paint, dumped some water from a pitcher on his hands to remove the residue of paint, and wiped his hands on a cloth.

He followed Albert along the narrow dirt road through the tiny village. A woman was using a hoe to soften the dirt to plant vegetables. Albert paused for a second to watch her.

"I'm sure you know, in Africa, many poor families rely on the land to survive. Luckily, each of these families own at least one goat. We teach them how to care for them. The goats produce lots of nutritious milk. The families drink and sell it to help pay for medicine and school books. Not to mention, the goats' manure is a great fertilizer for the crops."

"There were only a few goats in the village I stayed in," Clint said. They strode slowly down the dirt road for several minutes.

"Have you decided whether you plan to come with us?" Albert asked. "Back to the states, that is?"

Clint hesitated at first. "I . . . I'm a little low on cash."

"You won't need to worry about that. The captain of the ship is a good friend of mine and owes me a favor or two. My mother saved his niece's life many years ago. She caught a severe case of pneumonia and my mother nursed her back to good health. He never charges us for the trip. We'd fly, but mother says flyin' is for birds."

"Thank you."

Clint was humbled by the kindness of this stranger. In such a short time, he felt attached to Albert and his mother. They treated him with warmth and seemed to genuinely like him. But nice as they were, he felt a wave of unhappiness.

Albert looked at Clint, seriously. "You still worried about your friend . . . Abby".

"I'm afraid to leave . . . not knowing what's happened. If she's alive, she needs me."

I hate to say this son, but from what you've described, it would have taken a true miracle for her to have lived."

Clint glanced away. The words were too painful to hear.

"Like I said before, if she is alive, she might very well be back home by now."

Albert stopped and looked at Clint. "I know it's hard. Loss is almost unbearable, but sometimes you have to come to grips with it." His voice was compassionate yet stern.

Conflicting emotions whirled through Clint's mind. He fought to hold back the tears.

"I think you should go home."

He lowered his head and felt a lump in his throat. "I don't know if I have a home to go back to. I doubt my father would ever want to see me again. I know my brother doesn't."

"Why's that?"

In a low voice, Clint said, "I haven't spoken to him in three years. I didn't leave on good terms. That's not an excuse. My father is a good man. I never realized how good until now. He is kind, patient, and giving. He was a good father and I was a rotten son. I know my older brother hates me."

"If your father is the kind person you say, he'll be ecstatic to see you."

"I've made too many bad choices," Clint said.

"Have you ever heard of the story of the prodigal son?" "No."

Albert started to walk again, this time more slowly.

"There was a man who had two sons. The younger one told his father to give him his share of his estate. So he did. The younger son left home, eventually squandered his wealth, and ended up destitute. Finally, he came to his senses and decided to go home. He feared his father's reaction, but he had no other choice. The minute his father saw him, he ran to embrace him and told him he loved him. Luke 15, you should read it sometime."

"Your father may surprise you. I've only known you for a short period of time, but I believe your father would be proud of the person you've become. One of the hardest things for people to do is to let go of the past.

God does, regardless of what we've done. His love covers a multitude of sins"

Clint was silent, reflecting on what he was hearing.

"I had some trouble with my own faith. I was a deeply devout Christian for years. When my wife died, everything fell apart. I hated everything and everyone, including myself. When World War II broke out, I enlisted in the army and was sent to Africa. I nearly died twice from attacks by the Italian forces. I became increasingly disillusioned. I took to drinking and sank into depression."

Clint's eyes were fixed on him.

"But I decided I wasn't a quitter. I needed to finish the work my wife and I'd set out to do. I fell to my knees and sought the Lord. I let go of the bitterness I was holding inside, forgave, and accepted God's forgiveness. I was a broken man. God helped restore me. I know my wife would be happy if she saw the person I've become."

Albert looked directly at Clint. "I'm sure your father has given you many gifts, but the greatest gift is forgiveness. Clint, God has protected you and that's been for a reason . . . He loves you."

They walked several miles before stumbling upon two goats grazing in the open pasture.

Albert took one of them while Clint grabbed the other. They directed them back to the village inside a gate not far from Albert's house. Albert pulled down a hatch to lock the gate. They went back into the house.

Emma was sitting, knitting a sweater. "It's about time you two got back. What took you so long?"

"A couple of the goats got loose. We had to round them up. Clint's a good worker and a skilled craftsman. He fixed the fence and painted all of it in a half day. Albert took off his jacket and threw it on a chair. "I could use a good size bowl of that rice pudding you made."

She set the needles and sweater down. Before entering the kitchen she said, "Clint, can I bring you some?"

"Uh, no, thank you." He was covered in dirt and paint. "I think I'll take a bath."

He bathed and washed out a change of clothing in the small stream by the farm. After drying off, he put on a pair of clean pants and went back into the house. Albert was reading while Emma was still knitting.

"I'm going to turn in. I'm a little tired." "Good night," Emma said.

"Sleep well," Albert said. "Good night," he said.

When he shut the door and sat on the bed, he felt tears sting his eyes as he fingered the cup of water on the small dresser next to his bed. He meditated on the words Albert had spoken. *"God has protected you."*

A flashback of the Negro soldier pulling him to safety in Germany flashed through his mind. Then another of the car accident he had while racing; he saw an image of the car rolling down the hill, crashing. He saw the face of the gorilla that almost attacked him and a picture of himself falling down the hill to save Mardea. Then he saw himself crawling through the window where he'd been taken captive and running through the forest for his life.

Clint pulled out the bible out of his jacket and opened it to skim through the Book of Luke, stopping at chapter 15. He read the story of the prodigal son. When he was finished, he laid the bible down next to him. He took a deep breath, got on his knees, and spoke quietly.

"God, I'm sorry. I've made a mess of my life. I've done a lot of things I regret. Please forgive me." Tears slid down his face. "Give me strength to go on . . . I need you. And please, please let Abby be alive. I can't live without her. Please."

He lay down on the bed and cried harder.

The next morning, he took a walk along the river bank and paused to collect his thoughts. He knelt down. Using his hands as a cup, he filled them with water and splashed it on his face. It was early, but the weather was humid. After pondering long and hard, he made one of the hardest decisions of his life. He decided to go home.

Chapter 28

For two weeks, Clint labored diligently on the farm. He agonized over Abby every waking moment; tormented by the thought that he might never see her again.

Thursday morning, October 1948, he stepped into his room to pack his things. After sizing up the small space, he realized he had nothing to pack. He had left home a wealthy boy and was returning a poor man.

He strolled into the living room wearing the same faded black pants and blue shirt he'd worn most of his stay. Albert strode in dressed in a pair of clean gray pants and a blue cotton shirt. He set two old black suitcases filled with their possessions down.

"Let me help you," Clint said. He lifted the suitcases.

"Thanks. You can put them outside. A driver is waiting to take us to the river bank."

"I'd like to pay you back . . . for everything."

"We won't hear of it," Mrs. Watts said. She entered the room wearing a green dress, white shoes, and a wide-brim straw hat. "Clint, be a dear and grab the other handbag in the bedroom and put it on the cart when you're done loadin' those."

He took the two suitcases outside and onto the cart that had the appearance of a brown wagon. He returned inside and grabbed Mrs. Watt's bags.

"Thanks a million, Clint," she said.

She gave a round of hugs to the villagers. Albert and Clint said their goodbyes and got in the cart, driven by an African driver and pulled by two donkeys. Mrs. Watts sat up front.

The trip took almost twelve hours. They stopped only twice to eat and rest the donkeys.

They arrived at a small port near Lukapo and boarded a boat large enough to hold 40 people and traveled along the Kwango River.

Four days later, the boat arrived in Luanda. The crowded dock was filled with white men, some dressed in dirty trousers, others dressed in nice suits, with Negro men assisting them. Albert had mentioned that the port received 500 vessels a year and handled cargo such as iron, wood, oil, timber, ivory, cotton, and coffee.

Clint held Mrs. Watts' suitcase in one hand and grabbed the handrail with the other.

Albert and Emma, Clint right behind them, climbed aboard a 400 passenger ship. They were greeted by a pleasant plump man wearing a white sailor uniform. He had a strong lenient face and a mane of white hair covered by a white cap.

He smiled at them. "Albert, Emma, so glad you could make it." "Glad to be aboard," Albert said. He shook the man's hand.

Emma hugged him. "It's so kind of you to allow us to travel on your ship. Hope you don't mind, we brought an extra passenger."

"Clint, this is Captain Franklin Steele."

"Nice to meet you Clint, we're happy to have you aboard."

Clint shook his hand. "It's nice to meet you. Thanks for allowing me to travel on your ship."

"The more the merrier," said the captain. He waved his arm motioning to one of the cruise staff. "Take these bags to their rooms and see that this young man is put in nice cabin with a view."

"Thank you again, Franklin," Albert said.

"Anything for old friends. I'll look for you at dinner. I insist you dine with me."

"We'll look forward to it," Albert said.

Albert and Emma's room was on the first floor. Clint followed the young attendant to the second floor. His cabin was about 300 square feet; a small bathroom next door and a nice view of the ocean through a round porthole.

Clint walked on deck. He gazed out at the sterile coastal plain and a belt of hills and mountains behind a large plateau. He felt empty and hollow inside; as if a large hole had been dug in his stomach and nothing could fill it. He believed he was to blame for Abby being shot. He should have protected her. His heart told him to get off the ship and search the continent to find Abby, but his head convinced him to stay.

He remembered the first time he saw her in Wales, the stunning young woman at the top of the stairs. He recalled their walk along the beach, when he was so drawn to her. The image of her walking into the dining car on the train in a beautiful red dress, with a smile so graceful it filled the room, came to him. A vision of her caring for a weak elderly woman suffering from the fever, teaching bible study to young children, working in the garden, flashed through his mind. He especially remembered the night when he told her he loved her. She looked so beautiful. She told him she loved him too.

Fear threatened to overwhelm his emotions. Everyone he loved was gone. He wasn't ready to say goodbye to his mother, his brother, but most of all, Abby. All he had was a glimpse of hope that she could still be alive. He had to believe God would work a miracle. That soon, they'd be together again and he'd live the rest of his life with her.

It'd been a week on the ship. It was a little past eight. Clint sat across from Albert and Emma at the captain's table. Twelve guests had been asked to join him. The table was beautifully decorated with candles in crystal holders, on a red table cloth, crystal glasses, white china lined with gold and sterling silverware.

Clint had barely touched his food; wild salmon, red potatoes, sautéed string beans, and warm French bread. It was hard for him to eat. He felt as though he'd lost almost 20 pounds since he'd been in the village.

A stunning blonde dressed in a blue silk gown swept past his table and threw him a smile; her long blonde hair pulled away from her face. Clint merely looked the other direction. His thoughts were filled with Abby every waking moment. He felt powerless over his own emotions. At times, he felt the grief was too much to bear.

The captain, whose eyes were fixed on Emma and Albert said, "Did I ever tell you the story of the huge whale that almost sunk my ship?"

Albert set his fork down, still chewing on a medium rare steak. "Can't say that you have."

"The captain leaned into the table. "We were on an older ship that held about 200 passengers. I called her Lucky, cause she was my "lucky" vessel. I was one of the youngest captains, 23 years old.

"Lucky left the U.S. for a two-and-a-half week voyage off the west coast of South America. On the eighth day, about nine that morning, a whale rammed the ship. At first, I thought we'd hit a rock or something until I went on deck and saw it. It looked to be the size of a small submarine. It went under, battering the ship and causing it to tip from side to side.

"It surfaced close on the starboard side with its head by the bow and tail by the stern. The whale appeared to be stunned and motionless. I'll tell you what, once I got rid of the fear, I looked at that giant fish and said, 'I'll be darned if I let you sink my boat.'

"I told my first mate, Charles, to prepare to harpoon it from the deck. Then I realized that its tail was only inches from the rudder, which the whale could easily destroy if provoked by an attempt to kill it. I relented, fearing to leave the ship stranded thousands of miles from land with no way to steer it. The whale recovered and swam several hundred yards ahead of the ship and turned to face the bow."

All eyes were on the captain; you could hear a pin drop. Even Clint's attention shifted as he listened to the story.

"I turned around and saw him about a few hundred yards directly ahead of us, coming down with twice his ordinary speed. It appeared with tenfold fury and vengeance in his aspect. There was a continual violent thrashing of his tail. His head was about half out of the water as he came upon us, striking the ship again.

"The whale crushed the bow like an eggshell, driving the vessel backwards. I knew if it would have struck us again, it'd be pure destruction.

"We'd never had any trouble with whales. I asked myself, why in the world was this one attacking? Then, I saw a baby whale emerge. I think it was stuck beneath the surface of the ship. I realized it was a mother merely protecting her baby. We veered the ship left and saw the baby whale swimming in the opposite direction. The mother whale finally disengaged her head from the shattered timbers and swam off with her baby, never to be seen again.

"I tell you what, that was one scary trip. I thought for sure we were dead. We barely made it to shore. Took three weeks to repair the damage."

"What a mother won't do to protect her child," Emma said. "That's quite a tale. I'm sure you got more just like it," Albert said.

"I could go on for days," The Captain said. "There was another time when . . . ." before he could finish his thought, Clint, who had been slightly intrigued by the story, stood. "I'm going to turn in."

"Is everything okay, dear?" Emma asked.

"Yes. I'm a little tired, that's all." He looked at the captain. Thank you for the fine meal."

"You're welcome. Hope you'll join us for breakfast tomorrow. I'm giving a tour of the ship."

Clint nodded, "I'll try. Good night." Everyone said "Good night."

When Clint got to his room, he changed clothes and went right to bed. He lay down on the gold silk comforter and stared at the ceiling.

Once in Texas, he planned to begin searching for Abby. If she's alive, she could be home. But first, he had to see his father. Ashamed, he felt a deep sense of regret. He sighed. Confusing thoughts whirled through his mind.

My father probably hates me. Paul probably never wants to see me again.

He rolled over to his side. What would he say? How would he apologize? Why would his father forgive him? Should he ask for a job on the ranch? He'd be willing to do anything even though he didn't deserve it.

Clint pondered long and hard. He was different, but would his father see that?

The past few months he'd been surrounded by people who had sacrificed their lives to help others. They were noble, gallant, and kind. They knew God and were graceful, compassionate, lovely, and hopeful. They taught him a lot. The once selfish boy, absorbed in greed and lust, was returning a mature man.

Clint prayed to God with such intensity that he could share his life with Abby. He decided if fate dealt him a horrible hand in losing Abby, he would spend the rest of his life helping others. It's what Abby would have wanted.

He turned over on his back, his eyes were blinded by tears. After a while, he drifted off to sleep.

The ship traveled on the Atlantic Ocean. After twelve days, the ship arrived in New York. Clint and the Wattses disembarked and stepped onto the wooden pier.

The pier was active with people walking and children playing. Vendors and restaurants lined the opposite side of the street, including a fisherman's pub.

Emma straightened her hat. "Would you care to join us for some fish and chips at the pub across the streets? It's one of our favorite restaurants."

"No thank you," Clint said, glancing in the direction of the restaurant. "I need to get home."

"That's probably best, son," Albert said. He patted him on the back. "I'm proud of you. You're doing the right thing. Everything will be fine . . . you'll see. There is nothing stronger than a father's love."

Albert hugged Clint. "I'll miss you both."

He hugged Emma. She felt like his mother.

"I can never thank you . . . for everything. I want to repay you for the train and food."

She narrowed her eyes and said in a stern voice, "Like I said, we won't hear of it. It's our gift. You make sure you stay in touch. We'll expect a letter in the near future."

Clint smiled. "Yes ma'am."

Clint hugged them both again and headed a few blocks north to catch a trolley to the train station. The train was scheduled to leave at five p.m. Once he arrived, he pulled out the Browns' telephone number he had stashed in his bible. His hands began to shake when he lifted the receiver. A feeling of dread overtook him. *What will I do if her parents answer the phone and tell me she's dead?*

The phone rang seven times, but there was no answer. *I'll try again when I get to Texas.*

Albert had given him enough money for food, so he grabbed a sandwich and milk and boarded the train.

Chapter 29

The train arrived in Dallas Tuesday early afternoon after a four day trip. Clint took a bus through town and walked the rest of the way home. After a seven mile walk, he stared up at the large oak sign that said, "Edison Ranch". Everything looked the same. Hundreds of cattle were grazing on open brown fields. Fall leaves of orange, red, and yellow covered the ground. A blast of cold air whipped up forcing him to turn up his collar.

When he saw his house, he began to breathe anxiously. His father was sitting at the glass table on the patio. Clint moved slowly. From a distance, he looked different, like he'd aged.

Trip, Clint's golden retriever, emerged from behind the house. The dog dashed towards him, leaped on him and licked his face.

Clint laughed, trying to control him. "I missed you too, Trip." He knelt down and wrestled with the dog.

Once the dog calmed down, Clint stood. Fear shot through his bones as his father rose. They stood staring at one another, immobile. Finally, James reached for a cane and slowly moved down the stairs. Clint walked towards him.

James began to run, using his can. Clint noticed a slight limp. Once he reached him, he wrapped his arms around Clint and wept hard for a long time.

"I'm sorry, Dad. I'm so . . . . sorry," Clint said, crying.

James looked at Clint with his deep red and swollen eyes, filled with tears that were streaming down his face. "I can't believe you're home." His speech was slightly slurred. "I prayed for you every day and God answered my prayer. My precious son is home."

Clint's voice quivered as he said, "Please forgive me."

"There is nothing to forgive. You came home. You are my son and I love you."

They held one another again. Clint wrapped his arm around his father's waist and helped him up the stairs. They sat next to each other.

James touched Clint's face. "I can't believe it. I was scared that something had happened to you and I would never see you again. I'm so happy. To have you back safe is the greatest gift God could give me."

"Are you all right, Dad?" His father looked as though he had aged 20 years. His hair was completely gray and the left side of his face seemed slightly distorted. It was obvious that his father had suffered a stroke.

"I'm fine . . . especially now."

"I should have been here for you," Clint said, distressed.

"You are here now. I can tell you've changed, not just physically, but mentally. You've matured." He rubbed his hands against Clint's unshaven face. "I like the beard. It looks good on you."

"Thank you. I have so much to tell you."

Camellia walked out on the porch. "Oh my goodness." Clint stood and hugged her.

She held his face with both her hands. "Is it really you? You've come back to us. God has answered our prayers." She hugged him again.

"I've missed you, Camellia."

"I've missed you," she said, crying. "My precious Lord and Savior has brought you home. I will give thanks to him all day and night. You must be starving. I'm going to fix you something to eat . . . something special. Praise the Lord," she said, before entering the house.

As Clint was sitting, he asked, "Where's Paul?"

"Picnicking in the park with his wife and son. They live in a nice home about five miles south of here."

So Paul is married, he thought. *I don't imagine he'll want to see me.*

"I wish I could have attended the wedding."

"She is a wonderful girl. You will love her. Her father works for my oil company." James leaned back. "So tell me, Clint. Where have you been? I want to know everything."

"There's so much to tell. I don't know where to start. Do you mind if I get cleaned up first. I'm tired and haven't showered in a while."

"Oh course, of course. Go to your room and freshen up. Camellia will prepare a feast, I'm sure. We'll talk at dinner."

"Thanks."

He went inside. His gaze went directly to the telephone sitting on a small mahogany table. His heart began to beat faster. He started to race to the phone and call Abby's home but realized it would be two in the morning there.

That evening, Clint insisted Camellia join him and his father for dinner. They ate fried steak, mashed potatoes, string beans, and corn bread. Clint had missed Camellia's southern cooking. He had two helpings.

He spoke of his adventures on the French Riviera, the places he went, the people he saw, and the companions he met along the way. He told them Ted had committed suicide and why he felt responsible. His father showed compassion and assured him he wasn't to blame.

When he spoke of Abby, his father's face lit up. He smiled when he told of their time in Wales, her wonderful parents who made him feel at home, and his good friend, Frazier.

Clint talked about the trip to Africa, saying it was like nothing he'd ever seen: the amazing train ride, animals, and scenery. Camellia wore a look of astonishment on her face while she listened and James seemed surprised too.

He spoke about the mission trip: building the medial facility, helping the sick, planting crops, and fishing. The people had a strong faith and he attended weekly worship services, he'd learned so much. They were kind and generous, he said. James looked pleased.

Tears came to James's eyes when Clint talked about saving Mardea's life and how Freeborn, the little four year old boy, was miraculously found. He told them he'd fallen deeply in love with Abby and planned to spend the rest of his life with her.

When he told them that the village was attacked by rebels and Abby had been shot, Camellia looked horrified.

"Is she alright?" James asked, stunned.

"I don't know," Clint said, his voice lower. "I was taken captive by the rebels, but I'm okay. They didn't hurt me and I managed to escape. That's when I met Albert and Emma Watts, missionaries from Arizona, who helped me get home."

"Clint, the thought of you being held prisoner in a foreign land by dangerous rebels is horrifying. It's a wonder you made it out alive. God truly protected you."

"This is true," Camellia said, who was still in shock. "He saved my life."

Clint leaned forward, his elbows on the table. "I have to find Abby. I have to believe she's alive."

"Yes, we must believe the best," James said.

"I plan to call tomorrow morning. I'd call now but it's too early." He looked at his dad. His mood was grim. "If she's not there, I'm going back to Africa. I can't rest until I find her."

"I understand." James rested his hand on Clint's hand. "I will do whatever I can to help you. I can see you truly love this girl and she sounds like a wonderful person. We can only hope and pray that she is alive. I believe in miracles. I'm looking at one.

"Clint, you have been through an eventful and dangerous journey, and I can see it has changed you. I am very proud of you."

"You told me I'm the only one who can control my happiness. I didn't understand then, but you were right. I didn't find it by running. I still can't believe I'm alive, but God was with me and I fell in love." He bent his head. "I can only hope and pray by some miracle she's still alive."

They were silent for a moment before Clint spoke again. "I am sorry . . . . for everything, Dad. I haven't been a good son."

"The past is irrelevant. What's important is the man you've become. I've never been so pleased. This is the greatest gift God could have given me. You have become the man I hoped and prayed for".

Clint hugged him.

They ate peach pie for dessert. Clint took a few bites and then went to bed early.

He was up at dawn. He flew downstairs and eyed the telephone.

He dialed the number three times, but there was no answer. He decided to try again every half hour.

James entered the kitchen. Clint was sitting at the table drinking a glass of orange juice.

"Did you reach Abby or her family?"

"No, I've tried and there was no answer. I'll keep calling." "Good. Let's have some breakfast."

Camellia made Clint's favorite dish: huevos rancheros.

James talked about life on the ranch over the last three years. He spoke fondly of Paul's in-laws and his beautiful grandchild. Clint was looking forward to meeting them.

Clint thought James was doing remarkably well, but the strain of the past few years showed in his face and eyes.

He made several more attempts to reach Abby's family, but was still unsuccessful. The waiting was agony. Not knowing if Abby was all right was killing him.

Late that afternoon, dressed in a warm jacket, Clint sat outside. He'd been gazing into the open fields for hours. Memories of the last three years occupied his mind.

Why hasn't Frazier called me? Maybe he can't find my phone number. Then he remembered. *Frazier probably thinks I'm still in Africa, stranded in the forest. Or worse, he probably thinks I'm dead.*

Paul drove up to the house in a new black truck. Clint stood. Paul gave him a stare, got out of the truck, and walked around to the passenger side. He picked up a little boy who looked to be two years old, and then climbed the stairs.

"Hey Paul." Clint was smiling. "Good to see you." "You too."

Paul set the boy down and reached out his hand out to shake Clint's. Clint shook his brother's hand and then gently wrapped his arm around him. "This is my son, William." Paul ran his hand through the boy's thick black hair.

Clint knelt down and smiled. "So, I have a nephew." He looked up at Paul, "William . . . perfect name. How old is he?"

"Seventeen months."

Clint picked him up and stared into his slanted eyes. "You're a nice lookin' kid."

Paul sat down. "It's great to be a dad." "I can see why."

Clint sat William in a chair. He studied Paul for a moment. His hair was longer and lighter, a sandy brown. His skin had darkened, but he looked the same.

"So where is your wife?"

"She's at the house, resting. She's four months pregnant." Clint smiled. "Congratulations."

"Thanks."

Paul seemed gracious, yet Clint sensed aloofness in his emotions.

"Dad called me last night and told me you came home." Paul hesitated for a moment. "So were ya been? You left suddenly and never bothered to write. Dad had a stroke and I had no way of getting in touch with you." The tone of his voice had changed, almost irritated.

"I know and I'm sorry. I should have called or written." "Should have . . . . why didn't you?"

Clint glanced at the cold cup of coffee in front of him, unsure of what to say. "I don't have an answer. There's no excuse. I'm sorry I wasn't there for Dad. First, I lived on the French Riviera. Life was good. I was having the time of my life. My good friend got killed and then I traveled to Wales for a brief stay. As life would have it, I ended up in Africa. It started out fun and ended in tragedy. It's a long story."

Paul seemed unmoved.

Just then, James walked outside. "Paul. Good, I'm glad you're here. I hope the two of you have had a chance to catch up."

James sat down. Camellia walked outside holding a glass of chocolate milk. "Good morning Paul."

"Mornin'."

"Can I bring you anything? Perhaps some coffee?"

"No thanks. We can't stay long. Thought I'd stop by to say hi."

She sat the milk down in front of William and smiled. "Here you are my little sweetie. Drink your milk."

Little William picked up the class of milk, took a few drinks, then squirmed until Paul lifted him out of the chair and put him down. He ran towards the side of the porch where a few of his toy truck and cars were in a small box.

"Having you home has been a dream come true, Clint, so I've decided to throw a party to celebrate your homecoming."

At first, Clint was at a loss for words. "I appreciate it, but . . . a party?"

"I'll invite a few friends over to celebrate."

Clint could see the cold look on Paul's face.

"I'm really not up to it, Dad." He said politely. "Besides, I'm leaving as soon as I hear anything from Abby's parents."

"I understand, but I've been without you for over three years. I want to have a small gathering on Saturday. Then I will buy you a ticket anywhere you want to go. You can leave on Sunday. That's only four days away. Please, let me have a true celebration to welcome you home."

Clint felt uneasy. A gathering of friends was the last thing he wanted, but he hadn't so much as written his father or bothered to call. It was the least he could do.

"Alright. But just a few friends."

Paul leaped up out of his chair. "I need to go. I have some important work to finish up."

Clint could tell he was annoyed.

He lifted his son up and jolted down the stairs. "See you, Dad. Clint, welcome home."

"Thanks. It's good to see you."

"Paul, we'll see you for dinner tonight."

He nodded.

That evening, Paul entered the house with a woman with flawless white skin, thick long black hair, and slanted eyes. She was holding his son.

Clint thought, *That must be his wife. She's beautiful.*

Behind them was a short Asian couple, both with pure white hair. James, who had just walked into the hallway, shook their hands. *They must be her parents.*

Clint strolled over to them. "This is my wife, Aiko," Paul said. Clint shook her hand. "Hi, it's nice to meet you."

She hugged him. Her belly was bulging. "It's very nice to meet you." Her voice was kind and sweet. "I've heard a lot about you. I'm sure your father is very happy now that you are home. This is my father Hiro and my mother Kameko Yoshi."

"Mr. Yoshi, it's a pleasure." Clint shook his hand. "It's very nice to meet you, Mrs. Yoshi."

"You too."

"Let's go into the living room," James said. "Dinner will be served soon."

They talked for hours. Clint found the Yoshis kind and polite. Aiko was not only beautiful but intelligent. She was attending college at the University of Texas and working part-time in a legal office with plans of becoming a lawyer. She shared stories from her work. Clint could see why Paul had fallen in love with her. Her strength and compassion reminded him of Abby.

He'd tried calling the Browns for two days, but there was still no answer. It took every inch of strength to keep from packing his bags and leaving. Feelings of regret tormented him. *Why aren't they answering? Are they still in Africa? Should I have stayed? Could I have found her?*

Clint's days were spent working on the ranch, sometimes for ten hours. It kept him preoccupied.

On occasion, he visited old friends; mainly Eddie. He worked as the mechanic of a car shop in downtown Dallas. Although Eddie had somewhat matured, Clint knew their friendship would never be the same.

Chapter 30

It was Saturday morning and Clint was standing next to the barn. He reached over the corral fence to stroke the neck of a Texas longhorn. He planned to spend the day helping Bo and a few other ranch hands move cattle to a ranch up north. The owner had purchased 200 of their Angus cattle.

Clint didn't mind the work. Staying busy kept his mind and emotions stable when confusion set in. It had been over a month since she was shot. *If Abby didn't survive, then surely her family would be home. She must be alive, but where?*

Clint's plan was to purchase a ticket to Wales the next day. If the Browns didn't return home within the week, he'd travel to Africa and hire a guide to take him to the village. He was determined to find her, even if he had to search the entire continent.

He climbed the stairs, strode into the house, and went into the kitchen. Two glass bowls sat on the countertop: one filled with a dozen eggs and the other with six peeled potatoes. Cooked bacon, ham, and sausages were piled high in a plate on the stove.

"It looks like you're getting ready to feed an army, Camellia." "Your father invited a few people over for breakfast."

Clint shrugged. He shook his head. "I already agreed to a party that I'm dreading, but company, now . . . why?"

"Your father is excited. You must have patience and let him enjoy this moment?

He reached up in the cabinet, grabbed a cup, and filled it with hot coffee. After taking a drink, he glanced at Camellia, who was bent over taking a pan of biscuits out of the oven.

"Would you like a cup of coffee?"

She looked at him, surprised. "No, but thank you for asking."

She placed the biscuits on the stove. "He worried so much for you just as he did when you were in Germany, fighting. He feels very blessed to have you home."

"I just have a lot of my mind."

He grabbed a hot biscuit, poured some honey on it, and took a bite. "Where is Dad, I notice his car was gone when I was out front?"

"He had to run an errand before the company arrived. He said he would be back shortly."

"Can I help?"

Camellia looked at Clint. "Your father was right. You have become a young mature man. Oh course you can help. The potatoes need to be sliced."

He took a knife from a kitchen drawer and began to slice the potatoes. Minutes later, he heard his father's car pull up into the driveway.

Camellia pushed the yellow curtains to the side and glanced out the window above the sink. "Your father is here with some guests."

Clint didn't respond.

She smiled. "Don't you want to see who is here?" "Not really."

Seconds later, Clint heard his name being called.

Camellia glanced out the window, again. "Your father is calling you." Clint set the knife down, drank the last of his coffee, and went outside.

Once he stepped onto the porch, he felt his heart almost leap out of his chest. His body froze. His gaze went directly to her. *Am I dreaming?*

There she was, dressed in a sweater, and a pair of brown slacks. Her hair was tied back with a little brown ribbon.

He yelled, "Abby!"

He ran down the stairs, flew to her side and held her. "Are you okay? Is it really you?" There were a hundred questions whirling in his mind. He started to cry.

Keeping her gaze locked on his, she shook her head. "I'm fine."

He wrapped his arms around her and buried his face in her neck. They stood motionless in each other's arm for a long time. He felt her tears fall on his neck.

It was hard for him to talk, but he tried to compose himself. "I thought I'd never see you again. I didn't know if you were alive. What happened? Where have you been? I tried calling your home at least 30 times."

"We've . . . me and my family that is, have been in Africa this entire time."

"I knew I shouldn't have left," he said, still crying.

He held her for a long time before finally letting go. His eyes were overflowing with tears. Feelings of relief and excitement over took his past emotions of dread, grief, and fear. It was as though his life had been given back to him. Nothing mattered but her.

"I knew I should have stayed. My life has been agony these past weeks. What happened? How did you get here?"

"I have so much to tell you."

Before she could say another word Frazier, who was standing on the other side of the car holding Freeborn's hand said, "Cheerio."

His parents were next to him.

Clint hugged Frazier. "You don't know how glad I am to see you." "Me too, Clint. This is an answered prayer."

He knelt down and hugged Freeborn. He picked him up and whirled him around. Freeborn laughed vivaciously.

Alistair said, "Clint, we're pleased to see you." "Sir, I'm glad to see you." He hugged Alistair.

"We're relieved you're all right," Sarah said. She gave him a big hug. "What a horrible ordeal you've been though. I'm so happy you're safe and home." She looked past him. "And a beautiful home at that." Clint's eyes met his father's. "How? When?"

"I called your father four days ago," Frazier said. "I planned to tell him the horrible news; that you'd been taken captive by rebels and we didn't know if you were dead or alive. You can't know how thankful I was when he told me you were home safe."

James was smiling broadly. "I wanted to surprise you so I flew them here to see you in person."

Clint hugged Abby again. He didn't want to let her go.

James motioned towards the house. "Let's go inside. Don't worry about the suitcases. I'll have someone bring them in."

Clint led Abby up the stairs, his right arm wrapped around her. Camellia greeted them at the door.

"This is our housekeeper and friend, Camellia," James said. "Hello," she said, wiping her hands on her apron. "Breakfast will be ready in about 15 minutes."

Mr. and Mrs. Brown followed James into the dining room. Sarah took Freeborn with them while Frazier followed Clint and Abby into the living room.

Abby slipped her arm in his as they sat nestling closely together on the couch.

Frazier took the chair opposite of the couch.

"Abby, not knowing if you were okay was torture. I wasn't sure if I'd ever see you again. What happened?"

"Claude tried to get the bullet out of my chest, but he said it was lodged in too deep. He bandaged me up and did everything he could to rid me of the high fever I had. He planned to get me to a hospital as soon as possible. I lost a lot of blood. The next day my brother and Kpassi arrived back in the village. Gamba told Frazier the whole story. I didn't remember a thing because I was unconscious most of the time."

Frazier leaned forward. "We . . . Me, Kpassi, and the Abneys that is, took her to the hospital in Kinshasa. It was a miserably long trip. Some of the roads were washed out because of the storm, so we had to take several detours. At one point, I thought we'd lost her because her breathing was low and her blood pressure had dropped, drastically. Claude stayed by her side the entire time. It's truly a miracle that she's alive."

"The doctors performed surgery right away," Abby said. "My parents flew to Africa to stay with me. I was in a coma for eight days. Everyone thought I was going to die, but God worked a miracle and spared my life. My family had me moved to a hospital in Angola. Claude knew they had an excellent intensive care unit that specialized in treating gunshot wounds and felt I would have a much better chance of recovering there. Kpassi, Frazier, and the Abneys went back to the village to look for you."

"We searched high and low for you, Clint," Frazier said. "You're like a brother to me. I was scared for your life and prayed for your safety. By the eleventh day, we decided to leave. Although Gamba and many of the men in the village had agreed to continue searching for you, we thought for sure the rebels had killed you. It was a horrible day."

"I needed to get back to Abby. Kpassi and the Abneys went back to Wales. I knew that Abby would have wanted me to bring Freeborn with me, so I did.

"I found your journal by your cot in the hut. It had your father's telephone number in it. I called him once I arrived in Angola. Like I mentioned earlier, I planned to give him the bad news. But he told me you'd made it home a day earlier. It was an answered prayer and true miracle."

"I'd almost fully recovered," Abby said. "When Frazier told me you were home, in Texas, it was the happiest moment of my life. I was so worried," she said, looking intently into his eyes. "I couldn't sleep and it was hard to eat. I thought of you day and night. I don't know what I would have done if anything had happened to you."

"I feel the same way," Clint said, gripping Abby's hand tighter. "Is Mark okay? How's his head?"

"He's fine. We took him to the hospital in Mbandaka. One of the main roads was washed out so we had to travel by boat much of the way. That's what took us so long. It was close, but by the grace of God, he survived. He's home."

Frazier placed his elbows on both knees and arched his eyebrows. "Where did they take you, Clint? How did you escape?"

A troubled look crossed Abby's face. "Yes, what was it like? Did they hurt you?"

"They held me in a remote village for about six or seven days. I've never been so scared in my life. I thought for sure they were gonna' kill me." By some miracle, I managed to escape." He glanced at Abby, "And no, they didn't hurt me.

"I didn't think I would make it out of the forest alive, but I guess God was looking after me. I made it to a small village in Zambia. I met some missionaries, Emma and her son, Albert. I was dehydrated and weak. They nursed me back to health. I stayed with them for two weeks."

"I wanted to search for you right away, but they convinced me to go home. I didn't know where to start and had no money. I didn't know how to get back to the village. I wasn't sure if you were alive and if you were, I thought you'd be back in Wales. From listening to your story, I made the right decision. I would have never looked for you in Angola."

Abby leaned into Clint. "When I think of you lost and alone in Africa, it makes my heart hurt. I'm so happy you're okay."

He could hear the relief in her voice. He touched his forehead to hers. "We traveled from Africa by ship and then a train to Texas. Like I said, once I arrived I called your home more times than I can count. I was planning to fly to Wales tomorrow. I wasn't gonna' rest until I found you."

He stroked her face.

Camellia said, "Breakfast is ready."

After breakfast, James and Clint gave everyone a tour of the ranch. Clint and Abby spent most of the day walking, talking, and holding one another. It was the happiest day of Clint's life.

Chapter 31

Clint stepped into his party at the reception hall at 7 that evening. Five round tables large enough to seat 10 people were covered in white linen and accented by antique silver vase centerpieces packed with white and cream flower bouquets. The dinnerware was elegant yet simple, with each place setting adorned by silver flatware and crystal glasses holding folded green napkins.

Clint walked over to a small table with a large cake that said, 'Welcome Home Clint' written in green letters.

James arranged for the Browns and Yoshis to be seated at their table. Other invited guests included Eddie and his girlfriend, James Pastor, and a few friends from the church.

Camellia swept into the room carrying a large platter of smothered pork chops. She positioned them next to bowls of mashed potatoes, string beans, and a plate of corn bread. James entered the room. Clint wasn't sure whether to hug him or yell.

"I wish you would have told me as soon as Frazier called, Dad. You knew the torture I was going through." His voice was gentle but stern.

"I wanted to surprise you. I figured you'd already waited this long, a few more days wouldn't hurt. I realize I should have told you, now. I'm sorry. Can you forgive me?"

Still frustrated, he nodded. "All that matters is that Abby's here with me and she's alright."

"Speaking of Abby . . . ." as James pointed with his outstretched arm. Clint turned around.

Abby's hair, which had grown longer, fell softy down her back. Her beautiful white dress seemed to drift around her like a soft cloud. Her shoulders and arms were bare. He flew over to her.

"You're gorgeous."

"Thank you," she said, smiling graciously.

Frazier, dressed in a pair of black slacks and a cream shirt, came into the room. Freeborn wearing a pair of black pants and white shirt was next to him.

James walked over to them. "Where are your parents?" "They'll be down in a jiffy," Frazier said.

Eddie arrived at six thirty with a skinny, pretty girl with blonde curls. Clint introduced them to Abby.

When everyone else arrived, they were all seated for dinner. They talked and reminisced about old times. James spoke of his life over the past twenty years on the ranch and shared stories about cattle, oil, and raising three strong-willed sons.

Alistair leaned forward. "One time, Sarah, and I went away for the night. It was our anniversary so we dined at a fancy restaurant. Frazier was 15 at the time. We'd gotten a second vehicle, a truck. We were planning to use it to sell vegetables at the market. I made the stupid mistake of leaving the keys on the table."

Frazier set his fork down, shaking his head. "Oh, not this story."

Alistair went on to say, "Frazier took the truck. The boy didn't even have a license. He wasn't three blocks away when he wrecked it. You can only imagine how furious I was. Could have killed the lad."

"I had to wait another year before I could get my license. Not to mention the extra chores I was forced to do . . . for the next three months!"

"Be glad you got off that easy."

"I would have rather been beaten," Frazier said, jokingly.

Clint laughed. He hoped his father wouldn't tell them about the last time he wrecked his car.

"He's not the only one to turn to occasional acts of rebellion." Sarah glanced at Abby.

"Oh Mother," Abby said, annoyed.

"Abby was only 16, but she and a friend apparently thought they were old enough to venture out on their own. They decided they would skip school one day.

"They took a boat to London. Unlucky for her, there were problems with the boat." Her voice got louder, "It didn't arrive back till midnight. Can you believe it? I was worried sick. We put her on restriction for a month."

Abby glanced at Clint and shook her head. "I couldn't go out with my friends and was forced to spend every waking moment working. You would have thought I had robbed a bank."

"I'll tell you what. She never did that again," Alistair said.

Although their mishaps didn't begin to compare to his unruly and rebellious childhood, Clint was happy and relieved to learn they weren't always perfect.

Clint held his breath, hoping James wouldn't chime in.

After dinner, James cleared his throat and stood. "I'd like everyone's attention." Silence overtook the room.

James spoke slowly. "I want to thank all of you for coming to welcome my son Clint home. I'm thankful you were able to make this wonderful occasion."

He glanced at the Browns. "And I'm very grateful the Browns are here to share this precious, glorious homecoming."

Clint grabbed Abby's hand.

"As some of you may know, I've been unable to run the company to full capacity ever since my stroke. The board has done a remarkable job, especially with the help of Hiro." James bent his head and smiled at him.

"But there comes a time when I must do what's best for the company and my family. This business has been like my child. I can't think of anything better than putting my child in the hands of the people I love."

James paused for a few seconds. "This is why, I've made a decision . . . I've decided to turn over my entire company, including the ranch, to both my sons.

"As of November 6, 1948, Paul and Clint will manage the Edison estate and oil company."

Everyone applauded. Clint was shocked.

Abby's mouth flew open. She looked at him with amazement. "Congratulations, that's wonderful."

"Yes Clint, I'm sure it's well deserved. Congratulations," Alistair said.

Clint shook his head in disbelief and glanced at Paul, whose face had turned a deep red.

"Everybody, please have dessert. Let's celebrate." James sat down.

Paul threw his napkin on his plate, got up, and stormed out of the house. The door slammed behind him.

James was getting ready to stand but Clint motioned for him to stay. Clint rose from his chair and went outside. He shivered from the cool breeze, searching for Paul. He entered the barn. The pungent odor of hay and horse manure filled his nose.

Paul was leaning against a rail stroking a beautiful chestnut horse. Clint strolled over to him. He fidgeted, searching for the right words. Paul's anger cut through him like a flaming fire.

"You have every right to be mad," Clint said. "I don't deserve this."

"No, you don't!" His voice deep, eyebrows arched. He said, "You've been nothing but problems from the very beginning. You've been kicked out of two schools, barely graduated the last. You've never done a decent day's work on the ranch and you treated our father like a pile of horse manure. You leave town, we didn't hear so much as one word from you in over three years. Dad had a stroke. He could have died and I had no way to reach you." Paul's voice got louder and louder as he spoke. "You've been a disgrace to this family. I work 10 to 12 hours a day. You come home one week and Dad is giving you half of everything! No, Clint! You don't deserve it. I don't know why Dad didn't cut you off years ago!" He was almost yelling.

"You're right," Clint said, calmly. "I've been a disgrace to this family. I lived my life angry and resentful—for no reason. I had everything money could buy, but I was too selfish to notice." Clint took a deep breath. "I squandered most of my inheritance on the French Riviera, gambling and partying. I had more women then I knew what to do with. There wasn't a day I went without a drink. I meant to call, but truth is . . . I didn't care. I lost a good friend who killed himself due to my selfishness."

Paul looked at Clint, he was still angry.

"I decided to visit Frazier in Wales. He and his family taught me a lot. I went to Africa with them." Clint leaned on the rail. "It was life-changing. I learned the value of hard work. I met people who had very little but were some of the most thankful people I'd ever known. They were caring and willing to risk their lives for one another. I almost died in a storm and got captured by rebel forces that almost killed me. But worse, I came close to losing the only woman I ever loved." Clint fought to hold back the tears. "She is a lot like Aiko: strong, beautiful, kind. Anyone can see how wonderful she is . . . and she loves God. I still can't believe that she's here and with me. God changed me and he used Abby to do it. I learned that loving money leads to an empty existence. Real love is not selfish, but giving. It's being thankful for everything you have and doing for others."

Paul looked at Clint, his gaze softened.

"I don't care about money or material things anymore. God spared my life more than once. I can't understand it, but I know he loves me. I was headed towards self-destruction, but I've been given a second chance now." Clint paused. "I don't deserve anything . . . especially the ranch. Honestly, I don't want it. I just pray someday you could find it in your heart to forgive me."

Silence emerged between them. Paul reached over and hugged him. "You're forgiven. Welcome home Clint . . . . welcome home."

Clint cleared his throat. "I'm planning to ask Abby to marry me. Would you be my best man?"

Paul patted Clint on the back. "I'd be honored."

They went back into the house and joined the others.

Chapter 32

The next day, Clint knocked on the Brown's door.

"Yes," Mrs. Brown answered.

"Um, it's me . . . Clint."

The door opened, Mrs. Brown stood, dressed in a pink nightgown and curlers in her hair. "What is it love, is everything okay?"

"Oh, yes. I was wondering . . . can I speak to Mr. Brown."

"He's downstairs. I imagine stuffing his mouth with Camellia's grand cooking."

"Thank you."

He planned to ask Alistair for Abby's hand in marriage. As his hands gripped the banister to make his way down the stairs, his legs began to shake. He'd never been so nervous. *This isn't a big deal, Clint. Get a grip,* he thought to himself. *People do this all the time.*

When he stepped into the kitchen, his eyes peered straight to Alistair. His nerves shot through his spine, making him feel like running to the other direction.

Alistair took a sip of coffee and said, "Good morning, Clint." "Good morning. Sleep well?"

"Excellent. I'd take that bed home if I could."

Clint slightly laughed, trying to control his nerves. Just then, Camellia walked in.

"Good morning Clint. Breakfast will be ready in 30 minutes. Would you like some coffee?"

"No thank you. Where's Dad."

"He's taking his morning walk. It takes him a lot longer now."

Get this over with, Clint. You can do this.

"Is there something the matter?" Alistair asked.

"No. I was wondering if I could speak to you . . . . alone."

Camellia bent up from checking on the biscuits in the oven and glanced at Clint. "I'll leave you two alone."

Clint sat down directly across from Alistair. He started to perspire.

"I want to thank you for being so good to me. You and Mrs. Brown have become like second parents."

"And you've become like a son to us."

He took a deep breath. "I love your daughter . . . very much. He paused. "I would like your permission to marry her."

Alistair leaned forward and gently gripped Clint by the neck. "I would be proud to have you as a son-in-law. Permission granted."

Clint hugged Alistair. "Thank you. I'll make her very happy." "I know you will, son."

Later that day, Clint took Frazier and Abby to one of his favorite burger joints. It was the first time Abby had a cheeseburger and fries.

That evening Clint and Abby went for a long walk. It was a cold autumn day and the grounds were waxed in a thick layer of leaves. The sunset sky exploded with orange, pink and blue. Hundreds of cattle grazed on the open fields.

"Cheeseburgers and fries have become my favorite food. I can't remember when I enjoyed a meal so much. I'm still stuffed." Abby's hand was on her stomach.

Clint had his arm draped around her neck. "I can't believe you ate the whole burger and had a second helping of fries. One thing we do like to do in Texas is eat."

"I guess I'd better prepare to gain a pound or two. Although walking on your property will certainly help keep it off. The land seems to go on forever and it's so beautiful."

Clint looked around. The soft wind blew the autumn leaves, scattering them everywhere. "I never realized how fresh and beautiful everything is."

"I've never seen anything like it. I can't believe it's yours."

"Me either. My father's worked hard his whole life. Sad to say I never appreciated it until now."

Clint sighed loudly. "I'm not sure I have the skills to run this place."

Abby's eyebrows narrowed. "You're more than ready, Clint. Your father is a smart man. He would only do what's best."

"Honestly, it isn't important. I don't care what I do as long as we're together. I could spend my life helping others . . . with you."

A cool breeze caused Abby to shiver. He pulled her close, rubbed her arms, and they walked towards the lake. The dock creaked under their feet as they stepped onto it.

"It's so peaceful here."

"I come down here a lot. I love being close to the water. I spent a lot of time alone."

"I can picture you fishing, reading, and swimming here."

Clint turned towards her. "I can see you here too . . . with me." A gentle light shone in her eyes. She was wearing a smile. His expression changed from happy to serious.

He knelt down on one knee. "Abby, I love you and I can't live without you. Will you marry me?"

She looked surprised. She shrugged her shoulders and smiled. "Yes, yes, of course. I love you. Yes, I'll marry you."

He leaped up, wrapped his arms around her, and kissed her.

Three weeks of planning went by and the wedding day had arrived. Though it was cold, the sun was shining in a cloudless sky. The wedding was scheduled to begin at three o'clock. Clint glanced at himself in the mirror. He had shaved off his beard that morning and his hair was shorter. He stood bare-chested with a thin but muscular stomach. He shook his head.

I can't believe this day has come. I never dreamed I'd ever get married, especially at age 23, but it's really happening. And I'm marrying the girl of my dreams.

He dressed in a two button, black tuxedo jacket. He tightened his cummerbund, slipped into his shiny new shoes, and went downstairs. James was sitting in the living room.

James wore a black tailored suit. He stood and smiled when he saw Clint. Leaning against his cane, he said, "What a good-looking son I have. You get your looks from me."

Clint grinned.

"You are marrying a wonderful girl. I'm happy the two of you found each other."

"Me too, Dad . . . nerve-racking, but happy."

James laughed. "Take a deep breath and relax. It will be over soon enough. Try and enjoy the day."

They arrived at the church at two thirty. Abby and her family were already there. Clint had rented a limousine to pick them up.

Two hundred guests were invited to the wedding. The church was large enough to hold 500 people.

They walked into the church. They passed a credence table with a centerpiece of white lilies in a crystal vase, and a registration book for guests to sign. Clint went into the sanctuary first, followed by James. White roses and yellow tulips hung on the ends of each pew. The slender minister was standing under a canopy of white and yellow roses, tulips, and lilies. James had been attending the church under his leadership for over 25 years.

They slowly walked towards him. Clint stood next to the minister while James sat on the front right pew. He glanced nervously at the guests sitting on the pews.

"You look very nice, Clint" said the minister. "Thank you."

He adjusted his gold framed glasses, leaned towards Clint and whispered, "I knew I'd get you in here one way or another."

Clint laughed. His nerves were spiraling out of control and skin was perspiring. This was exciting and frightening.

He watched Paul enter the sanctuary dressed in a three-button tuxedo and black cowboy boots. Camellia had her arm wrapped in his. She was holding a handkerchief. Her eyes had already begun to tear and the service hadn't even started.

Frazier entered next. He led his mother, beaming with happiness in her long, yellow silk gown, to the front left pew. Freeborn, wearing a black suit, walked in only a few steps behind them.

Both Paul and Frazier joined Clint in the front of the church.

Clint nodded and smiled when he saw his friend Nick who he met in Germany during the war. He was sitting on the fourth row with his wife and two children, ages two and six months. The black soldier who had saved Clint's life sat next to him. Clint had kept his address. He sent him a telegram a few weeks earlier. Clint insisted on paying for the train ticket from Hattiesburg, Mississippi. It was important to Clint that the people who made a significant impact in his life attend his wedding.

Albert and Emma Watts were sitting in the fifth row. They were like his surrogate parents. Emma beamed with joy when Clint glanced at her. Albert winked. Clint smiled.

Kpassi, the Abneys, and Mark were sitting on the second row, behind Mrs. Brown. Clint glanced over at them. Jacqueline smiled; her eyes were filled with tears.

Clint glanced at James. He knew this was a proud day for his father. Once the processional music began, Mark's wife, Abby's bridesmaid, walked down the aisle dressed in a yellow, classic sleeveless gown. Aiko, who was the maid of honor, followed dressed in the same gown.

Everyone stood as Abby entered. She glowed in her elegant vintage gown with her arm nestled in her father's arm. The train of the skirt was accented by hand-beaded floral arrangements. Her hair was styled in loose curls covered by a two-tier cathedral length veil. She carried a hand-tied bouquet made with white and yellow lilies. Clint beamed with excitement when he saw her.

She moved next to him and clutched her arm. Her eyes roamed over his face. He whispered in her ear, "You look beautiful."

"Thank you," she whispered back.

Clint knew their love story was real. He was completely committed to Abby, and he knew their love was pure and honest, and would be together forever.

They shared their vows—a solemn, eternal covenant with each other before God. Clint placed a four carat, princess shaped diamond ring on her finger. He bent down and kissed her before the preacher said "you may kiss the bride".

They drove back to the ranch for the reception.

Clint walked into the hall holding Abby's hand. The radiant crystal chandelier brightened the room. Twenty-five tables were draped with yellow linen table clothes and floral arrangements in elegant crystal vases. A long rectangular table decorated with candles, orchids, hydrangeas, and roses was placed in the center of the room for the wedding party.

Musicians played by the entrance. Butlers and maids hovered over the tables quietly and efficiently, assuring everything was perfect.

A stunning three-tier cake sat in the center of a table covered with a yellow white linen tablecloth with five satellite cakes surrounding the center cake. A feast with BBQ tri tip, turkey, potato salad, roasted corn an assortment of salads, and corn bread was served for dinner.

Clint and Abby sat next to James. A distinguished looking gentleman with silver hair walked up to James and patted him on the back. James smiled.

"Don't get up."

"Nonsense. I want to greet our great governor, properly." James shook his hand. "I'm so glad you could come."

"Thank you for inviting me."

"Clint, this is Governor Allan Shivers."

Clint stood up and shook his hand. "Hello sir, it's an honor to meet you. Thank you for coming."

"Hello. You were only five years old when I first met you. Your father and I go way back. Welcome home and congratulations. Your father tells me you were in Africa. What was that like?"

"It was amazing. The most beautiful place I've ever seen." "Must have been quite an adventure," the governor said. Clint nodded and smiled, "To say the least."

"Please, sit down," James said.

"I've got to catch an early flight in the morning. It was a beautiful service. Thank you for the invitation, James. It's always good to see you. Let's keep in touch."

"Oh course, and thank you again for coming." James shook his hand again.

They ate, drank, and danced all night.

Clint and Abby stayed the night at the Ritz-Carlton in Dallas. The next day, they took a plane to Maui, Hawaii for their two-week honeymoon. They were the most memorable two weeks of his life.

Chapter 33

The large reception hall at the Governor's Mansion was filled with some of the richest and most powerful people in the state of Texas, including the governor and several senators. The crowded room echoed with the voices of people talking and laughing. Everyone had gathered at the Grand Gallo event held at the Governor's Mansion to celebrate the wonderful contributions made by the Edison family.

Clint, now 33, dressed in an expensive black tailored suit, sat next to his thin, frail father. James's health had deteriorated as he had suffered a heart attack two years earlier. His face had grown old, but his spirit was still strong and determined. Although he'd been fully retired for years, he asked about business affairs and still wanted to be informed of major changes.

Abby sat next to Clint along with their three year old son Phillip James, their seven year old daughter, Liberty Frances Edison, and now, fourteen year old, Freeborn. Phillip's sandy brown hair was wavy and looked just like Clint's. Frances's beautiful black hair and stunning blue eyes mirrored her mother's.

The Yoshis, Paul and Aiko with their children, the Browns, including Frazier and his wife with two year old son, were also invited.

Freeborn, looking tall, young, and handsome propped his elbows on the table with his cheeks resting in the palm of his hands. A belligerent shrug lifted his shoulders. "Dad, I'm bored."

Clint seemingly sympatric pointed to the long rectangular table to the far side of the room holding an array of desserts. "Why don't you and William go and get some dessert."

Freeborn and William, Paul's twelve year old son, jumped out of their seats, dashed across the room and returned with large pieces of chocolate cake.

Abby slipped her hand into Clint's. "This is a grand day. It's been a wonderful life. I love you."

He smiled broadly. "I love you."

The music stopped and the governor stepped onto the stage.

"Ladies and gentlemen, we've gathered here today to celebrate and honor a family for their years of service and numerous contributions, including the orphanage here in Dallas, large enough for 150 children, and funding of the new pediatric wing at Parkland Memorial Hospital."

The governor went on to say, "James Edison and his family have contributed to the health and well-being of people all over the world: building schools, hospitals, and orphanages. It is seldom to find a family so willing to devote much of their lives in helping others. And it is for that reason that we gather together to honor them and say thank you. Ladies and gentlemen, I give you . . . James Edison."

A clap of thunder echoed through the room. James grabbed his cane and slowly rose to his feet. Clint wrapped his arms around James and helped him climb the stairs, and made their way onto the stage. James leaned against a podium and spoke directly into the microphone. "I can't believe it." A moment of silence. "I can't believe I actually made it up those stairs."

There was a roar of laughter.

His voice was hoarse and soft. He spoke slowly. "I'm honored that you would take this day to honor me and my family. God has truly blessed us and given us the grace to assist so many. It is He who should receive all the glory. We are merely his servants." The audience applauded again.

Clint leaned next to his father and put his mouth to the microphone. "Like my father said, we are very honored. Though there have been difficult times, we are grateful to have the ability to help change the lives of others for the better. Many of you have worked alongside us assisting so many people in the United States and all over the world and we'd like to say, thank you. I am thankful my father has been a wonderful role model to me and so many others. His wisdom and grace have taught me that to give is better than to receive. That was a lesson that took me a long time to learn; through many hardships and trials, I might add. But he was right . . . it's truly rewarding. God has blessed us and now we have the chance to bless others. So again, on behalf of my father, wife and extended family, thank you."

Everyone applauded and stood to their feet.

Clint and Abby drove there father home. They had hired a live in nurse to assist him. They then drove five miles to their own 200-acre spread.

He stopped by the bright blue mailbox on the way to their three-story, 7,000 square foot brick house, surrounded by a green lawn and a lush rose garden. A large oak tree shaded the deck.

They entered the house. Abby climbed up the carpeted stairs carrying Phillip, who was sound asleep. Freeborn and Frances were right behind her. The house had eight bedrooms, including a master bedroom with a bathroom. Abby had turned one of the rooms into a study for Clint.

Clint went into the large kitchen, opened an oak cabinet, fixed himself a cup of herbal tea, and strolled into the living room. It was decorated with apple green walls, a tangerine and lemon rug covering the hardwood floors, a natural stone fireplace. There was also a collection of African art they'd collected over the years such as candles, ebony carvings, and paintings.

He fanned through the mail stopping at a letter from Democratic Republic of Congo. It was from Chiamaka. He was 26 now. They wrote one another often.

Eight months prior, Clint and Abby spent three weeks in the village, now a prominent town with over 1,000 residents, working to establish an orphanage. Chiamaka, who had received a degree in Business Management at Cardiff University, would manage the orphanage.

Clint set his tea cup down on the glass table and opened the letter. He leaned back in his chair.

Dear Clint. It was so good to see you and Abby. We miss you. My wife sends her love as does my son. He just had a birthday. He is four. Time seems to go by quickly. Things are well here. The construction team has begun work on the orphanage as planned. It should be complete in five months.

My sister sends her love. She returned yesterday from college. She loves living in London, and visits the Browns often. She decided to become a teacher. Mother and Father are very proud. Father is better now, as you know; he suffered a very mild heart attack. Mother has him resting most of the time, but it's difficult. He is stubborn.

How are the children? I can't believe Freeborn is 14. I look forward to coming to America in the summer to see your children. My wife can hardly wait. She'd start packing today if she could. My son looks forward to learning to ride a horse.

Clint smiled.

I must go. The town is having a social gathering to celebrate the wedding of my cousin. Be sure and write soon. May God continue to bless you and your family.

Chiamaka.

Clint set the letter down. He had a flashback of the energetic, kind 16 year old boy who he had met so many years ago. It seemed like yesterday. He had become one of Clint's best friends.

Abby walked into the room. She moved up behind him, wrapped her arms around him and kissed him on the cheek. "The children are all in bed. What are you doing?"

"I was reading a letter from Chiamaka." Excited she asked, "How is he?"

"Doing well. Everyone is fine. He's looking forward seeing us soon."

"Good. I'll read it in the morning. I'm exhausted. I'm going to bed."

She started to walk away. "Are you coming?" "I'll be up soon."

He watched her climb the stairs. She was still slender and beautiful after ten years of marriage. He was more in love with her now than he was when they married.

He glanced outside. *How did I get so blessed?* he thought. So much had changed. Clint managed the ranch while Paul took on the position as CEO of Edison enterprises. He'd become quite the business man. Clint preferred working on the land.

The Browns visited often, including Frazier and his family. He, Abby, and the children often vacationed in Wales and traveled to Africa at least twice a year on mission trips. They planned to adopt another child.

Life had been full of surprises. He pondered on the past; remembering the selfish boy who had left home many years ago looking for an adventure. A flashback of him walking the narrow path with Albert, listening to him share the story of the prodigal son entered his mind. He remembered the words Albert spoke.

"God has protected you Clint and that's been for a reason . . . He loves you."

My life is definitely an example of God's great grace. I should be dead, but here I am, married to a wonderful woman, doing incredible work, and living an invigorating life.

He leaned back in his chair. *One thing I know for sure . . . God's love covers a multitude of sins.*

In the Pit

The dark prison cell smelled of decay. Joseph lay back on an old bed soiled from years of use. Wires from the springs in the mattress stuck into his back like pins. He had been locked up in this tiny brick cell for almost eight years. The cell was eight-by-eight with a toilet in one corner and a five-foot-long bunk bed in the other. Joseph slept on the bottom bunk.

He stretched his legs in an attempt to relieve some of the stiffness. He pulled the thin, moth-eaten blanket up around his chin to try to get warm and rested his head on the smelly pillow. He imagined sitting by the fireplace in his parents' house to escape the freezing cold air.

A guard strolled by silently with confidence, peering in on occasion before passing on down the hallway. Joseph reached down on the floor next to his bed and grabbed the journal his sister had given him. He began writing a story his father had told him about his grandfather, who had traveled on foot from Persia to Italy. Writing gave Joseph a brief diversion from his life in captivity. After an hour he put the journal down on the table. He picked up the gold pocket watch his father gave him as a graduation present and checked the time.

It was five p.m. and the year was 1914. Thoughts of his family flooded his mind. It had been so long since he last saw them. Joseph thought of the times he came home from fishing with his best friend, Martino. His mother would have dinner on the table. Her pot roast melted in his mouth. He remembered the long walks he used to take with his older sister Rebecca. He smiled as he remembered the excited look on his brother Benjamin's face when he came home from school. Ben was only two then, but they were inseparable.

When he was fourteen, Joseph took a trip with his father to Toscana, an ancient city nestled in the mountains in Italy. The hills were covered with grapevines and olive groves. Sunflowers bloomed on the hillsides. They strolled through a museum filled with beautiful paintings. He would never forget that trip. He'd always been close to his father. Knowing he would never see him again filled him with despair.

Joseph wondered how God could have let him end up in a place like this. He prayed to God for his freedom. Suddenly the cell door flew open. He rolled over and saw a stocky guard. Standing next to him was a skinny, sickly pale young man with red hair.

The guard pushed him into the cell.

"Here ya go, boy. Your home for the next ten years. Get used to it!"

The guard slammed the door shut with a cold, heartless clank that echoed through Joseph's mind for several seconds.

The young man glanced around, dazed and nervous. He shrugged and took a few steps forward. He set a small brown sack containing his belongings on the floor. Joseph sat up on his bed and studied the young man. *Who is this poor boy*, he thought, *and what's he done to be brought here?* He rolled off the bottom bunk and put his feet on the cold concrete floor.

"I'm Joseph," he said.

The young man looked at him for a moment. He stood still, staring wide-eyed at Joseph, his hands trembling. Finally he said, "My name's Gilbert, but everyone calls me Gil."

"Good to meet you, Gil. I hope you don't mind, but I sleep on the bottom."

"Sure, that's fine," said Gil, still somewhat bewildered. He threw his bag onto the top bunk.

"Where are you from?" Joseph said.

Gil opened his mouth to respond when a loud bell sounded. "What's the bell for?"

"Dinner. Let's go."

The same stocky guard opened the cell door. Joseph quickly stepped into line. Gil followed. Down the line was a sea of men dressed in black and white prison uniforms. They looked identical, down to the white socks and black shoes and anger and hatred in their faces.

"Face forward!" the guard yelled.

Joseph glanced out the corner of his eyes and saw Gil spin around. He had a terrified look on his face and avoided making eye contact with the guard.

The guards led the men down what seemed like an endless corridor until they finally reached the dining hall. Hundreds of men sat at long rows of tables. Joseph handed Gil a tray, then he picked one up for himself. A large blond-haired inmate shoved Gil. Gil turned around. The man shot him a hateful look and walked away. Joseph put his hand on Gil's thin back to calm his nerves. Gil was small in size and ordinary in appearance with a round face, bushy red eye brows, and damaged teeth. Gils' pale face had reddened and Joseph felt him shiver as they stood on the cold concrete floor. Gils' breathing was labored and his heart was pounding.

They shuffled through the line. The prisoner serving them placed a foul-smelling piece of meat the size of a fist onto their plates along with a handful of potatoes, some wilted lettuce and a chunk of stale bread. Joseph looked around the room for a place to sit. He spotted two empty chairs on the far right. "Over there," he said.

Joseph moved among the men to get to the other side of the room. Gil followed close behind him. Joseph set his tray on the table and was about to sit down when someone shoved him from behind. His head hit the floor. He sat up and reached for the leg of the chair to help him stand, but a big fat black-haired man flattened him again.

"Sorry, didn't see ya there, Jew boy." It was Joseph's nemesis, Max. Max stared down at him and sneered.

"One day I'm gonna teach you a lesson you'll never forget. You'll wish you was never born, you stupid Jew."

Gil watched in terror as Joseph lay there. Joseph tried to remain calm. He stayed still and glared at Max; his eyes were hard. Max grabbed the chair and walked away snickering.

Joseph got up off the floor, grabbed his tray, and moved to another table with Gil right behind him. Disoriented from the fall, Joseph sat down and rubbed the back of his head.

"You okay?" Gil asked. "Fine."

"Who was that?" "No one."

Gil looked back and saw Max staring at Joseph from across the room. His hatred for Joseph was apparent.

"I take it he's not a friend," Gil said.

"It's no one important," Joseph insisted. He took a bite of his bread. He cringed from the stale bitter taste in his mouth. "So you never answered my question. Where are you from?"

"North Carolina."

"How long have you lived there?"

"Mostly all my life," said Gil. "I moved from Minnesota with my ma. She passed away a couple of years ago. Never knew my pa."

"So how did you end up here in New York?"

"I wanted to sow my oats and venture into new territory. I ran a little low on cash, and I got in some trouble with the law. So here I am." Gil took a few bites and pushed his tray aside. "My stomach's already sick. This slop will make it a whole lot worse."

"You'll get used to it." Joseph glanced at the plate in front of Gil. "Where ya from with that accent and all?" Gil said.

"Italy. I'm Jewish. My family moved to Italy when I was two." "Long way from home aren't ya?"

Joseph paused. "Yes, it's a very long ways from home." "How'd ya learn to speak English so well?"

"When my father lived in Persia, missionaries from America taught him English. He taught all of his children. My English was minimal; but after eight years in prison, I speak it fluently."

"So what's the story with Goliath?"

Joseph slightly smiled. "Actually, I don't know; guess he never really took to me."

"What's he in for?"

"I'm told he beat a man to death."

"Why is it I find that easy to believe," Gil said somewhat sarcastically.

Joseph was almost done eating. Using his hand, he gently wiped the crumbs of bread from his mouth before taking one more drink of water. He lightly set the glass down and then took one more bite of potatoes.

"So, what ya in for, Joseph?"

Joseph paused while his mind searched for something to say. He hesitated for a moment, and then grabbed his tray and headed for the doorway. Joseph could hear Gil's tray scrape across the table.

"Joseph, hang on. I'm comin' with ya."

They piled their trays on top of a high stack of dirty trays on a scarred, food-stained wooden table. Two guards escorted them outside to the yard.

The dust-filled yard was about half a mile wide. It was surrounded by a barbed-wire fence fourteen feet high. The fence loomed like a tower. The guards walked the yard heavily armed with guns and iron poles.

Although it was a far cry from his life in Italy, the fresh air and view of the cloudy gray sky offered a reprieve from the horrific stink and confinement of life inside the prison walls.

Gil and Joseph stood about ten feet from the gate. They watched as an inmate ran several yards to catch a football. Men on both sides of the yard cheered him on.

After half an hour, a large inmate started yelling at another inmate who was smaller than him. The larger inmate pulled out a knife from under his shirt and stabbed the other guy in the chest. He fell to the ground, blood pouring out of his chest. Another inmate reached down and grabbed a thin wire out of his sock and drove it into the larger inmate's neck. He fell to the ground screaming, his blood spilling everywhere.

Alarms went off. Guards tried to break up the fighting. Gil and Joseph stared in horror, unsure what to do. Joseph wanted to run but there was nowhere to go. More inmates joined in the fray. Many lay on the ground bleeding profusely from stab wounds in the chest, legs, or stomach. Soon other guards arrived. They stumbled and clashed with the inmates.

Joseph looked at the gate. Max was only a few feet away. He punched a skinny bald man in the face. The man fell flat on his back. Max walked away.

Joseph turned to Gil. "Try and run to the gate to get out of the yard. I'll be right behind you."

Gil tried to maneuver his way around several fighting inmates. One of them banged into him from behind and knocked him to the ground. Gil swung his fist and kicked him from the ground. Once he found his feet again, he got up and kept running.

Joseph wasn't far behind. He ran toward the gate, but slipped and fell on a twelve-inch iron pole. He looked up and saw a large man stumbling toward him with ripped clothing drenched in blood. The man collapsed on top of Joseph. Unsure what to do, Joseph lay there. He tried to crawl out from under the man when he saw Max running up to them.

"Frank, Frank!" Max cried. "What'd ya do to my brother?"

The rage in Max's eyes stabbed Joseph like a knife. Joseph clenched his teeth in terror as Max approached him. Just when Joseph thought Max was going to kill him, a guard grabbed Max and threw him to the ground before handcuffing him.

"I'm gonna kill you! Just wait! I'll get you for killin' my brother! You'll pay for this; you low-down, good for nothin' scum!" Max yelled as the guard dragged him away.

Joseph finally managed to roll Max's brother off of him. He touched the man's cheek to see if he was breathing but could feel no air. There was nothing he could do for him now.

Joseph quickly got up and bolted to the gate where Gil was waiting. "You all right?" Gil said.

Joseph nodded. "I'm okay."

He was exhausted and covered with blood. Max's threat played over and over again in his mind like a phonograph. Joseph had managed to get away this time, but he knew he could get killed any day now since Max was waiting for him.

Later that night, Gil was rummaging through some old photos while Joseph lay on the bottom bunk and stared at the ceiling, completely lost in thought. Visions of Max infiltrated his mind. Max had been thrown into solitary confinement for only two weeks. One thing was certain: Max wouldn't stop until he made good on his threat to kill him. Joseph prayed silently to God to save him.

"You okay?" said Gil. The violent outbreak had shaken him up. "I'm fine."

His voice shaking, Gill asked, "That happen often?" "Only once in a rare while."

"I thought we were goners."

Joseph didn't say anything. He thought it'd be a miracle if he were still alive in a month.

"You never answered my question. How'd you end up in prison?" "It's a long story."

"I got all night," Gil said.

Joseph paused for a few seconds, his heart pounding at the thought of Max's threat. Perhaps changing the subject would bring him some relief, if only for a moment. He sighed. "Where do I begin?" Joseph replied.

"My family lived in Italy most of our lives. We are Jewish and originally from Persia. We owned a farm in a small town called Umbria. We grew mainly corn, wheat, and grapes. My oldest brothers did most of the farming. The land flourished, as did everything we produced. It always yielded a good crop. My father said that God has favor on our family and that is why we were so blessed financially. We had horses, chickens, and a donkey on the farm. My mother loved animals. We were taught to appreciate everything we had. My father, Jacob Solomon, was successful, strong, determined, and faithful. Though he was only five foot five, he was the strongest man I've ever known. He was also the wisest. Faith was important to him. It came before everything. My father was passionate when he spoke of the Lord. We were very close. You might say I was his favorite child. That's probably why my brothers despised me.

"I have five brothers and one sister: Judah, Samuel, Luke, Matthew, and Rebecca from my father's first marriage to his wife Carolyn. She passed away many years ago. My brother Benjamin and I are from my father's second marriage to Rachel, whom he truly loved. My mother was a beautiful and gentle, caring woman. She lived life to the fullest. It took several years for her to become pregnant with me, but she never lost hope. She told me I was the completion of a promise from the Lord. My brother Judah was the oldest. He had a quiet inner strength. My brothers looked up to him. He and my father didn't get along. Actually, none of my brothers got along with my father. Samuel was the second oldest, and the intelligent and reserved one in the family. I spent some time with him every so often, but I remained distant from the others. They were jealous of my relationship with my father. They hated me. Luke was the strongest of all my brothers. He was arrogant and used to getting his own way. He had the hardest time with my father, perhaps because he had the quickest temper. I think he and my father are a lot alike. He had a stubborn streak so thick you could cut through it. My brother Matthew was the handsome one in the family. He loved only two things: girls and parties. He could build almost anything. My sister Rebecca was the last child born to Carolyn. She was beautiful and shy. We were very close. I was fifteen years old when my mother was pregnant with my brother Benjamin. It seems like a lifetime ago. I can still hear my mother calling my name . . ." Joseph trailed off.

http://www.janiceparkerbooks.com